# "FRANK" AND I

Next morning, "Frank" got down to breakfast
before me, and when I entered the room she
welcomed me with a smiling face, looking, in spite
of her boy's dress, so fresh, rosy, and pretty, that I
felt inclined to take her in my arms and kiss her red
lips. 'How is *it*, this morning?' I asked, in a joking
way. This question made her blush a little, but she
answered readily that 'it' was much better, she
could sit down comfortably; but that the ___ rks
were still very ___

C000162285

*Also in this series*

# "FRANK" AND I

## Anonymous

NEXUS
*published by*
the Paperback Division of
W. H. ALLEN & Co. PLC

A Nexus Book
Published in 1983
by the Paperback Division of
W. H. Allen & Co. PLC
Sekforde House, 175-9 St John St.
London EC1V 4LL

Reprinted 1988, 1989

Published by arrangement with Grove Press Inc., New York

Printed and bound in Great Britain by
Courier International Ltd, Tiptree, Essex

ISBN 0 352 31339 0

This book is sold subject to the condition that it shall
not, by way of trade or otherwise, be lent,
resold, hired out or otherwise circulated without the
publisher's prior consent in any form of
binding or cover other than that in which it is published
and without a similar condition including this
condition being imposed on the subsequent purchaser.

# "Frank" and I

## Volume One

## I

A STRANGE MEETING.———RUNNING AWAY TO SEA.
———THE GOOD SAMARITAN.———"FRANK" AND HIS
NEW CLOTHES.

Twenty years ago, on a beautiful evening in the month of
September, I was plodding along a tree-bordered road in
Hampshire, on my way home after a long day's partridge
shooting. I was looking forward to the good dinner awaiting
me, and I was feeling perfectly satisfied with everything,
for I had had splendid sport; the "birds" had been plentiful,
my dogs had been staunch, and I had missed very few shots.

I was thirty years old; a bachelor,—I am one still—
and I lived, with a number of male and female servants, in
a rambling, old, red brick mansion which had been in the
possession of my family for several generations.

It was past six o'clock, and the rays of the setting sun,
streaming between the trunks of the lofty trees, cast alternate
lines of golden light and deep shade athwart the dusty white
road. The hush of evening was over everything; no sound
broke the stillness but the twittering of unseen birds; while
the only living thing in sight was the solitary figure of a lad
who was walking slowly along the road about a hundred
yards ahead of me. As I was walking fast, I soon overtook
the boy, and was about to pass him, when he asked me to
tell him the time.

I did so; then slackening my gait, I entered into conversation with him, and we walked along side by side at a slow pace, for the boy was evidently footsore. He did not talk much at first, but he was not at all shy or awkward, and he seemed to be glad of my company on the lonely road. He was apparently about thirteen years old; a slenderly built, good-looking lad, with small hands and feet; short, curly fair hair, and blue eyes. He was dressed in a Norfolk jacket and trousers of dark tweed; neat, laced boots, and a white straw hat, but I noticed that his clothes, though almost new, were dusty and travel-stained. His manner was quiet and self-possessed; he expressed himself well, speaking with an educated accent; and he appeared to be in every respect a little gentleman.

"You seem tired," I remarked.

"I *am* rather tired. I have walked fifteen miles to-day," he replied.

"That's a long walk for a little chap like you. Where are you going?"

"I am going to Southampton. I want to go to sea," he answered, without the least hesitation. "Oh, indeed," said I, very much surprised at his answer; especially as we were quite twenty miles from Southampton.

"You don't intend to walk all the way," I observed, in a chaffing way.

"Yes, I do. I have not enough money to go by train," he said, getting a little red in the face. I thought to myself, that he had run away from school. However, it was no business of mine; moreover, I felt pretty sure that no skipper would take such a slight, delicate-looking lad on his ship; and therefore the runaway would soon have to communicate with his friends.

"How old are you? I don't think you are strong enough to be a sailor yet awhile," said I.

"I am going on for fifteen, and I am stronger than I look," said the boy.

I did not believe he was so old. He certainly did not look it.

"Well, anyhow, you can't go much further to-night. What are you going to do for food; and where are you going to sleep?" I inquired.

"I have a little money, and I intend to buy some bread and cheese at the first public-house I come to; and I shall sleep in a haystack—as I did last night," replied the little fellow, bravely.

I laughed, but at the same time I admired the lad's pluck.

"I suppose you have run away from school. Don't you think your parents will be angry, and alarmed when they hear what you have done?"

He looked up in my face, and replied, with a catch in his voice, "I have neither father nor mother; and I have not run away from school."

"Well, from relations, or friends then," said I.

"I have no relations, or friends," he said, huskily, his eyes suddenly filling with tears, which he at once brushed away.

"But you must have been living with someone until now. Tell me all about yourself. Don't be afraid of me. I won't interfere with you. And perhaps I may be able to help you along, if you are determined to go."

He hesitated for a moment, and then spoke: "My father was an officer in the army, and both he and my mother died in India five years ago. I was sent to a school near London where I remained until six months ago: then I believe the money which had been left for me came to an end, and I was taken away from the school by some people with whom I lived until the day before yesterday. I do not want to tell who they are, or where they live. I do not know why they kept me, for they were not paid to do so, and I have no claim upon them in any way. I had never seen or heard of them until they came to the school and took me away.

They were not unkind to me until lately, and then, because I refused to do a certain thing they wished me to do, they ill-treated me, and told me that if I did not consent to do what they wanted, they would turn me out of the house. I still refused, and after a few more days had passed, they told me they would not keep me any longer, and that I was to go away at once. So two days ago I left the house, quite determined to make my way to Portsmouth, and go to sea."

This story appeared to be a highly improbable one in every way, but he told it without hesitating, in a most straightforward manner, and there was a ring of truth in his voice. I looked searchingly at him, and cross-questioned him, trying to make him contradict himself in some way; but he did not get the least confused, nor did he alter his original story in the smallest detail, and he politely, but firmly, refused to give me his reasons for leaving the people with whom he had been living. He evidently noticed that I seemed rather incredulous, for he raised his head and said proudly, his face flushing and his lips trembling a little as he spoke: "I am not a liar. I have told you nothing but the truth; and I have not done anything wrong."

His face was so open, and his candid blue eyes met mine so unflinchingly, that I began to think that his story might perhaps be true. If it was true, he was very much to be pitied, for it was very hard that a young, fragile, and apparently gently nurtured lad like him should be thrown alone on the world to make his own living. At any rate there was some mystery about the whole affair, and I began to feel an interest in the lad; so I determined to take him home with me, give him some dinner, and put him up for the night.

I said, "Well, anyhow you may as well come home with me to dinner, and I will give you a bed for the night. Then in the morning I will see what I can do for you."

The boy's sad face brightened, he gave me a grateful look, and exclaimed earnestly:

"Oh! thank you! Thank you very much. You are very, very kind."

"Well, that is all settled. Let us walk a little faster. My house is close by," said I.

We stepped out briskly; the boy's manner became more confidential; he informed me that his Christian name was Francis, and confessed that he had only sixpence left, and that he had not had much sleep in the haystack the previous night. In a short time we reached my lodge gates, and walked up the long, winding avenue leading to the house; the first sight of which seemed to impress the boy very much, for he evidently had an eye for the picturesque.

"Oh!" he ejaculated, "what a fine old house, and such a splendid lawn!"

I was pleased with his artlessly expressed admiration, for I was proud of my quaint old place, with its irregular gables, corner turrets, and deeply mullioned windows, and its heavy oaken door on which was carved the arms of my family.

When we entered the hall, my man Wilson was in readiness to take my gun. He was an excellent servant, who always accompanied me wherever I went, and he was quite accustomed to all my ways, which were sometimes, to say the least, very irregular; so when I told him to take the dusty young stranger up to a bedroom, get him a bath, and attend to him; the man showed no surprise. I, also, went to my room, had a bath, dressed, and then went down to the drawing-room, where, in a short time, I was joined by the boy, who was ushered in by Wilson.

Frank, as I already called him in my mind, looked fresh and clean after his bath, and his clothes had been brushed, and his boots polished.

Dinner being immediately announced, we went into the dining-room and took our seats at a round table which was placed in a snug recess at one side of the large, oak-panelled apartment.

Frank gazed round the room, apparently struck by the rather sombre splendour of the old-fashioned furniture, and also by the display of silver plate on the sideboard; and I think he was a little impressed by the appearance of my solemn old butler. However, the lad was too well-bred to show any signs of astonishment, and he was evidently faint with hunger, so he concentrated his attention on his dinner. I gave him a glass of champagne, which he relished very much, as he had never before tasted the wine, and under its exhilarating influence he began to chatter freely; and I found that he was a well-educated lad, who talked nicely, and who was possessed of a quick sense of humour, a thing rather uncommon in boys of his age. But his head soon began to droop a little, as he was thoroughly worn out, and by the time dinner was over, he could hardly keep his eyes open; so I told him that he had better go to bed, which he gladly did, after again thanking me for my kindness.

Lighting a cigar, I sat down in an easy chair to think over the whole affair, which had interested me strangely, and somehow or other, I could not divest myself of the idea that the boy's story was true; then I thought of his slight *physique* which utterly unfitted him for the rough life of a common sailor; and finally, by the time I had finished smoking my cigar, I had decided to keep the lad in my house for a few days, provide him with a complete outfit, and then try to get him some employment more fitted to his capabilities than going to sea before the mast. Having settled all this in my mind, I smoked another cigar, drank a glass of whisky and water, and then went to bed, as I was feeling tired after my long day's tramp over the stubbles.

Next morning, at breakfast, Frank turned up, looking very fit; his cheeks, which had been pale overnight, were now rosy, and his eyes had lost their wearied look.

He greeted me with a smile, and, in answer to my inquiries, said that he had slept most soundly, never waking until called, and that he was quite strong again.

When breakfast was over, and my trim parlour-maid Ellen, who had waited on us during the meal, had left the room, I lit a cigar, and turning to the lad, said: "Now Frank, I want to have a little talk with you. To begin with, I must say to you that I believe all you have told me about yourself."

"Oh, I am so glad you believe me," he ejaculated, clasping his hands. I went on: "Though I must say it seems very strange that people whom you say you did not know, should have taken you into their house and kept you for six months without any remuneration; and then have suddenly turned you out."

"It was very strange. But it all happened just as I have told you," he said. Then after a moment's pause, he added, flushing slightly: "I think I know now why they took me into their house."

His last remark did not make any impression upon me at the time, but I remembered it afterwards. I continued: "I feel interested in you, and I do not consider you are at all fit to be a sailor; so I think you had better stay here for a few days, so that I can get you properly fitted out with clothes, and then I will try and procure you some employment on shore."

He gazed at me for a moment as if he could hardly grasp the meaning of what I had said, then a joyful look came to his face and his eyes grew moist. "Oh!" he exclaimed, "you are so kind and good to me: I do not know how to thank you. I shall be only too delighted to stay. I really do not want to go to sea. I hate the very idea of it! But when the people turned me out, my only thought was to get away from them as far as possible. That was why I thought of going to sea. Oh, thank you again for giving me the chance of escaping such a horrid life! I will do anything you wish, I should like to stay with you always. I have not a single friend, and I am so lonely," he added, with a little sob, the tears overflowing his eyes and running down his cheeks. I am by nature rather inclined to be sympathetic, and I had all along felt strangely drawn to the poor little fellow, but now my heart went out entirely to him, and I said to myself that I would keep him in the house for the present; he would be company for me, in a way, when I was at home—then, after a time, I would send him to school, and make arrangements for his future career. There was no reason why I should not do so. I was well off, and there was no one who had a right to question or interfere with me.

"Well, Frank, you shall stay with me always, if you like," I said.

His face beamed with happiness, and running over to me, he seized my hand, kissing it in a transport of gratitude, and thanking me over and over again, till I was so embarrassed by the fervour of the feelings he displayed that I was obliged to tell him to go and sit down.

When I make up my mind to do a thing, I set about doing it at once; so ringing the bell, I told the maid who answered it, to send up Wilson. When he appeared, I informed him that Master Francis was going to remain with me; then I told him to order the dog-cart to be got ready, and that he was to drive the boy to Winchester,—the nearest town—have him measured for some suits of clothes, and to buy him underclothing, shirts, boots, and the other things necessary for the complete outfit of a young gentleman. My well-trained servant made no remark, but bowed gravely and left the room. In a short time he returned, saying that the dog-cart was at the door. I gave him a sum of money sufficient to meet all expenses, then I put Frank into his charge, and the two went away. As soon as they had gone, I got my gun, went to the kennel for the dogs, and started off to have a pop at the "birds," and as the sport was good, I remained out all day, getting home just in time to change my clothes before dinner.

When I got down to the dining-room, Frank was waiting for me, looking very smart in his well-brushed clothes, clean shirt, large turned-down collar, and neat tie; he had on a pair of patent leather shoes, and I again noticed the smallness of his feet. During dinner he was in high spirits, and, boy-like, seemed very pleased with all the new clothes and other articles which Wilson had bought for him; he told me all about the shopping and how they had lunched at a confectioner's. Altogther, he seemed to have enjoyed his day in Winchester, and he did not forget to thank me. After dinner, we played draughts, at which game he showed a fair amount of skill, and at ten o'clock I sent him to bed.

## ·⟨· II ·⟩·

A TIMID BOY.——LESSONS TO LEARN.——A CARE-
LESS PUPIL.——A MYSTERIOUS SPANKING.——THE
THREAT OF THE ROD.——THE CHASTISEMENT.——
POOR "FRANK'S" BOTTOM.——ARE GIRLS
EVER BIRCHED BY MEN?

A couple of weeks passed. Frank never made the slightest
allusion to his past life; he seemed to be perfectly happy,
and he had become as much at home as if he had always lived
with me at Oakhurst, but he was never forward or presuming
in any way. During the time that had passed, I had been
able to form an estimate as to the boy's character and disposition. He was straightforward, and perfectly truthful;
his nature was affectionate, and he appeared to be fond of
me, for he always liked to be in my company, either in or
out of the house; and he was always very sorrowful when
I went out to dinners or to parties at the neighbouring
houses. But he never would accompany me out shooting;
he said he could not bear seeing the birds killed. I thought
that weak and silly on his part, and I frequently chaffed
him about his squeamishness. It was strange that a boy who
had had pluck enough to run away to sea should have
shrunk from seeing a partridge shot. I had been right in
thinking that he was quite unfit to be a sailor.

He had many winning ways. I got quite attached to him, and never regretted having taken him under my care. Of course he was not faultless. He was indolent, he had a hasty temper, he liked having his own way, he was sometimes inclined to be disobedient, and he was rather disposed to treat the servants—the female ones especially—in an imperious way. This trait in his character I attributed to his having had to do with native servants in India during the first ten years of his life.

The days slipped away rapidly and uneventfully; I shot, hunted, and occasionally took a run up to town for a night, and so things went on, until the end of October, when I made up my mind to send Frank to school at the beginning of the new year. Not that I wanted to get rid of him, but because I had an old-standing engagement with a couple of friends to go on a yachting trip to the Mediterranean, and we were to start early in January.

I did not tell Frank that I was going to send him to school, as I knew the idea would make him miserable, and I did not want to have him moping about the house. I had lately been thinking a good deal about his future, and it struck me that I was not acting rightly in allowing him to run wild about the place as he had hitherto been doing. I remembered the old saying about "idle hands and mischief," so I determined to set him some lessons which would keep him employed for part of each day. I at once looked up a number of my old schoolbooks, and when he had had his lunch, I told him that in future I wished him to study every day for a few hours, and I also informed him that I would set him various lessons and exercises, and that I would examine him upon them in the evening when I was at home.

He looked surprised and rather dejected on hearing my announcement, but said he would learn any lessons I chose to set him.

Next morning, before going out hunting, I marked various tasks for him, and sent him into the library to study them, telling him that I expected him to stick to his work, and not to go out until he had learnt all his lessons. I had a capital run with the hounds, and did not get home until seven o'clock; but as soon as dinner was over, and I had lit my cigar, I made Frank bring me his books and papers; then I examined him, and looked over his exercises, finding that he had done all his tasks fairly well. Then we chatted, and played draughts until it was time for him to go to bed. Everything went on pretty well for some days, and then I began to notice that he was chafing under the regular routine which I had laid down; and he got so careless in writing his exercises, and he learnt his lessons so imperfectly that I had often to scold him. On these occasions he was always penitent, promising to be more diligent, but in a few days he would again grow idle and careless, and at last became positively disobedient. So I came to the conclusion that I should have to adopt severe measures with him; as I did not mean to let him have his own way entirely. I am a bit of a disciplinarian, and I believe in the efficacy of corporal punishment; moreover I think all boys require a flogging occasionally. I was often birched when I was at Eton, and I am sure the punishment was good for me. So one evening, on finding that he had been more than usually idle during the day, I spoke sharply to him, saying: "You have been extremely inattentive to your work of late, and to-day you do not appear to have made an attempt to learn your lessons. I am very angry with you, and if you do not apply yourself more diligently to your tasks, I shall be obliged to flog you."

He started, turned very red, and gazed at me with a frightened expression on his face, saying: "Oh, I am so sorry to have made you angry! I know I have been very idle lately; but I will work hard in future. I will indeed. Oh, I hope you will never flog me," he added, fervently.

"That depends on how you go on. If you persist in not learning your lessons, I will certainly give you a flogging with a birch rod," I said.

He gave a little shudder, and clasped his fingers tightly together.

"Have you ever been birched?" I asked.

The colour deepened in his cheeks. he cast down his eyes, and after a moment's hesitation replied in a low voice: "No, I have never been birched, but Mrs."—he checked himself, and did not pronounce the name which had been on the tip of his tongue—then he went on: "One of the ladies at the house where I lived spanked me three times to try and force me to do a certain thing I had refused to do. I told you that they had ill-treated me."

I laughed, and said: "Well, I am very much surprised. I thought you had more spirit than to allow yourself to be spanked by a lady. And you say that you are over fourteen years of age?"

His face grew redder, he moved uneasily in his chair, and stammered out: "Oh—you—don't—understand. I—could—not help—myself. These—were—two—ladies. I—am—not,"—he stopped, and wrung his hands, looking utterly miserable and confused.

I laughed again: "Oh, you need not tell me any more about it," I said, taking up a book and beginning to read. He also began turning over the leaves of a book, but I noticed that he appeared very ill at ease, and after a short time he bade me "good night," and went off to bed.

Master Frank was thoroughly frightened by my threatening him with the rod; he had evidently not thought that I would be so determined with him, and for some days afterwards I often noticed him looking at me in a timid sort of way; but in time his fear appeared to wear off, and he began again to give trouble in many ways. He developed a waywardness of conduct, and his temper became very variable; at one time he was lively and talkative, and at another time sulky and depressed; he was often disobedient, and occasionally gave way to fits of passion. I could not make out what had come over him. His behaviour was tire-

some, and it annoyed me, and though he was always sorry
after he had misbehaved, I saw that he needed a taste of the
birch to bring him to his senses; so I determined to flog him
the next time he offended in any way.

Before another week had passed, he had received a
birching.

He wrote a very good hand—which I do not—and one
morning I wanted a manuscript copied; so I gave it to him,
telling him to make a fair copy of it as soon as possible, as I
wished to post it in the afternoon. It was not a long job, so
I told him to have it done in an hour.

At the end of that time I went to the library expecting to
find him there with the copy ready for me, but he was not
in the room, nor had he even begun the work, for I saw the
manuscript lying on the table beside a blank sheet of fools-
cap paper. I felt very angry, and resolved to birch him as
soon as he made his appearance. I had not got a rod, but
there were several birch trees growing in the grounds, so
I went out and cut a few long, slender, sappy, green twigs,
and soon made a first-rate rod; and, as I swished it in the
air to test its flexibility, I said to myself: "Ah! master
Francis, this will make your bottom smart." I went back to
the library, put the rod in a drawer, and taking up a novel in
which I was interested, I settled myself comfortably in an
easy-chair beside the fire, and began to read.

In about an hour's time Frank came into the room. I
put down the book and rose from my seat. "Why have you
not copied the manuscript?" I said sternly, looking him full
in the face, as he stood before me.

"Oh, I couldn't be bothered," he replied flippantly. I was
very much astonished, as he had never answered me in
such a saucy way before.

"You have deliberately disobeyed me, and you have
answered me improperly. I am going to birch you," I said,
angrily taking the rod out of the drawer, and holding it
up for him to see. He was quite taken aback at the sight

of it, and very much frightened; his face became scarlet. and he began to tremble.

"Oh! don't birch me! Please don't birch me!" he exclaimed, bursting into tears, and stretching out his hands towards me, with an imploring gesture.

"Let down your trousers, and lie across the end of the sofa," said I, sharply.

"Oh! Oh! Oh!" he cried. "I know I deserve to be punished, but please don't birch me. Punish me in any other way but that."

"I will not punish you in any other way. Let down your trousers at once. I did not think you were a coward."

"I am not a coward. I am not afraid of the pain. I can bear it. But I am ashamed to let down my trousers before you," he sobbed out.

"Don't be silly! When the lady spanked you, you had to let down your trousers; and it is more shameful for a boy to let down his trousers before a woman, than to let them down before a man. Now unbutton! Look sharp!"

"Oh! don't make me let down my trousers," he again said, beseechingly. I lost patience. "If you don't at once obey me, I will send for Wilson and get him to take down your trousers, and then hold you on his back while I flog you," I said, in a loud voice.

"Oh! don't do that. Don't do that!" he cried out, in terrified accents, with a look of horror on his face. "I will let down my trousers."

He turned half aside, and with trembling fingers, unfastened his braces, and unbuttoned his trousers, letting them slip down to his knees; and then he laid himself across the end of the sofa, with his hands resting on the floor at one side, and the tips of his toes on the other side, thus bringing his body into a curve with his bottom well raised up in a splendid position for receiving the rod. I could not understand why he had made so much fuss about letting down his trousers. It seemed very absurd.

Standing at the end of the sofa, I rolled up the tail of his shirt, then tucking up his undershirt, I bared his bottom, and as I did so, he uttered a choking sob, covered his red face with both his hands, and a shudder passed over his whole body.

"Now let me see how bravely you can take a birching. Don't attempt to rise from the sofa, or to put your hands behind you," said I, raising the rod and making it hiss in the air over the doomed bottom, the flesh of which was instantly contracted in dread of the coming stroke.

I gave him eight strokes; not very severe ones, but they marked his bottom a great deal and turned it a deep red colour all over; for his skin appeared to be of delicate texture. He winced at each cut, twisted his hips from side to side, and cried with pain, the tears rolling down his cheeks; but he clenched his teeth, and never once bawled out; nor did he attempt to shield his bottom with his hands. In fact he took his punishment in a plucky manner, considering it was the first time he had felt the sharp sting of a birch.

He was not a coward after all. I told him to rise, adjust his dress, and go to his room; and he got up, standing with his face averted, holding his trousers up with one hand, and brushing the tears from his eyes with the other; then after a moment or two, he buttoned up, and walked out of the room sobbing, with his handkerchief to his face.

I put away the rod, and then went out to make some calls in the neighbourhood. I did not see Frank again until we met at dinner, and as he took his seat opposite to me at the table, he glanced at me shyly, and a deep blush spread over his whole face. As the butler was not in the room at that moment, I said laughingly: "Well, Frank, I suppose you feel a little tender behind. But what are you blushing so for, you young donkey? You are not the first boy who has had a birching. Most boys get a birching occasionally. They require it. I was often birched when I was a boy. It is nothing when you are used to it."

He gave a little shiver. "Oh, isn't it," he said, in a very doubtful sort of way; then went on with his dinner.

I could not help laughing at the way he spoke, but as he appeared to be low and wretched, I gave him a glass of wine. When the meal was over, and I had drawn an easy-chair up to the fire, and lighted my cigar, he came and sat near me in his usual manner, but did not speak; so I chatted to him and rallied him until he brightened up and began to talk. He had not a sulky temper, and he did not appear to bear me any malice.

After being silent a short time, he suddenly asked me, again blushing very red as he spoke: "Do you think that girls are often birched?"

"Not as often as they should be," I answered, laughing, "but many a girl does get birched by her mother, or governness."

"Did you ever know of a girl being birched by a man?" was his next question.

"Well, I can't say I actually know of a girl being birched by a man; but I have often heard that such a thing is by no means uncommon. And I have no doubt that some fathers birch their daughters."

My answer appeared to have given him a certain amount of satisfaction; and he asked no more questions, but sat staring at the fire, in deep thought. He did not seem inclined to talk much, and he went early to bed.

# ❧ III ❧

THE POWER OF THE ROD.———THE ST. JOHN'S WOOD
VILLA.———A WEEK'S FUN.———"FRANK'S" PRANKS.
———THE HOUSEKEEPER'S REPORT.———A SEVERE
BIRCHING.———THE DISCOVERY.———THE SECRET
AND ITS SENSUAL EFFECT.———THE SIGHT OF A
SORE BOTTOM.———A PLEASANT DRIVE.

After that everything went on well. Frank for some days
was rather shy with me, often blushing when I looked at
him; but as time went on he gradually seemed to forget
all about the birching, and he became bright, cheerful and
quite his old self. He was obedient, and there were no more
fits of ill-temper: moreover he studied diligently, being
always perfect in his lessons whenever I happened to examine him. Wonderful is the persuasive power of a birch rod,
properly applied! A week more passed; then I thought I
would run up to town, and spend a few days with a young
lady named Maud, who lived in a pretty little villa in St.
John's Wood. The expenses of the establishment were borne
by me. Frank was rather disconsolate when I told him I
was going away; but he promised to study for three hours
every day during my absence. I committed him to the care
of my old housekeeper, Mrs. Evans; a most worthy old lady,

who had been at Oakhurst in various capacities for twenty-five years.

Then I drove to Winchester, and caught the afternoon train to London. On my arrival, I put my portmanteau and myself into a hansom, and went straight to the little villa; where I was received with kisses by Maud, to whom I had written the previous day. It is a great mistake for a man to pay a surprise visit to the young lady whose rent he pays.

She gave me a cup of tea in her prettily furnished little drawing-room, and we chatted for a short time; then she went away, returning in half-an-hour dressed well, but quietly, and looking very nice. She was a pretty, plump, little woman, with a lot of fair hair, and soft, brown eyes. She professed to be fond of me, and was, I believe, tolerably faithful. We went out, and had a good dinner with plenty of "fizz" at a West-end restaurant; then we patronized a theatre; had some supper; returned to the villa, and went to bed.

I remained a week at the villa with Maud, and we had a pleasant time; going about all day; dining at various restaurants, and visiting the theatres. I especially enjoyed the nights, revelling in Maud's naked charms; her bubbies were large, round, and firm, with pretty little, pink nipples; she had a big, plump bottom, and her skin was very white, soft, and smooth; moreover she was a very good poke, and also skilled in all the "arts of love." I was sorry to have to go back to Oakhurst so soon; but I had a dinner engagement which I did not wish to put off: so I started for Winchester by a morning train, and arrived at home about two o'clock. I was surprised to find that Frank was not in the house to receive me, and after waiting a short time I sat down to lunch, wondering what had become of the boy, and beginning to think that he had been up to some mischief. Just as I had finished lunch, a knock came to the door, and my housekeeper, Mrs. Evans, sailed into the room, gorgeously arrayed in her best black silk dress and white lace cap, with open-work mittens on her hands and a gold chain round her neck. Curtseying to me in the old-fashioned way, she said that she wished to speak to me. I was fond of the good old woman who had been in the house since I was five years old. She had originally come to our family as nurse, and I can quite remember that she used to spank me, and my brothers and sisters, when we were small children. I gave her a chair, saying that I was ready to hear what she had to say.

"It is about Master Francis," she said, smoothing the folds of her gown.

"I thought so," said I to myself. She was a verbose old woman, who liked hearing herself talk, so she took some time to tell her story; but I will condense it, and merely relate the main points.

During my absence Frank had behaved well, and given no trouble until that morning, when he had taken it into his head to make a raid upon the store-room and help himself to jam and various other good things. The store-room maid, who had charge of, and was responsible for the things, happening to see the young marauder, remonstrated with him, and told him to leave the room; but he refused to do so, and on her attempting to put him out, he lost his temper, struck her thrice in the face, and pulled down her hair. The woman, who had been somewhat hurt, and a good deal frightened by Frank's violence, ran crying to the housekeeper, and complained. Frank had been sorry for what he had done, and had apologized to the woman; but she had insisted upon my being told, and so the old lady had been obliged to report the affair to me.

I was much vexed on hearing of his ungentlemanly conduct, and I felt very angry with him. He deserved a flogging, and I meant to give him one. I went to the library, after giving orders that Frank was to be sent to me as soon as he returned to the house.

In about half-an-hour he came into the room and greeted

me quietly, but he looked as if he were rather ashamed of himself. He was pale and nervous, and he kept his eyes cast down.

I said: "Frank, I am very sorry to hear how badly you behaved this morning. I should not have taken notice of your pilfering things from the store-room, though that was a contemptible act for a boy of your age: but I am grieved to think that you should have so far forgotten yourself as to strike Jane. It was cowardly and ungentlemanly. I did not think you could have done such a thing. You ought to be ashamed of yourself. I intend to punish you severely. Prepare yourself at once," I added, getting out the rod. He glanced at it with a look of fear, and a hot flush rose to his cheeks.

"I am ashamed, and very sorry for what I have done. I expected to be punished," he said in a low voice, his eyes filling with tears, and his lips trembling Then, without another word, he let down his trousers, and placed himself in position across the end of the sofa.

I tucked his shirt up and began to apply the rod, and as I was angry with him, I laid on the cuts smartly, raising long, red weals all over the surface of his white bottom. He wriggled, writhed, and cried as the stinging strokes of the birch fell with a swishing sound on his plump, firm flesh, striping the skin in all directions; but I went on flogging him, till at last he could no longer suppress his cries, and he began to scream in a shrill tone, at the same time putting both his hands over his bottom. I seized his wrists and held them with my left hand, while I continued to apply the rod with a little more force, extorting from him louder screams, as well as piteous appeals for mercy and entreaties to me not to flog him so hard. He drew up his legs one after the other and then kicked them out again, he jerked his hips from side to side, and rolled about in pain, half turning over on to his side for a moment, so that I saw the front part of his naked body. And what I saw paralyzed me with astonishment, causing my uplifted arm to drop to my side, and the rod to slip from my grasp. In that momentary glimpse, I had caught sight of a little pink-lipped cunt, shaded at the upper part with a slight growth of curly, golden down.

*"Frank" was a girl!*

This most astounding and totally unexpected discovery made my brain whirl, and for a moment I stood utterly confounded.

As the cuts of the rod were no longer falling on her red, striped, quivering bottom, she had ceased struggling, and lay on the sofa wailing piteously.

I took a long look at the half-naked body lying before me, and I was amazed that I had not discovered her sex on the day I had first seen her figure exposed; for the broad hips, the swelling curves of the plump bottom, and the rounded thighs, were those of a fairly well-developed girl about fourteen or fifteen years of age. And as I realized the fact that I had just been birching, and that I was at that moment looking at the naked bottom and thighs of a young female, I got a most tremendous cockstand. What a sensitive thing is the sexual feeling, and how quickly it is excited!

But while all these various thoughts and sensations were passing through my mind, the girl was lying sobbing on the sofa, and I had to decide as to the course I should take with regard to her. I did not hesitate, but at once resolved not to let her know that I had noticed anything; and I felt pretty sure that she had been in too great pain during the flogging, to be aware that she had revealed her sex in her contortions.

I now told her that she might rise from the sofa; and she struggled to her feet, and slowly adjusted her dress; her whole body shaking with sobs, the tears streaming down her scarlet cheeks, and her lips quivering.

She had received a severe birching, and her bottom must have been smarting and throbbing most painfully. I pitied her, because she was a girl, but I should not have pitied a boy who had received an equally severe flogging

for the same offence. At that moment, as she stood before
me in her male attire, with short cut hair, it was astonishing
how boy-like she was in appearance; she looked just like a
lad about thirteen years of age. I felt very much inclined
to laugh, but that would never have done; if I had even
smiled she would have known that her secret had been
found out; so I kept a stern countenance. and addressed her
in a cold, hard voice, saying: "Now, Frank, you may go.
You have had a severe flogging, but you deserved it. I
hope you will never be so ungentlemanly as to strike a
woman again."

She wiped her eyes, from which the big tears were
still slowly trickling, and walked stiffly out of the room, in
perfect ignorance of the fact that her true sex had been
discovered.

When the door had closed behind her, I felt rather
relieved; for the startling discovery had been so sudden,
that it had somewhat bewildered me, and I wanted to be
alone, so that I might collect my ideas, and settle upon what
I should do with the girl in future. I can always think best
while smoking, so I lit a cigar, and took a seat in a comfortable arm-chair. Then I thought over everything that
had happened since "Frank"—as I still called her in my
mind—had become an inmate of my house; and in the light
of the knowledge I had just acquired, I understood the
meaning of many things which had puzzled me at the time
they had occurred. It was perfectly clear to me now why
"Frank" had been so confused when I laughed at "him" for
submitting to be spanked by a lady: and I could well understand why she was ashamed to let down her trousers before
me; why she was so shy with me after I had flogged her;
and why she had always blushed on the slightest provoca-
tion. I was also able to account for her curious behaviour
some time previously, when she had been so queer and
wayward, alternately lively and depressed, and so liable to
fits of anger. No doubt this state of nervous excitement had

been owing to her having come to puberty, and been unwell with her courses for the first time. I wondered how she had managed to hide all the tell-tale signs from the eyes of the female servants, who are generally so quick to find out anything of that sort. But she had undoubtedly contrived to conceal her sex, and I was convinced that no one in the house but myself knew her secret.

Then I wondered by what means she had procured male attire, and what could be her object in passing herself off as a boy. Where had she come from? Who were the mysterious ladies who had taken her into their house without remuneration? What was the thing she had so obstinately refused to do, in spite of three spankings? I got quite bothered pondering over these various things, not being able to explain them in any satisfactory way; but I had no doubt that in due course of time I should find out all about them.

I had definitely made up my mind to keep the girl at Oakhurst; moreover as long as she chose to conceal her sex, I would let her do so; and, on my part, I did not intend to let her know that I had found out she was a girl.

What the end of it all would be, I could not foretell, but in the meantime everything should go on as before; and I must say, I liked the idea of always having about me, a good-looking young girl dressed in boy's clothes; and the fact that no one but myself was in the secret, added piquancy to the affair. Besides, it was pleasing to know that I should occasionally be able to treat myself to a sight of her half-naked figure; for it was my intention to birch her whenever she was naughty; not severely, but just with sufficient force to raise a rosy blush on the plump, white cheeks of her pretty little bottom.

It was a delicious idea, and as I thought of it, my cock grew quite stiff. I have always been extremely fond of looking at feminine bottoms; but I had never, till that day, whipped one in any way. I knew that many men were fond of applying the birchrod to young females; but I hitherto had never had the least inclination to birch a girl;

now, however, I felt conscious that to do so would always in future give me pleasure. In fact, I had become, almost in a moment, a lover of the rod. I remained in the library for an hour, turning over various things in my mind, and settling my plans. I decided to write to my two friends, saying that circumstances would prevent my going yachting with them. I could not leave the girl alone in the house; and in fact I did not want to go away from her at all at that moment; I had always liked her when I thought she was a boy, and now I had a tenderer feeling for her; not exactly love, but a slight feeling of sensual desire. However, I resolved not to harm her or try to debauch her in any way; I would whip her when she deserved punishment, and at the same time enjoy the sight of her nakedness, but nothing more;—for the present, at any rate. But I could not help thinking that the affair would end by my poking her some day or other, when she had grown a little older. I now suddenly remembered my engagement to dinner, and as the house I was going to was a few miles from Oakhurst, I had not much time to spare; so I hurried to my room, dressed, and drove off in my brougham, arriving just in time for dinner. The repast was well cooked, the wines excellent, and I had taken into dinner a pretty girl who turned out to be lively and full of chat, so I had a pleasant time with her. I wonder what she would have thought had she known that a few hours before, I had severely birched the naked bottom of a member of her own sex. I did not get home till late, and as "Frank" had gone to bed at her usual hour, I did not see her that night.

Next morning, when I sat down to breakfast, the girl was not in the room, but in about ten minutes she made her appearance, looking rather sad, though otherwise fresh and well. She shyly bade me "good morning," with downcast eyes, and blushing cheeks; and I looked at her face with a new and keener interest now that I knew she was a girl. She certainly was very pretty, and if her golden hair had been long, and she had been dressed in the garments of her sex, she would have been perfectly charming, for she had a good complexion; large, limpid blue eyes, and a delicious, kissable, rosebud of a mouth. Strange I had never taken any notice of her good looks before. Then I closely scanned her figure to see if I could trace the feminine outlines through the clothes she was wearing. She had on a doublebreasted P-jacket, which came well down over her hips, concealing their contours effectually, but I fancied I could see the slight swell of her budding bosom under the jacket.

However, she could easily pass as a boy at that moment, but I wondered how much longer she would be able to wear male attire without exciting suspicion. When she took her seat in her usual place opposite me, I noticed that she sat down carefully and did not rest the full weight of her body upon the chair; which showed that her bottom was still very tender. I pitied her, but I had to keep up appearances; so I nodded carelessly to her, saying, with a smile, "You don't seem to be able to sit down very comfortably this morning."

She glanced at me for a moment, then dropped her eyes, making no remark; but I was glad to see that she was able to make as good a breakfast as usual. In fact, ever since she had been at Oakhurst, she had been in perfect health; her skin was clear, and her cheeks were always rosy, for she was fond of open air and exercise, and she used to take some of my numerous dogs for a run every day.

When breakfast was over, she went and stood in front of the fire, resting her elbows on the broad, low mantelpiece, and looking at her face in the mirror.

"Well, Frank; is your bottom very sore?" I asked lightly.

Still keeping her back turned towards me, she replied, dolefully, "Only when I sit down, now; but it smarted dreadfully nearly all night. I could not sleep."

A sudden desire to see her bottom, and also the marks of my handiwork upon it, came over me at that moment. "Come here and let me see your bottom," I said, taking my seat in a chair near the window.

She turned round, blushing furiously, and hesitated for a moment, but evidently she thought she had better obey my order, so without a word, she came over to where I was sitting; then, turning her back to me, she unbuttoned her trousers, letting them slip to her feet, and stood quite still, holding down with both hands the front part of her shirt, so as to completely hide the secret spot. I smiled, and lifting up the tail of her shirt above her waist, I took a good look at the girlish figure, naked from loins to ankles, standing before me; and as I gazed, my tool swelled, and I felt a strong inclination to put my hand between her round white thighs and feel her small slit. However, I restrained myself. Then I inspected the ravages which had been made by the rod on her prettily shaped bottom, finding that the entire surface of the skin was still very red, the weals having gone down, but both her plump, firm buttocks were covered all over with long, purplish stripes, crossing, and recrossing each other in all directions. Poor little girl! I must have flogged her more severely than I had meant. She must have suffered a great deal.

I laid my hand gently on her bottom, which was hot and rough; she shrunk away, exclaiming: "Oh, don't touch it! It is awfully sore!"

Then, as she buttoned up, she said in a rueful voice, looking at me reproachfully: "Oh! you flogged me very hard."

I was really very sorry, and I said to myself that I would never birch her so severely again, unless she did something exceptionally bad.

I said, smiling: "Never mind; the marks will all be gone in a couple of days."

Then I added: "You shall have a holiday. I will take you out for a long drive after lunch; and we won't come home to dinner, but stay and dine at a hotel in Winchester. Would you like that?"

Her face brightened at once, a faint smile curved her

red lips, and she answered that she would like it very much. She then left the room, and after I had sent my orders to the stables, I sat down to read the paper, and smoke my after-breakfast cigar.

At two o'clock, my mail phaeton with a pair of horses was brought to the door; then "Frank" and I put on our overcoats, took our seats, and drove off. It was a cold day, but the sun was shining brightly, and there was no wind; the roads were hard and dry, but not dusty, and as we rolled swiftly along, the fresh, keen air filled our lungs, exhilarating us both, and making our cheeks glow, and our eyes sparkle. The girl's spirits rose; she began to talk, and in a short time she was laughing and chattering away in her usual manner, for as a rule she was merry, and light-hearted.

When the shadows began to lengthen, I turned the horses' heads in the direction of Winchester, arriving there at six o'clock, and putting up at a comfortable, old-fashioned hotel where I was well-known. Then, after a wash and brush-up, we sat down to a nice little dinner, and I ordered a bottle of Burgundy, of a brand which I knew to be good. I gave my companion a glass, asking her if she had enjoyed the drive and if she liked the dinner and the wine. She answered in the affirmative, looking frankly at me now, without a trace of shyness, and without a blush.

We drove home at a rattling pace as it was a bright moonlight night, reaching Oakhurst a little after ten o'clock; then I sent "Frank" to bed, and went into the smoking room to have a quiet cigar, and a glass of whisky and water before retiring for the night.

# ·IV·

CHRISTMAS FESTIVITIES.——THE WISH TO WHIP.
——MAUD'S INITIATION.——THE ROD AND THE
RESULT.——A BLUSHING MILKSOP.——THE EROTIC
BOOKS.——HOW CURIOSITY WAS PUNISHED.——A
SERMON AND A SPANKING.——HOW TO PREPARE
THE VICTIM.——"FRANK'S" BOTTOM WELL
SLAPPED.——AN EXQUISITE SENSATION.——
THE EXPOSURE OF THE BUTTOCKS.——
"FRANK" AND THE SECRET
OF THE SPANKING.

Next morning, "Frank" got down to breakfast before me,
and when I entered the room she welcomed me with a smiling face; looking, in spite of her boy's dress, so fresh, rosy,
and pretty, that I felt inclined to take her up in my arms
and kiss her red lips. "How is it, this morning?" I asked, in
a joking way. This question made her blush a little, but she
answered readily that "it" was much better, she could sit
down comfortably; but that the marks were still very plain.
After breakfast when I set her the tasks for the day, I changed
the whole of her studies, making them less abstruse, and more

suitable to a girl. She seemed to be glad of the change, and went off cheerfully with her books to the library.

So everything went on as usual; time passed, and Christmas week arrived when, according to my custom as head of the family, I had a large party of relatives of both sexes to stay with me; every bedroom in the old house being filled. "Frank,"—whom I introduced as a young friend come to live with me for a time,—soon became a favourite with the ladies, who all said, "he was such a pretty boy"; and her quiet, well-bred manner made her popular with the gentlemen. Not one of my guests ever had the slightest suspicion that my young friend was a girl.

That year, it happened to be what is commonly called an "old-fashioned Christmas," that is, there was plenty of frost and snow; the children of the village sang carols, and the waifs played at midnight in a most dismal way. The great hall, with its trophies of arms and the chase, was decorated with holly and mistletoe, under which the usual kissing took place. I know I kissed several pretty cousins. There was a yule-log burning on the queer old hearth, with its massive carved brass dogs; we had a wassail bowl; we had the inevitable turkey, and plum pudding; and we all, I think, eat more than was good for us; and in short, we went through all the usual rather dreary festivities which are thought proper at that season of the year.

The week passed over pleasantly, but I was glad when all was over, and my relatives had gone away. I had got so accustomed to living by myself in my old house, that the presence of a number of people put me out of my way; and, as I was not a family man, I had found the constant talk about domestic matters, carried on by my female relatives, most decidedly tiresome. So with a feeling of relief I returned to my usual habits, amusing myself by day hunting or shooting, and on the nights when I was at home, I always had "Frank" to amuse me with her lively chatter, and quaint remarks on things in general. She was sometimes idle, and occasionally a little wilful, but she never committed an offence of sufficient gravity to necessitate a whipping; and though I often felt very much inclined to take a look at her bottom, I had determined never to make her let down her trousers unless she really deservèd punishment.

I frequently went up to town for a day or two, on business, or pleasure, and on those occasions I stayed with Maud, who always appeared glad to see me; and, as I had now become a "lover of the rod," it was not long before I introduced it to the notice of my young lady. On one of my visits, I took with me a nice little birch, prettily tied up with bows of blue ribbon, which I hid under the pillow when we were going to bed at night. Maud had not noticed anything, and she was soon locked in my arms in a close embrace. Then we had a little talk, followed by another embrace, after which we both fell asleep lying on our sides, spoon fashion, Maud's warm, soft-skinned bottom being closely pressed against my belly, while my tool lay between her thighs. When I woke next morning, it was broad daylight, and I had a splendid erection. Maud was still asleep, but I soon roused her, and when she was fairly awake, I told her how I had lately taken a great fancy for inflicting corporal punishment; then, producing the rod from under the pillow, I asked her to let me give her a slight birching.

She sat up in bed and stared at me with her big, brown eyes, in utter astonishment for a moment; then she began to laugh; saying that she had never heard of such a thing; that she could not understand why I should take pleasure in giving her pain. I said that I would not hurt her much, only just make her tingle a little; and as she was a good-natured little woman, she soon consented to let me birch her.

She laid herself down at full length, and I pulled down the bedclothes, and rolled her night-dress up to her shoulders so that her pretty, plump, white body was entirely naked. Then I birched her gently till a pink tinge showed on her skin, and she rolled over on to her back saying that she had had enough, and that her bottom was smarting.

I was very much excited, and my prick was rampant,

so I put my arms round her, as she lay with outstretched legs, and gave her the lustiest poke I had ever given her, making her bound under me, and wriggle her bottom in rare style; and when all was over, and she had recovered her breath, she remarked with a laugh, that I had never done it to her with such vigour before, and she added, she never would have believed that I could have got so excited by merely birching her bottom. I laughed, gave her a kiss, and told her that it was a well-known fact that the sexual powers of men are always increased by whipping females, or by see-ing them whipped.

After that, whenever I spent a night with her, I always gave her a touch of the rod, so that in time she grew accus-tomed to it, and was able to take a tolerably smart birching. And I got fonder of it than ever as I found it always in-creased the pleasure of the poke, which, as a matter of course, followed the application of the rod.

But though I enjoyed using the birch in fun, I was al-ways wishing for a chance to use it in reality.

All this, however, is by the way.

One night, after dinner, we were as usual, sitting by the fire; I was smoking and "Frank" was reading; when, just to hear what she would say, I said: " 'Frank,' I think I must send you to school. It will do you good to mix with other boys; and you will learn more."

A look of fright came to her face, and the colour rushed up to her cheeks.

"Oh," she said earnestly, "don't send me to school. I don't want to mix with other boys. I am very happy here with you; and I am sure I am learning quite enough."

"You ought to be out every day playing football with lads of your own age."

"Oh, it is such a rough game. I should not like to play it."

I laughed, saying, with affected sarcasm: "I am afraid you are rather a milksop."

The tears came into her eyes, and she looked so dis-

tressed, that I did not chaff her any more; so she soon recovered her equanimity, and then we had a game of chess.

A few days after this, I had the double pleasure of seeing her bottom, and whipping it for an act of gross disobedience.

My library is an extensive one, containing a large col-
lection of standard works on all subjects, and a great number
of novels. I also had at that time, several books of the most
erotic description, illustrated with coloured plates. These
books were kept separate from the others, locked up in a
small bookcase, the key of which was always in my possession.

"Frank" was fond of reading, and she had the run of the
whole library, with the exception of the locked-up books.

I knew her to be a perfectly innocent girl, and I meant
to keep her so for the present. She had several times asked
me why I kept the books locked up, and she also frequently
begged me to let her see them; but I had always refused,
and I had also warned her not to attempt to open the bookcase. No doubt her curiosity was aroused by my refusal, and,
with the wilfulness of her sex, she had made up her mind
to see those particular books, although all the other volumes
in the library were open to her.

One morning, I had gone out hunting, fully expecting
to be away the whole day; but my horse cast a shoe, and
went lame, so I had to lead him home, where I arrived at
two o'clock. After I had changed my things, and had my
lunch, I went up to the library, finding that the door was
open, and on looking in, I saw my young friend standing in
front of the locked bookcase, holding in her hands a bunch
of keys, and trying to find one which would open the lock.
I watched her unsuccessful attempts for a moment or two,
then I went into the room. On seeing me, she was utterly
taken aback,—for she had thought me miles away,—she
dropped the keys on the floor, turned pale, and stood staring at me, apparently quite unable to say a word.

"Aha! you naughty boy. I have caught you nicely!" I exclaimed. "How dare you attempt to open that bookcase, against my express orders?"

I was angry with her, but at the same time I was glad she had given me an excuse for baring her bottom. I did not intend to birch her, as I thought it would be more exciting to take her across my knees and spank her.

She could see from my face that I was angry, and no doubt she guessed that I was going to flog her; but as she was a plucky girl, she did not whine, or beg to be let off; she merely cast a deprecating look at me, and stood silently awaiting her fate—blushing of course.

"I will not birch you this time, but I will spank you. Take off your coat. Come here," I said, seating myself on a chair.

She seemed to be rather relieved on hearing that she was not going to be birched, and at once took off her jacket, and came up to me.

Taking hold of her, I laid her across my knees in the orthodox position for receiving a spanking. I then began to prepare her for punishment. And I may here remark, that to a "lover of the rod," the preparing of a culprit for punishment is always a most pleasing task, which should be done as slowly as possible. It is a great mistake to lay bare at once the posteriors of the victim.

If the subject to be operated upon happens to be a female, her dress should be first turned well up, then her petticoats one by one, and lastly her chemise; then her drawers should be quietly unfastened and pulled down to her knees. But to proceed. I unfastened her braces back and front, unbuttoned her trousers, and pulled them down to her ankles; then carefully rolling up her shirt, I tucked the tail under the back part of her waistcoat. Then I gazed with a strong feeling of sensual pleasure, and a very stiff cock, at her pretty bottom, thighs, and legs, all of which seemed to have grown bigger since I had last seen them. I was in no hurry to begin the spanking; so I lectured her on her disobedience, while feasting my eyes on her naked charms and I could not resist passing my hand two or three times over her milk-white, satin-like skin, at the same time gently pressing the swelling hemispheres of plump flesh; but I resisted my desire to thrust my hand between her thighs, which she kept tightly pressed together. It was delicious to touch her cool, soft skin, but it would be still more delightful to watch the lily-like surface changing to a rosy red under the slaps of my hand. All this time she had been lying quietly,—though no doubt in dire suspense—in a curved position across my thighs, her hands resting on the floor, and the middle part of her body pressing against my upright tool which felt as if it were going to burst through my trousers.

Placing my left arm over her loins, I held her firmly in position, then, raising my right hand, I brought it down upon the middle of the right cheek of her bottom; a loud "smack," resounded through the room, and though I had not applied the slap with any great force, the marks of my four fingers and thumb were instantly printed in red on her white, delicate skin, and she flinched, uttering a slight ejaculation of pain. Again my hand rose and fell, this time on the left cheek, which also at once became marked with the red imprints of my fingers, and again she shrunk under the slap, a slight moan escaping from her lips.

I went on spanking her, smartly but not severely, striking alternately the right and left cheek of her bottom; my hand each time rebounding from her firm elastic flesh. Her skin grew redder and redder, and as the smarting pain increased, she burst into tears, and began to wriggle about on my lap, and in her wriggles her naked belly rubbed against and pressed my tool, which was sticking up inside my trousers, as stiff as a bar of iron. This friction excited in me an intensely lascivious feeling, and I held her tightly pressed down upon my thighs so that I might feel the writhing of her body as much as possible. The sensation was exquisite!

But I was soon obliged to stop spanking her, for had I gone on, the rubbing of her belly against my prick would have made me "spend," which I did not wish to do. Besides I did not want to punish her severely.

I had given her a couple of dozen smacks, which she had borne very bravely; for though her bottom must have smarted considerably under the slaps; judging from the way she had wriggled and cried, she had never attempted to put her hands behind her, nor had she once screamed.

I let her get off my knees, but as I was not yet tired of looking at her nakedness, I told her to kneel upon a chair, with her back towards me, and her trousers down. Holding her open trousers with one hand, she shuffled over to a chair, placing herself in the required position, without uttering a word; and again I admired her shapely young figure, and her rose-red bottom which contrasted so strongly with her milk-white thighs. After gazing at the charming spectacle for a minute or two, I told her to button up, which she did with her head hanging down, her tearful eyes fixed on the floor, and a very red face—her bottom was redder though.

I told her she might go, and she quickly scuttled out of the room.

I leant back in my chair, feeling very randy, and I would have given anything to have got hold of a woman at that moment. There were plenty of "Polls" in Winchester,—some of them very nice,—but it was hardly worth while going to the town; for, by the time I got there, all my excitement would have passed off. So I fell back on the soothing weed; and lighting a big cigar, I settled myself in an easy-chair for a comfortable smoke; and by the time I had finished the cigar, my desire was no longer keen.

I did not see the girl again until we met at dinner, when she took her seat quite comfortably, apparently none the worse for the spanking. She was rather quiet and subdued at first, but after she had had some soup, and a bit of fish, and had drunk the glass of wine I gave her, she began to talk.

When the butler had left the room, I put a few leading questions to her, and she told me, shyly, that the spanking I had given her, was not so severe as the spankings she had received from the lady; she also informed me that the three spankings had been inflicted with a thick-soled slipper on three successive days; and her bottom in consequence had become so bruised, that it had turned black and blue, remaining so for some time.

Then, after one or two more questions, she told me that though the spankings had been severe, they were not nearly so painful as the birching I had given her for striking Jane. She clasped her hands, and seemed to shudder at the recollection of that flogging.

I tried to get her to tell me what had caused the lady to spank her so severely; but she would not give me any information, and she looked so distressed when I pressed her, that I ceased questioning her on the subject.

I then told her to get the novel we were both interested in at that time, and read aloud to me, a thing she often did, for I liked listening to her, as she had a musical voice, and she read well, with good intonation, and proper emphasis. She got the book, curled herself up in an arm-chair opposite me, and in a short time we were both deeply interested in the story, which happened to be the "Moonstone," by Wilkie Collins.

She read to me for an hour, and then I sent her to bed.

# V

"FRANK'S" DEVELOPMENT.———MAUD'S BIG BOT-
TOM.———AN AFTERNOON IN THE ARBOUR.———HOW
TOM WAS SPANKED AND HOW "FRANK'S" HAND
WANDERED.———THE MOTHER'S COMPLAINT.———
"FRANK" PAYS THE PIPER.———A SEVERE FLOG-
GING.———BOUND AND BIRCHED.———THE
ANNIVERSARY.———"FRANK'S" GRATI-
TUDE.———THE CURTAIN STILL
NOT LIFTED.

I will now pass over a space of time. It was the middle of
June; "Frank" had been with me over nine months, and she
said she was between fifteen and sixteen years of age. She
had grown a little taller, and the contours of her figure had
become rounder, but she still looked quite like a boy, in her
male attire; for I had taken care that she should always be
dressed in long loose jackets which concealed the swell of
her bust, and the breadth of her hips; and so far, the secret
of her sex was known to no one but myself.

During the past months, I had the pleasure of taking
down her trousers,—though not as often as I should have
liked,—and each time I saw her half-naked figure it appeared

to have become more developed; the bottom broader, and plumper, the thighs rounder, and the calves of the legs larger; and while looking at these uncovered charms, I could quite believe she was the age she represented herself to be.

I never birched her now when she committed an offence, because I preferred to spank her while she lay over my knees, on account of the intense sensual pleasure I experienced where her belly rubbed against my tool, in her writhings. For, though I never spanked her severely, yet the smarting pain always made her twist herself about in a lively manner; causing me once, much against my will, to spend profusely; thereby cutting short my pleasurable sensations.

She always bore her punishment pluckily, she would cry, and wriggle, but she never made a noise by squealing out loud; and after the smart had passed off, she would become quite composed, never showing the least sulkiness, nor did she blush, or look shyly at me as she formerly had. In fact, she appeared to take her occasional spankings as a matter of course; knowing that I never gave her a whipping unless she deserved it. Whenever I did happen to take her across my knees, I really believe I was the more moved of the two— in a different way, of course—for I am sure that I was always more affected by the tickling of my prick, than she was affected by the smarting of her bottom.

I had grown fond of her, and I think she had begun to have a tender feeling for me, for she would sometimes sit on a stool at my feet, and nestle close up to me, resting her head against my knee in quite the girlish way, and looking up at me, with an affectionate smile. On those occasions, I had some difficulty in preventing myself taking the dear little creature up in my arms and kissing her all over, at the same time telling her that I knew she was a girl.

But I always managed to restrain myself. There was no hurry, and I intended to wait some time longer before attempting to "pluck the rose."

I frequently went away, for a few days at a time, to

London or other places, and whenever I returned home, "Frank" always welcomed me most warmly, her eyes sparkling, and her cheeks flushing with pleasure; she would take my hand and press it between hers; and I am sure, had I given her the least encouragement, she would have kissed me. But I used merely to shake hands with her in the ordinary male way, and ask her some trivial questions.

The weather at this time was glorious, and the country was in its full summer beauty, so "Frank" and I spent a good deal of our time in the open air, walking, or driving. I had wished her to learn to ride, but she always refused, and I think I knew the reason of her refusal. She did not like to ride astride, which she would have been obliged to do in her character as a boy.

And so the days slipped by; the girl being my constant companion, and I thought I knew her disposition and tastes completely; but, later on, I found that I did not know quite everything.

Towards the end of July I went up to London, where I spent ten days very pleasantly, as I knew numbers of people, and always had plenty of invitations of all sorts; moreover, there was Maud. I slept with her every night, and in the mornings I always renewed my vigour by birching her big, white bottom till it turned as red as a rose; the smarting pain making the tears come into her eyes. But she was very plucky; she would bury her face in the pillow, and allow me to go on whipping her till at last she could bear no more. Then she would roll over on to her back, and with outstretched legs, flushed cheeks, and her eyes sparkling through the tears that filled them, she would wait for the furious assault which was soon made upon her by me.

On my return to Oakhurst, "Frank," as usual, was delighted to see me, and she hovered about me all the evening in a most affectionate way. But I was destined soon to see a curious phase in her character, one hitherto unknown to me. About a week after my return, on a beautiful afternoon, I took a book and went out into the grounds, intending to go and read in an arbour which had been built under two large oak trees at some distance from the house. This arbour was a favourite resort of mine on a hot day, as the place was always cool and shady, being constructed of lattice work, and covered with creepers of various sorts. It was furnished with a couple of low, round, Moorish tables for holding coffee cups; there was a long cane chair well-cushioned, and on the floor there were two or three Persian rugs.

On approaching the arbour, I heard voices: one being "Frank's," and the other was the voice of a child. Now, as I had never before known "Frank" bring a child of any sort into the grounds, I felt rather curious, and I wished to see what was going on inside the arbour, without being seen myself. So I did not go into the place, but slipped quietly round to the back, and peeped in through the creeper-covered lattice work. "Frank's" companion was a little boy between nine and ten years old, whom I recognized as one of the children of a most respectable woman named Mrs. Barker, the wife of a gardener who lived in a cottage near my lodge-gates, but who was not in my employ.

I was aware that all Barker's children were known by "Frank," but I did not think she would have associated with any one of them.

The boy, Tom, was a good-looking little fellow, with dark eyes, and curly, brown hair; he was clean, and was neatly dressed in a knickerbocker suit.

"Frank" and he, apparently on very friendly terms, were sitting side by side on the long chair. I watched, and listened attentively. The first thing I heard "Frank" say, astonished me. She put a question to the boy.

"Have you ever been spanked?"

"Yes, Master Francis," replied Tom. "My mother often gives me a spanking."

"Then you know what it feels like?"

"Oh, yes. I knows very well. Do you, master?" said little Tom, grinning.

"Never you mind," said "Frank," shortly. Then she went

on. "I will give you six-pence if you let me spank you. I won't hurt you."

I pricked up my ears, and smiled, on hearing the cool request made by "Master Francis." Tom laughed, but at once agreed to let himself be spanked; stipulating, however, that he was not to be hurt.

I looked on with increased interest. The little affair was getting exciting.

"Master Francis" lost no time, but at once laid the little boy across her knees, unbuttoned his knickerbockers, pulled them down to his knees, and tucked up his shirt, as coolly and methodically as if she had been accustomed to the job. I laughed silently at the girl's deliberate way of setting to work at her strange task. The boy had a chubby little bottom, which she looked at for a moment or two; then, with her right hand she stroked and squeezed the boy's flesh,—exactly in the same way as I had often stroked and squeezed hers —and at the same time she put her left hand under his belly, and kept it there, her fingers, no doubt, touching his little prick.

I saw her face suddenly flush, her bosom heaved, and her eyes sparkled.

"Aha, Miss!" I said to myself, with a chuckle, "you have your hand on it for the first time in your life, but not for the last, I'll bet!"

The boy did not move; and after a moment or two, she took away her hand; then putting her arm over his loins she held him in position, and began to spank him; gently at first, but she seemed gradually to get excited, and she spanked harder and harder, redding the boy's skin at each smack. He began to cry loudly, and writhe, but she held him firmly down, and spanked away vigorously, making the urchin scream, kick up his legs in pain, and put his hands behind him. She stopped for a moment, seized his wrists, and put her right leg over his legs, then went on spanking the boy, in spite of his yells and struggles, until his bottom was crimson. Then she ceased, and let him roll off her lap on to the floor, where he lay on his face, howling lustily, with his knickerbockers down, and his scarlet bottom bare. He evidently never had had such a spanking in his life.

"Frank" was quite out of breath; her face was very much flushed, and I could see her bosom rising and falling, under her jacket. She was obviously agreeably excited; there was a pleased expression on the face, her eyes twinkled, and her lips were curved with a slight smile.

Rising from her seat, she lifted the squalling child on to his feet, buttoned up his knickerbockers, and tried to soothe him, but in vain. His bottom must have been smarting considerably; he was thoroughly frightened, and he sobbed and cried, vowing that he would tell his mother. Then, without waiting for his sorely earned sixpence, he ran off as fast as he could.

I had been extremely amused by the scene I had witnessed, but I was very much surprised at "Frank's" proceedings. I did not think she would have been up to such tricks. Leaving her in the arbour, I slipped quietly away, walked back to the house, and went up to the library, where I sat down to think over the whole strange affair.

After turning over everything in my mind, I came to the conclusion, that the whippings the girl had received from me, had raised in her the desire to inflict corporal punishment on some one else. Such is often the case. And as she had come to puberty some time previously, her sexual instincts had awakened, and she, naturally, as a female, had chosen a boy as her victim, not only for the pleasure of spanking him, but also that she might make herself acquainted, by touch, with the male organ.

I expected I should soon hear more about the affair; as the boy would certainly tell his mother how he had been treated by "Master Francis," and the woman would most probably come to me and make a fuss.

In about half an hour's time "Frank" came into the

room, looking a little pale; and her manner was nervous. She took a chair near the window, sitting silent and thoughtful, but glancing every now and then at me, with a queer look in her eyes.

I had a strong inclination to laugh, and to tell her that I had seen her spanking Tom, and feeling his little tool; and I also had a desire to let her feel what a full grown prick was like. But I restrained myself.

"Where have you been?" I quietly asked.

She started, looked confused, and blushed. "I have been in the arbour."

"What were you doing there?" I inquired mischievously, suppressing a smile. She grew redder, and more confused, hesitated, and at last stammered out, that it was a very cool place to sit in. Then she took up a book and began to read, as if to avoid further questions.

I also began to read, and nothing more passed between us at that moment.

The windows were open, a cool breeze was blowing into the room, the leaves on the tree were rustling softly, and the birds were singing; everything was calm and peaceful, except "Frank," who was restless and fidgety.

I think an hour must have gone by, when a knock came at the door, and one of the maids appeared; saying, that Mrs. Barker was in the hall, and that she wished particularly to speak to me.

"Frank" put down the book, and stood up, looking very uncomfortable; no doubt guessing that Mrs. Barker had come to make a complaint.

I went down to the hall, where I found the woman in a great state of indignation; and she at once poured out her story; telling me how Master Francis had cruelly spanked her little boy Tom, for no reason whatever; that his little bottom was very sore, and as red as fire; that she would have the law of Master Francis; and all that sort of thing.

I soothed the justly irritated woman with soft words,

gave her a sovereign, and told her that I would punish "Master Francis" for what "he" had done.

Mrs. Barker was a sensible woman; she thanked me for the money, and took her departure, perfectly satisfied.

I was sorry the affair had occurred, as I did not want to have any scandal about "Frank," and I was afraid the woman would talk, although she had promised to keep silence.

I was not a bit angry with "Frank"—quite the contrary. In fact, I had a sort of fellow-feeling with her. She liked spanking; so did I. Besides I could not help thinking that it was my whipping her, that had made her want to whip. Nevertheless, I should have to punish her, as I had promised to do so.

I went back to the library, where "Frank," looking very woebegone, was waiting for me. I put on a stern face, saying: "I suppose you can guess what Mrs. Barker had to say to me?"

"Yes," she replied in a low tone.

"Well, you are a nice boy, I must say. What on earth induced you to spank the unfortunate child?" I said, feigning great indignation.

She shifted her feet uneasily, blushed, twisted her fingers together nervously, and replied, in faltering accents: "Oh, I —can't—tell—exactly. You have—often—given me—a spanking; and I—I—think it has made me feel—a wish—to—spank some one too. I can't explain why."

"But why did you spank him so severely? His mother tells me his bottom is red and sore."

"I did not intend to spank him so hard, but somehow or other I got excited and hardly knew what I was doing. I am sorry I hurt him so much," she said blushing more hotly, and looking more confused and uncomfortable than ever. Then she added, with a catch in her voice, and with tears in her eyes: "I suppose you are going to flog me."

"Yes. I must birch you this time. Fetch me the rod," said I, handing her the key to the drawer in which the instrument of punishment was kept. I was sorry for the girl in one way; but on the other hand I was delighted at the idea of birching her; I had not had the pleasure of seeing her bottom for some time, nor had I birched her since the day on which I had flogged her so severely for striking Jane.

She went to the drawer, unlocked it, and brought me the rod, and as she handed it to me, she looked beseechingly at me, while the big tears overflowed her eyes and began to slowly trickle down her cheeks. "Oh, please don't birch me so hard as you did the last time," she pleaded. Then without another word, she took off her jacket, let down her trousers, and heaving a deep sigh, extended herself at full length on the sofa. Taking my handkerchief I tied her wrists together, a proceeding which frightened her; and in a quavering voice she said: "Oh, why have you tied me? I will lie quietly if you do not flog me very hard. Oh! please don't flog me very hard."

"I am going to give you a dozen smart cuts, and I have tied your wrists to prevent you putting your hands over your bottom in the middle of the punishment," I said, turning up her shirt, and tucking it well out of the way.

She gave a little sob, buried her face in the sofa cushion and a slight tremor passed over her. She dreaded the rod!

I took a long look at her plump, well-shaped bottom, exposed in full nakedness before me. The swelling cheeks in their milk-like whiteness were very pretty, but I thought they would look more sweet when they were blushing rosy red under the stinging kisses of the rod. I passed my hand caressingly several times over her cool, smooth, soft skin; and then, laying my hand firmly on her loins, I held her down, and began to birch her smartly; but not so severely as on the previous occasion. She burst into tears, and at each cut she gasped and shuddered, drawing in the cheeks of her bottom; and as the strokes continued to fall, her flesh began to twitch, she writhed and twisted, and cried bitterly with pain. Then, raising her head, she looked over her shoulder, and fixed her eyes, dilated with fear, on the dreaded rod each time it rose in the air; and each time the cut fell on her shrinking bottom, she flattened herself down on the sofa, throwing her hips from side to side with impatient jerks, and uttering little shrieks,—but not loud ones,—until the twelve strokes had been inflicted.

On the whole, she had borne her punishment fairly well, for it had been rather a severe one; her bottom being extremely red, and a good deal striped, when all was over.

I must confess that I had thoroughly enjoyed birching the girl, and, as a natural consequence, I had a very strong erection. I am not a cruel man under ordinary circumstances; but latterly, whenever I had seen the girl's bottom reddening and writhing in pain under my strokes, I had felt no pity for her sufferings; my only sensation being one of intense desire. Consequently, on this occasion, I was, as usual, full of lust, and I was strongly tempted to clasp the half-naked, crying girl in my arms, press my lips to the glowing cheeks of her pretty bottom, and finish the whole affair by turning her over on to her back, and taking her maidenhead then and there. However, I curbed my ardent desire; and to rid myself of the temptation, I untied her wrists, telling her she might go away.

She got off the sofa, standing for a moment or two with an expression of pain on her face, crying silently; her trousers hanging about her feet, and her legs bare. Then she buttoned up with trembling fingers, put on her jacket, and walked out of the room.

I sat down in an easy-chair, and lighting a cigar, began to smoke, thinking to myself that I had passed a rather exciting afternoon.

It was then five o'clock, and as I did not feel inclined to go out, I remained in the library, reading until it was time to dress for dinner.

When I reached the dining-room, "Frank" was not there, and as she had not made her appearance when the soup had been put upon the table, I sent one of the maids to find out what was the matter. In a short time she came back and told me that "Master Francis" was not coming down, as he had a bad headache. On hearing that I smiled, saying to myself that the poor little girl was suffering more from a bottom-ache than a headache. She did not come down at all that night, and I quite missed her as I sat by myself after dinner.

However, at breakfast next morning, she turned up, bright and fresh, greeting me quite in her usual manner, without the least sign of either sulkiness or shyness. On my making a few tender inquiries, she informed me that her bottom was still a good deal marked, and though it was a little sore she could sit down in comfort. Then she took her seat, smiling at me as if to prove her words, and ate her breakfast with a hearty appetite. She was, without doubt, a high-spirited, lovable girl, and I longed to kiss her.

A week passed without incident, and then I went to the seaside, leaving the girl at Oakhurst, very disconsolate, though she had not asked me to take her with me. No doubt she thought her secret would be more likely to be discovered if she left home.

I was away a month, and during the whole time I received a letter from "Frank," every three days; she wrote long, chatty letters, and I always liked reading them, for they showed that the girl was cheerful and happy.

I returned home in September, and by a curious coincidence, it happened to be the same day of the month, on which a year previously I had picked up "Master Francis." She had remembered the day, and after giving me a warm welcome in the hall, she followed me into the drawing-room, and, again taking my hand in hers, she told me how grateful she was for all my kindness; adding that she had been perfectly happy ever since she had come to Oakhurst; and she hoped I would let her remain with me. The girl had certainly always appeared to be happy; and moreover,

I think she had got to be very fond of me, in spite of the smart bottoms I had given her—perhaps she was fond of me because I *had* given her smart bottoms.

I settled down to the life I usually led at that period of the year; riding or shooting every day; going out to dinners or parties in the neighbourhood, and paying occasional visits to London.

"Frank" still continued to keep her true sex concealed.

# VI

THE CHOICE OF A PROFESSION.——THE STRUGGLE
TO BE SILENT.——HOW ANNA LEE STOLE THE
WATCH.——HORSED AND BIRCHED——THE MAN
WHO LOOKED ON.——BLOOD ON A BOTTOM.——THE
EFFECTS OF THE BIRCHING VIEW.——LUCY THE
HOUSEMAID.——AN ENJOYABLE ENCOUNTER.
——SHORT AND SWEET.——"FRANK"
PUTS A FEW QUESTIONS.

And now, to avoid unduly lengthening this veracious record
of events, I will pass over a period of many months; re-
suming the thread of my story at the time when "Frank"
had reached the age of seventeen-and-a-half years. She had
attained her full height, which was five feet, five inches; she
was prettier than ever, and her figure was well developed.
I could vouch for the lower half of her body, but I had not
as yet seen the upper half naked. Being now quite "grown
up," she always wore coats with long tails, and as she made
a very good-looking young "man," I often noticed my
parlourmaids casting admiring glances at "Mr. Francis," as
she was now called by the servants.

I always treated her as a lad, and had never allowed her to suspect that I had discovered her secret, as I was determined to wait until she herself made known her sex to me. I felt sure she would tell me some day; and then, most likely something would happen.

I was now really fond of her, and I could quite plainly see that she loved me, for she showed her affection in many little feminine ways, of which she was unconscious, but which would certainly have betrayed her secret, had I not already known it.

During the period which had passed, I had often been away from home, occasionally for a month at a time; but "Frank" had always remained at Oakhurst, never manifesting the least desire to leave the old place, even for a day. She had no girlish accomplishments, but she was fairly well-read, and on the whole, better educated than nine out of ten girls of her age; and though I no longer set her lessons, I still kept her under discipline, taking her across my knees, and spanking her, whenever her conduct gave me a reasonable excuse for doing so. And she was occasionally very wilful. And I must confess, that now she was a full-grown, well-developed young woman, I enjoyed, more than ever, taking down her trousers, and reddening her broad, plump bottom. I never spanked her severely, though I always took care to bring a blush to the white cheeks, and the smart was sufficient to cause the tears to rise to her eyes, and to make her squirm a little against my stiff prick; the friction invariably giving me extreme pleasure.

Big as she was, she never made the least objection to my taking her across my knees, and she did not appear to mind the punishment much.

Moreover, with the quick instinct of a woman she had, of late, seemed to divine that I liked spanking her; and I really think that she now and then behaved wilfully, merely that I might have a reason for whipping her. But it never seemed to strike her, that a young man between seventeen

and eighteen years of age would never have allowed me to
spank him like a child. She was not very consistent in her
impersonation of a young gentleman.

I do not know whether she had ever spanked any more
little boys, but I dare say she had; for when the desire to
inflict corporal punishment is once raised in a person, male,
or female, the passion generally remains. And she certainly
was possessed of the desire at the time she had spanked little
Tom.

She had quite lost her rather imperious way of dealing
with the servants, and they had all become devoted to her;
especially my own man Wilson, who somewhat neglected
me, while he looked carefully after everything belonging
to "our young gentleman," as he called "Frank" when speaking to her. I sometimes felt rather disturbed at the thought
of the scandal that would arise if the girl's secret was discovered; and it might be discovered at any moment. How the
ladies, young and old, in the neighbourhood would talk
about me, and lift up their hands in horror at the idea of my
having kept for three years at Oakhurst, a young girl dressed
up in boy's clothes. I do not much care what people say
about me; but for the sake of a quiet life, I did not want my
neighbours to find out anything about "Frank." Of course,
I should eventually have to send her away from Oakhurst,
but I intended always to take care of her. In the meantime,
she amused me, and I was looking forward to the moment,
when, all disguise thrown off, I should clasp her in my arms
and embrace her as a woman should be embraced by a man.

There is a proverb which says "everything comes to
him who waits."

I had waited a long time, but I did not think I should
have to wait much longer. The girl was certainly fond of me,
her temperament was warm, she liked to touch me, and
when she was sitting on a stool beside me, she often glanced
up in my face with a yearning look in her pretty blue eyes.

All these little signs were significant, and I was almost

certain that she would have let me do anything I liked to her. But, before I touched her, I wanted her to tell me, of her own accord, that she was a woman.

Although she had as yet never hinted at her true sex, she, with a curious perversity, always seemed to be annoyed when I talked to her as man to man; and one night, out of mischief, I teased her so much, that she was on the point of declaring herself.

We were sitting in the drawing-room after dinner, and I said: "Frank, you are now a young man, and you should be thinking of taking up some profession. I will do all that is necessary in regard to money. What would you like to be? You are too old for the army; but there is the law, the church, and the medical profession. Which of the three will you study for?"

"Oh," she exclaimed, turning quite pale, "I don't know I have never thought about anything of the sort. I have been so happy here with you."

"What! in spite of all the spankings?" I said, with a laugh.

She smiled faintly. "Yes, in spite of the spankings I don't mind them much; and you never give me one unless I deserve it."

I again laughed, saying: "No, I don't. think I do And I am very pleased to have you with me We get on together very well."

"Then let me stay with you," she put in, quickly.

"But I may get married some day, and then all our old habits would have to be changed, and you might feel dis-contented. That is why I think you had better adopt some profession, so as to become to a certain extent independent."

The idea of my marrying seemed to move the girl deeply; she coloured up, her lips trembled, and she looked at me with a most pathetic expression in her eyes. "Oh, dear me!" she said in a broken voice. "I never thought of that. Oh, what shall I do!" she added, bursting into tears.

I was sorry I had agitated the girl, but I laughed, saying in a bantering way:

"You silly lad. You are too big to cry like that. One would think you were a girl." She looked at me, with the big tears running down her cheeks, and said: "Oh I know I ought not to cry; but I can't help it. I,—I am"—she stopped suddenly and buried her face in her handkerchief.

I thought I had pushed the joke far enough; so I told her not to cry; that after all, there was plenty of time to think over the matter, and that she need not bother herself about it for the present.

She seemed to be satisfied with what I had said; and she dried her eyes, smiling gratefully at me, and in a short time she was chatting and laughing merrily. She was a light-hearted creature, who evidently thought that "sufficient for the day is the evil thereof." She played a game of chess, and afterwards she read to me for some time; then we parted for the night, with the secret still untold.

A fortnight passed without anything happening worth recording. Then certain events occurred, the details of which I will relate, though "Frank" had no part in the affairs.

One morning, just after breakfast, I was in the hall, fixing on one of the panels a number of Eastern weapons; when a young girl came in, bringing me a note from one of my neighbours, who had left it at the lodge with orders that it should be taken to me at once. The girl, named Anna Lee, was fifteen years old; she was a friendless waif who had been left in the village by a band of gipsies, five or six years previously; and she would have been sent to the workhouse, had it not been for the charity of my lodge-keeper, Mrs. Grove, who took the deserted child into her cottage, and had kept her ever since. The note required an answer; so, telling the girl to wait in the hall, I went up to the library to write a reply. I hastily scribbled a few lines, and then I went back to the hall, gave the note to Anna, and told her to take it to its destination without delay. She went away, and I finished arranging the trophy of arms; then I went to the little table on which I had placed my watch before beginning my work. I looked about carefully, but the watch was not to be found.

It was a massive, old-fashioned, gold lever, which had belonged to my father, consequently I valued it very highly. As no one had been in the hall but Anna Lee, I felt quite certain that she had stolen the watch. I was very angry, and at once made up my mind to go after the girl, hoping to be able to catch her before she had time to hide her booty; so without saying anything to my servants, I started off. Hurrying down the avenue, I passed through the lodge-gates out on to the road, and looked up and down it, but the girl was nowhere in sight; so I thought I had better go back to the lodge and speak to Mrs. Grove.

She received me with great respect and ceremony, ushered me into her neat little sitting-room, and made me sit in the best chair, while she stood before me, waiting to hear what I had to say.

Mrs. Grove was about forty-five years of age; a good-looking buxom woman, whose husband had been lodge-keeper; and on his death I had allowed her to remain in charge of the lodge, as she was quite capable of performing all the duties of lodge-keeper, with the assistance of her grown-up daughter.

Mrs. Grove had been born and brought up on the estate, so she was devoted to me, and to everything connected with Oakhurst.

I told her what had happened, and asked her to keep an eye on Anna's proceedings, and if possible, find out what she had done with the watch.

The worthy woman was quite concerned on hearing of my loss, and she was furious with Anna, who was, she said, a naughty, troublesome girl in every way. Then, she went on: "Anna may not have hidden the watch anywhere as yet; perhaps she has got it on her person; so when she comes back I will search her, and if I *do* find the watch, I will give her the soundest birching she has ever had in her life—and she has had many a one from me."

I smiled at the emphatic way she spoke, thinking to myself that if the watch *was* found on Anna, she would get her bottom well warmed.

Mrs. Grove continued: "If you have time, sir, I should like you to wait and see what happens, and if I have to birch the girl, I should very much like you to be present. I think it would be a bit of satisfaction to you to see her well whipped for all the bother she has given you."

I was rather surprised at Mrs. Grove offering to let me see her birch the girl, but I was delighted with the offer; for since I had become a "lover of the rod," I had often had a wish to see a girl birched, and now there was a chance of my wish being gratified. It would be deliciously exciting to watch a bottom, that I had never seen before, reddening under the strokes of a birch-rod wielded by a buxom woman. My cock began to stiffen at the thought!

I said that I would wait and see the affair out, whatever happened; then I added: "I have no doubt that Anna is the thief, but if she has not got the watch in her possession when she comes back, we can do nothing. We cannot birch her without proof that she has stolen the watch."

"No, sir, I suppose not," said Mrs. Grove in a tone of regret.

She had hardly finished speaking, when we heard the outer door opened, and then closed, as the girl entered the cottage. Mrs. Grove called her, and she came into the little parlour, jauntily, but when she saw me, she started and looked rather uneasy for a moment; then she informed me that she had delivered the letter.

Anna Lee, as I have before said, was a little over fifteen years of age, a well-grown sturdy wench, not bad-looking, but her face had a saucy expression; she had a dark, olive complexion; black hair; and bold, black eyes; very white teeth; and red lips. She was supposed to have gipsy blood in her, and she certainly looked as if she had. She was neatly dressed in a cotton frock, with a white apron, and on her head she wore a linen sun-bonnet with scarlet ribbons. Altogether she was a nice morsel for the birch. She took off her bonnet, and was about to quit the room, when she was stopped by Mrs. Grove; who did not waste words, but at once came to the point. She said: "You were up at the house a short time ago. The master's watch was stolen out of the hall. I believe you stole it. I am going to search you." So saying, she caught hold of Anna, who was so taken aback that she never even denied the charge, but stood perfectly still during the whole time she was being searched. Mrs. Grove first felt in the girl's pocket; then she passed her hand down the girl's arms to see if the watch was hidden in her sleeves; then unfastening the front of her dress, she thrust her hand down her bosom, but she did not find the object of her search. So I began to think that Anna had not got the watch on her person, and consequently that I should not have the pleasure of seeing her bottom whipped.

But Mrs. Grove had not finished her search; and much to my surprise, she put both her hands up under the girl's clothes, and after a little groping, cried out in a tone of triumph, "I've got it, sir!" at the same time producing the watch, which Anna had managed to stow away in some of the mysterious recesses of her underclothing.

The culprit, thus caught almost red-handed, did not say a word. She turned a little pale, a sullen expression came to her face, and she stood twisting the hem of her apron between her fingers.

"Now, you hussy!" said Mrs. Grove, "you shall catch it! I'll make your bottom smart, you horrid young thief."

Then, going to the door, she called out to her daughter: "Come here, Fanny, and bring the rod with you."

The girl's black eyes flashed, and she darted a look of hatred at Mrs. Grove, saying, sullenly: "It is not right that I should be flogged before a gentleman."

"Hold your tongue, you bad girl! You ought to be

publicly flogged in the middle of the village!" said Mrs. Grove angrily.

At that moment, Fanny came into the room, carrying in her hand a formidable looking birch-rod, which she placed on the table. This rod was much longer, and bigger in every way than the one I had used on "Frank."

Fanny was about twenty-three years old; a tall, strapping, broad-shouldered country lass, as strong as an average man. Her mother briefly told her what Anna had done; adding: "I am going to flog her soundly. Take her up, and mind you hold her fast."

Fanny glanced at me, blushing a little, but said quietly: "All right, mother; I'll hold her tight. This will not be the first time I have hoisted her for you." She seized Anna's wrists, turned half round, and swung the big girl easily up on her broad back; then slightly separating her feet, and bending well forward, she brought the culprit's body into a curved position, with her bottom well thrown out, at a most convenient angle for receiving the punishment.

Mrs. Grove stepped forward, and rolled the girl's skirt up to her shoulders, doing the same with her petticoats and chemise, which, though coarse, were clean; then she carefully pinned up all the garments in such a way that they could not fall down while the culprit was being birched.

As Anna wore no drawers, she was now naked from her waist to the tops of her stockings. For her age, she was remarkably well developed; her bottom was broad and fleshy—there was plenty of room for the birch to play on—her thighs were large, and she had rather thick legs, which were encased in white cotton stockings, gartered above her knees with black ribbons. Her skin, clean, and wholesome-looking, was of an olive tint, rather coarse in texture, but quite smooth; and I at once noticed that both of her round, plump buttocks were marked with faint, pink lines, evidently the traces of a flogging which had been inflicted not many days previously. Mrs. Grove rolled up her sleeve, displaying a muscular arm; then, taking up the rod, she lightly touched the girl's bottom with the end of the twigs, pointing out the pink marks on her skin, saying: "There, sir. Those are the marks left by a birching I gave the wicked girl, only three days ago, for being saucy to me." A slight shudder passed over the culprit, as she felt the birch touching her bare flesh, but she did not utter a word.

"How many strokes shall I give her, sir?" asked Mrs. Grove, as she drew the rod through the fingers of her left hand, so as to separate the bristly twigs.

My eyes were fixed on the girl's fat bottom. I was greatly excited, and I had a stiff prick, so that it was as much as I could do to preserve a calm, judicial demeanour while I replied to the question.

"I think that eighteen strokes will be sufficient, if you lay them on well."

Mrs. Grove smiled, saying: "Never fear, sir. I will lay them on in a way that will astonish her. She is going to get a birching such as she has never had in her life before."

Anna moved uneasily on her "horse's" back!

Raising the rod high in the air, the woman laid on the first cut with considerable force. Anna's plump flesh quivered involuntarily, and long purplish streaks at once showed on her olive skin: she gave a convulsive start, contracted the cheeks of her bottom, threw back her head with a jerk, and drew her breath through her teeth sharply, with a hissing sound. Again and again, the stinging rod swept through the air, falling with a loud-sounding "swish" on the culprit's writhing bottom; the sharp pain seemed to take her breath away; she gasped, and made a gurgling noise in her throat; clenching her teeth so tightly that I could see the outline of her jaws through her cheeks, while the tears streamed from her eyes, but she did not scream.

Swish! Swish! Swish! She could no longer suppress her cries, and a long, shrill shriek followed each slashing cut a it scored her red buttocks.

Swish! Swish! Swish! Mrs. Grove birched slowly, pausing between each cut, so that the culprit felt the full sting of the stroke, before the next one was applied. She roared, and begged for mercy; and she struggled and plunged so violently, that Fanny, strong as she was, staggered once or twice. Swish! Swish! Swish! Swish! Her bottom was rough with weals, scarlet in colour, and speckled with livid dots. Screaming loudly, and entreating to be let off, she drew up her legs, and kicked them about in all directions, and arching her loins, she twisted her body from side to side, so that I occasionally caught sight of her small cunt, which was just beginning to be fledged with curly, black hair; and I noticed that the little, pink lips were gaping slightly, as if mutely sympathising with the smarting bottom.

Swish! Swish! Swish! Swish! The rod rose and fell, slowly and relentlessly; the girl's shrieks became piercing. She struggled hard, kicking vigorously, and a few small drops of blood appeared on each cheek of her crimson bottom.

Swish! The last cut fell on the quivering flesh of the shrieking girl: and Mrs. Grove, putting down the rod, wiped her hot face with her apron. Then she unpinned the girl's clothes, letting them fall down over her scarified bottom; which had looked very much like a great plum-pudding. Fanny let go the victim's wrists, and she stood on the floor, crying, twisting herself about, and actually dancing with the smarting pain of her well-birched bottom. Mrs. Grove smiled grimly, saying: "There, Anna, I don't think you will steal anything the next time you are sent to the house on a message. Go away."

The sobbing girl, with pain-drawn, scarlet face, trembling lips, and cheeks furrowed by tears, limped stiffly out of the room, with her hands pressed to her sore bottom.

I glanced at Fanny, noticing that she was smiling, and that her eyes were sparkling; but when she saw me looking at her, she became grave, and blushed; then taking up the rod, she hastily left the room.

Mrs. Grove turned to me, saying: "Well, sir, I hope you are satisfied with the flogging I gave Anna. She will remember it for some time. She won't be able to sit down comfortably for days."

I was now more excited than ever, and I had some difficulty in preventing myself showing my feelings, but I told Mrs. Grove, as calmly as possible, that I was perfectly satisfied, and also much obliged to her for the trouble she had taken. Then I left the lodge, filled with an intense desire; for, strange to say, I had been more inflamed by the sight of the whipping I had just seen inflicted, than I ever had been when whipping "Frank." The punishment had been so severe; the agonized contortions of the girl's naked body had seemed to me voluptuous: the quivering of her flesh; and the appearance of her blood-spotted bottom; the occasional glimpses of her little gaping cunt. All these things had set my blood on fire; my cock felt as if it would burst, and my balls ached. I hurried back to the house, went up to my bedroom, shut myself in, without taking notice of anything, and threw myself into an easy-chair; my tool still in full erection.

Then I saw that one of the housemaids, named Lucy, was in the room, dusting it. She was about twenty-five years old, a good-looking, and very plump young woman, with a quantity of dark brown hair, and big, hazel eyes. She had been a little startled by my very abrupt entrance, and she stood gazing at me. I, in my turn, gazed at her; and very "fetching" she looked to me, at that moment, in her clean, well-fitting, pink cotton dress, which showed off the swelling contours of her full bosom, and the breadth of her hips.

It had hitherto been my rule never to take liberties with my female servants; not, I must say, from any moral scruples, but simply because I thought the practice dangerous, and likely to lead to trouble of all sorts. Moreover, I am fastidious, and servant girls are not always so clean, either in person, or linen, as they should be.

But now, my standing prick made me forget everything
but the fact that I wanted a woman; and as there was one
in the room, I determined to make an attempt on her virtue.
I knew nothing whatever about her; she might be a virgin,
or she might not. If she was a virgin, she would soon repulse
me; if she was not, she would most likely let me "have" her.

All these thoughts passed rapidly through my head as
I looked at the trim housemaid. "Lucy," I said, "you are a
very pretty young woman."

She looked surprised, for I had never made such a
remark to her before; then she simpered, seemingly pleased
with the compliment. I then went boldly up to her, put my
arm round her waist, and pressed my mouth on her red lips,
in a hot kiss. She struggled a little, but I noticed that she did
not blush, or seem at all frightened at my sudden assault, so
giving her another kiss, I sat down on a chair, and pulled
her on to my knees.

She resisted in a half-hearted way, saying: "Let me go,
sir! Let me go!" But I held her round the waist with one
arm, and kissed her warmly, at the same time feeling the
outlines of her bubbies through her dress. Then I slipped
my hand under her petticoats, and took hold of the calf
of her leg; this made her struggle a little more, and she
exclaimed: "Oh, don't do that, sir! Take away your hand!
I won't allow you to do that!" But as she made no violent
effort to escape, I pushed my hand further up her clothes,
and opening the slit of her drawers, I thrust my hand between her closely-shut thighs, and with my forefinger,
tickled the "pleasurable spot," which was thickly covered
with soft, curly hair. She now ceased struggling, and leant
back against my shoulder; her face grew red, her bosom
began to heave, and a sensuous look came into her eyes.
The woman had, without doubt, felt a man's hand on her
cunt before, or she would not have been so quiet.

I tickled her a little more, making her stiffen herself,
squirm about on my knees, and giggle; her breath came and

went, she was evidently excited, so I thought the moment had arrived for me to finish the job. Lifting her up in my arms, I carried her to the bed, and laid her down upon it, without her making the least resistance; and she lay quietly on her back with her hands over her face. It was plain that she intended to let me poke her, and I was glad of it, for had she resisted, I think I should have raped her, so excited was I at that moment.

I got up beside her, slipped both my hands under her clothes, unfastened her drawers, and pulled them right off her legs; then my hands roved freely over her very plump charms. I squeezed the cheeks of her large and fat bottom, stroked her great, round thighs, tickled her cunt again, and gently pulled the hair. Then I unfastened the front of her dress, and plunged my hand as deeply down between her big bubbies as her stays would allow. Unbuttoning my trousers, I let out my rampant prick, then I turned up all her clothes above her waist, so that I might inspect her naked figure; but she did not like being looked at, for she at once covered her slit with one hand, and tried to pull down her chemise with the other; saying: "Oh, do not expose me so!"

It is strange that some women who will let a man feel them, and poke them, do not like to let themselves be seen.

I laughed, and pulling her hand away, took a good look at everything she had; finding that she was clean in every respect, and that her linen was of a very good description; her limbs were shapely, her skin was white, and the curly hair shading the "spot" was light brown.

Stretching out her legs, I got between them, and inserted the tip of my tool into her cunt, which was fairly tight; then, clasping her in my arms, I forced the weapon deeply into the sheath, and began to poke her vigorously.

She seemed to enjoy it, for she threw her arms round me, and bucked up well to meet my thrusts; but as I was so much excited, the fun did not last long; in a moment or two the spasm seized me, and I sent the hot fluid in jets up her vagina, while she wriggled her bottom, and squirmed about under me until she had received all I had to give.

I pulled down her clothes, and she looked up in my face, smiling. Her own face had a contented expression on it, and her eyes were glistening. "Oh, sir," she said, pretending to pout, "you should not have done that. You took me by surprise."

"Never mind, Lucy," I said, laughing. "You seemed to like it; and I am sure I did."

She giggled, and a slight blush appeared on her cheeks. Jumping off the bed, she calmly fastened up the bosom of her dress, and shook her petticoats straight; then going to the glass, she arranged her hair under her cap; and when she had settled everything to her satisfaction, she turned round, and looked roguishly at me.

I gave her a kiss, which she returned, and then she left the room, looking as fresh and tidy as if nothing had happened.

I performed some necessary ablutions, and sat down, feeling much better; and I said to myself that now the ice was broken, I would often amuse myself by poking my plump and pretty young housemaid.

That night, after dinner, I told "Frank" how the watch had been stolen, and how it had been recovered. She listened attentively while I was speaking, and when I had finished she began to question me.

"Was the girl punished in any way?"

"Oh, yes," I replied. "The girl was 'horsed' on Fanny's back, and birched by Mrs. Grove."

"Did you see her birched?" "Frank" asked, in a tone of great interest.

"Yes, I did."

"Oh, did you really!" Then, with a humorous twinkle in her eyes, she said, demurely: "Was it not rather strange that you should be present while the girl was being birched?"

I laughed, saying: "Oh no, I don't think there was anything strange in my seeing her punished. I have been present on other occasions, at the birching of a girl."

"Oh, indeed! You never told me that before."

Again I laughed. "I don't tell you everything I see or do, Master Frank."

"No, I suppose you do not," she said smiling. Then she went on: "Did Mrs. Grove birch the girl as severely as you once birched me?"

"I should rather think she did," I replied. "Why, the birching I gave you was nothing compared to the birching the girl received. There were drops of blood on her bottom when the punishment was over."

"Oh, how dreadful!" said "Frank," shuddering a little. "How awfully sore she must be at this moment. It was sore for hours after my birching, although there was no blood."

"Perhaps you have a finer skin than Anna. But she will soon get over the pain, she is a strong girl, and her bottom will be healed in a few days." The subject then dropped, but "Frank" seemed to have been moved in some way,— whether it was pleasantly, or unpleasantly, I could not make out—by our talk about the flogging; she became silent and abstracted, occasionally looking at me in a peculiar way, and I thought that perhaps she was going to tell me her secret. But she did not, so I rallied her for sitting so silent, and told her to get a book and read to me.

She smiled, and getting up from her chair, went away to the library, returning in a short time with a volume of Shakespeare; then, seating herself near me, she read "The Tempest," in a way that showed she possessed a large amount of histrionic talent. The time passed quickly, and it was late before we separated for the night.

# ❧ VII ❧

After the little affairs last narrated, things went on very quietly. The weeks passed; it was again springtime, and the grounds round Oakhurst were looking most charming. The fine old trees, from which the place took its name, were bursting into leaf, the garden was full of crocuses, violets, daffodils, and all the various spring flowers, and the mossy banks were everywhere starred with primroses.

"Frank" was just eighteen years old, she had become quieter in many ways, but she was more woman-like and affectionate in her manner towards me, so that I felt sure the day was fast approaching when she would declare herself to me as a loving girl.

I was as fond of whipping as ever, and I often longed to see, and to spank her pretty bottom; but latterly, I never could find the least excuse for taking down her trousers; she was just a well-bred, well-conducted young lady dressed in male attire. I sometimes used to spend a few days in London, and on those occasions I generally visited Maud, who was still under my protection, though she had informed me that she was thinking of getting married. When I was at home, I could always, whenever I felt inclined, "have" Lucy, who, ever since the day on which I had first poked her, had manifested an affection for me, which at times I found rather awkward, as I did not wish to be found out in an intrigue with one of my own servant girls. But yet I did not like to snub her, for I always thoroughly enjoyed myself when I *did* poke her; moreover she allowed me to spank her; and she had a bottom that was well worth spanking; it was so broad, so fat and dimpled; yet withal it was firm, and I revelled in it; especially as she could take a spanking better than any woman I have ever come across.

I sometimes spanked her till my hand was sore, and her bottom was the colour of beetroot, and as hot as fire.

I occasionally gave a dinner party to the neighbouring squires and their families, and on those occasions, it always amused me to see "Frank" in correct evening dress, looking quite the "gentleman," taking into dinner, with perfect composure, some young lady, or buxom matron.

"He" always got on well with the ladies, to whom "he" was most polite and attentive; but since she had grown up, she had become shy with women, and they, I think, considered "him" rather a duffer, as "he" did not smoke, or ride to hounds, or go in for athletic sports of any kind. It had always been a source of wonder to me that none of the servants had ever any suspicion as to "Frank's" true sex; but it is a fact, that during the whole period of her stay at Oakhurst, she managed to keep her secret from every one but me.

The time passed on; and at the beginning of July, I

found that I should have to go up to London for some days, on business connected with the estate. I had not been away from home for a couple of months, and when "Frank" heard that I was going to town for a time, she became sad and dejected; and on the day of my departure, she hovered about me the whole time, and I could see that she could hardly keep back her tears.

She had never before shown so much emotion at my going away; so I thought I would chaff her a little, in a good-humoured way; but I could not get her to smile; and she said, sorrowfully: "I shall not know what to do with myself, without you."

I laughed, saying: "Why, I have often been away before. You must amuse yourself as you have always done." Then I shook hands with her, and drove off, leaving her standing on the terrace, in an attitude of dejection. The girl was very fond of me; of that I felt sure.

I was detained in London longer than I had expected; but I received a letter nearly every day from "Frank," and I could see from the way she wrote, that she was pining for me, and longing for my return. I also wished to go back to her; I often thought of her, and I did not go near Maud, but lived in chambers close to my club.

At last the day came when I was able to leave London, and I felt quite glad to find myself in the train on my way to Winchester.

When I arrived at the station, my dog-cart was waiting for me and in a short time I reached Oakhurst, where I found "Frank" on the terrace, waiting to receive me. She welcomed me warmly, her face beaming, and her eyes glistening; but as we were under the observation of the servants, she had to suppress all outward show of emotion, but I saw that she was much moved.

As it was rather late, I proceeded at once to my room and changed my clothes, then I went down to the dining-room, and we took our seats at the table. During dinner,

"Frank" did not talk much; she appeared to be quietly happy, there was a soft light in her eyes, she did not bother me with questions, and she seemed perfectly content to sit and look at me. When dinner was over, and I had smoked a cigar, we went into the drawing-room. It was a beautiful evening; the sun had been set for some time, and it was beginning to get dark; the long windows were open, and a gentle breeze wafted into the room the sweet scent of the roses which grew in profusion in the garden. On a tree, not far off, a nightingale was just commencing to sing, giving forth every now and then a few mellow notes; all else was still. It was an ideal night for love-making.

I was sitting in a low easy-chair, and "Frank" was sitting on a stool beside me. We were both silent; the light faded, and the room grew darker. She put her hand on my arm, and nestling close up to me said: "Oh, I am so glad you are back! I have missed you dreadfully."

There was such a loving tone in the girl's voice that it made me think she was about to tell me her long concealed secret: so I put my arm round her waist in lover-like fashion, for the first time, and whispered in her ear:

"Why did you miss me?"

I could feel her tremble as I pressed her waist; she made no answer, but she rested her head on my breast and heaved a long, tremulous sigh.

"Why do you sigh? What is the matter with you, *Frank*?" I said, emphasizing the name.

Still she kept silent. The nightingale burst into full song, its liquid trills filling the air with melody; I pressed her closer to me, and bending over her, said coaxingly, "Tell me, *Frank*."

Then she suddenly threw her arms round my neck, murmuring in a voice choked with emotion: "Oh, don't call me Frank! My name is Frances, I am a woman, and I love you! I love you!"

My heart bounded with a feeling of joy and gratification. The confession had come at last! My patience was rewarded!

I lifted her off the stool on to my lap, and folding her in my arms, I kissed her passionately, on her eyes, her forehead, her cheeks, and her warm mouth. It was too dark to see her face, but as my lips pressed her soft cheeks, I could feel that they were hot with blushes; and she lay like a little child in my arms, her bosom rising and falling quickly.

After a moment or two, I said: "I knew you were a girl, Frances!" She started, and uttering a little cry of intense astonishment, asked: "How long have you known it? How did you find it out?"

"I have known it for a long time. I found it out by seeing something you accidentally showed me on the day I birched you so severely."

"Oh! Good gracious!" she exclaimed in a horrified tone. I laughed, and stopped her mouth with a kiss, saying: "What does it matter when or how I found it out. You have said that you love me, and I love you."

"Oh, do you really? I am so, *so* glad. I was afraid you would be angry with me. I have been wishing for a long time, to tell you I was a girl, but I never had the courage to speak," she said in a low voice, clinging close to me. Then, after a pause, she asked timidly: "Why did you not tell me that you had found out I was a girl?"

"Because it would have caused bother, and altered all my arrangements; besides I preferred to wait until you told me yourself. I felt sure you would tell me some day; and I am glad the day has come at last. You are now my sweetheart, you dear girl," I said, kissing her.

"Oh! how patient and good you have been to me all these years; and how happy I feel at being your sweetheart," she said, in a voice vibrating with emotion. Then she got off my lap, and sitting down on the stool, put her little hand on mine and pressed it warmly.

"Now," I said, "tell me when you first began to love me."

"Oh, I began to love you the day you took me into your house, when I was homeless and friendless, and ever since that time, my love for you has been growing greater and greater."

"Did you never feel angry with me when I whipped you?"

"No, never. Of course I did not like getting a whipping, as it was painful;—the rod was dreadful—but somehow or other, I seemed to love you more after you had given me a spanking." Then, after a pause, she added rather bashfully: "And I will confess to you, that at one time, I used to be naughty on purpose that you might spank me; for I liked to lie across your knees, and feel your hand stroking my bare skin; although I dreaded the pain that was to follow; for you always made me smart a great deal."

I laughed at this queer confession, but was pleased to hear it, for it showed that the girl had a rather voluptuous disposition. Then I said: "So it gave you pleasure to lie across my knees, and feel my hand stroking your bare skin? Well, I shall be delighted to let you have that pleasure now, if you like."

She made no answer, but gave my hand a squeeze, which I took as a sign of assent; so I at once lifted her up, placed her in position, and took down her trousers; which I had not let down for upwards of six months.

It was too dark for me to see her bottom, but nevertheless I had great sensual pleasure in passing my hand over the swelling hemispheres of plump, firm flesh, which I stroked, squeezed, and played with in all sorts of ways, for a minute or two.

"Did you like that, Frances?" I asked, when I had done paddling with her bottom. "Oh, yes!" she replied, still lying face downwards on my lap. "It was very nice. It gave me a most pleasant sensation."

I smiled; and to give her another sensation, I put my hand under her belly, and gently touched, for the first time, her virgin cunt. She started, and a tremor passed over her:

then I took away my hand from the "spot," as I did not wish to frighten her by going too fast. I intended, however, to take her maidenhead that night—and I did not think she would object—but I meant to do the job comfortably in my own bed later on; so I put her on her feet, kissed her, and told her to button up. Then I rang for lights, as it had become pitch-dark in the room. In a few moments, one of the servants came, and after lighting all the lamps, went away again. Then I looked at Frances, who was sitting demurely on a chair at some distance from me; and, as soon as she caught my eye, she blushed, but instantly came to me, and perching herself on my knees, laid her cheek against mine, with a low sigh of perfect contentment; saying: "Oh, how nice it is not to have any secret between us!"

"Yes; it is very pleasant. We are lovers now; so you must give me a nice kiss." She laughed softly and at once pressed her cherry lips to mine, kissing me warmly, and repeatedly. She had never kissed a man before, and no man but myself had ever kissed, or touched her in any way. It was most delicious to feel her virgin lips pressed against mine, and to inhale her fragrant breath: and it was also extremely pleasant to feel her soft bottom pressing against my upright prick, as she sat on my lap. I wondered if she could feel the peg underneath her!

I thought it was now time to speak plainly to my sweetheart. She loved me, and she was a clever girl, who had read a great deal; therefore she, no doubt, had a very clear idea of what generally happens when a man and a woman love each other. I said: "Frances, I have something to say to you. We love each other, and to-night we will set the seal on our mutual love. You understand what I mean?"

She blushed rosy-red, and hid her face in my breast; then, after a moment's hesitation, said in a low, but firm voice: "Yes. I understand. I love you, and will do anything you wish."

I raised her head, and kissed her on the lips, saying affectionately: "I love you too. You are a darling girl."

She slipped off my knees, and seated herself in a chair, looking at me timidly, and I saw that she was rather frightened at the thought of what was before her. And I must say, that under the circumstances, her timidity was only what one would have expected. Her "courtship" had been short; my "proposal" had been sudden, and the "marriage" was to be consummated that night. No wonder the girl was a little startled!

I did not bother her with talk, but I rang the bell, and ordered the servant to bring up a bottle of champagne, and some cake. In a short time, the cake and wine were placed on the table; then I told Frances to cut her "wedding cake," which she did, smiling a little, and we both ate a piece. Filling her glass with champagne, I made her drink it, and at the same time I drank her health as the "bride," making a joking little speech which amused her, and the wine exhilarated her, so her face soon lost its timid look; she again became the loving girl, and she seated herself beside me; not talking much, but holding my hand in hers, and occasionally looking up at me, with a soft, love-light shining in her pretty blue eyes, and a slight smile dimpling the corners of her ripe, red lips.

I do not know whether the "blushing bride" felt impatient, or not, but to me, the "ardent bridegroom," the time seemed to pass very slowly; and when the big ormolu clock on the mantelpiece chimed eleven, I rose from my seat, and tucking Frances' hand under my arm, said: "Come along dear; it is time to go to bed." Then I led her out of the drawing-room, and upstairs into the long corridor, off which both our bedrooms opened. To get to my room we had to pass her "virgin bower," but she never faltered as we went by the door, and in another moment we were in my room, where we were sure to be undisturbed, as all the servants slept in another wing of the old house.

My chamber was large, and was handsomely furnished as a bed-sitting-room, with tables, cabinets, sofa, and easy chairs: there were some good pictures on the walls, and the polished oak floor was partially covered with fine, old Eastern rugs. The bedstead was a big, brass one, with ample room in it for two persons. I turned up the flame of a tall, pedestal lamp, and I also lighted all the wax candles in two Dresden china candelabra, which were on the mantelpiece, as I wanted the room to be brilliantly illuminated, so that I might have a good view of my "bride's" charms.

But the fact of my "bride" being at that moment dressed as a man, made me feel rather inclined to laugh. However, the masculine attire would soon be off, and then the feminine figure would be revealed in all its naked beauty.

Kissing her as she stood bashfully in the middle of the room; I said: "Now, Frances, I want you to undress yourself, as I am longing to see the whole of your figure quite naked. You know I have often seen half of it bare." A little blush marked her cheeks, but she smiled, saying: "Very well. I will do as you wish." Then she quietly took off her coat and waistcoat, collar and tie; and sitting down for a moment, pulled off her shoes and socks; next she unfastened her braces, unbuttoned her trousers, and let them slip down her legs on to the floor; finally, after a moment's pause, she drew off her shirt and undershirt, and throwing them on the floor, stood before me, perfectly naked. She trembled a little, and her sense of modesty made her instinctively assume the attitude of the Venus de Medici: one arm stretched downwards, the hand hiding the secret spot, the other arm raised and held across her bosom; her head was turned aside, her eyes were cast down, and she was blushing scarlet from her brow to the upper part of her breast,—even her ears were red.

I gazed with admiration, and also with a strong feeling of lust, at the pretty, naked, virgin girl. Her skin was smooth and white as alabaster; she was as plump as a partridge, and her figure was beautifully proportioned in every way; her small, well-shaped head was gracefully poised on her slim neck; her arms were well-formed; her bubbies were fully developed, round as apples, and firm looking, standing well out from her bosom, and tipped with small, erect, rosebud-like nipples; her belly was broad, and smooth; and her little cunt, which she was trying to screen with her hand, was shaded with soft, silky, golden hair.

When I had sufficiently feasted my eyes on the front part of her charming figure, I turned her round, and looked with increased admiration at the hinder part of her body,— for to me the back view of a naked woman is more pleasing than the front view. Her shape, as seen from behind, was perfect. It presented the true line of beauty and grace, as depicted by Hogarth: the gently sloping shoulders, the smooth, white back, curving slightly in to the fine loins; then the rounded contours of her broad, plump bottom, swelling out in grand curves, and sweeping down to her splendid, round, white thighs, which tapered to her beautifully shaped legs. Her ankles were small, and she had tiny feet without blemish, the toes tipped with little pink nails.

I did not touch her, and she let me inspect her, standing quite still; like a beautiful statue; only instead of the lovely figure being cold marble, it was warm flesh and blood.

Putting my arms round her, I lifted her up, carried her to the bed, and stretched her upon it at full length; then, after I had undressed myself, I put out the lamp and most of the candles, but I left several burning, so that the room was still well lighted.

The girl never moved, but lay just as I had put her, flat upon her back, on the outside of the bed; she had covered her blushing face with both her hands, and I noticed that every now and then a slight tremor passed over her whole body.

However, before making the grand assault, there was a final preparation to be made; and that was to spread something on the bed to prevent it being stained by her blood; so I got a couple of large bath towels, and put them doubled, underneath her loins, bottom and thighs.

The victim was on the altar, ready for the sacrifice!

Burning with a fierce desire, I got on the bed, clasped her lithe, yielding body in my arms, and pressed my hand in all directions over her deliciously smooth, satin-like, white skin. I toyed with her beautiful, round, firm bubbies, squeezing the elastic flesh, and gently pinching the tiny, pink nipples which seemed to stiffen slightly at the touch of my fingers. I stroked her soft belly; ran my hand up and down her thighs; and felt the calves of her legs. Then turning her over on to her face, I played with her magnificent bottom in all sorts of ways; I smoothed it, I pinched it gently, and I spanked it slightly; I put my hand in the division between the cheeks and separating them a little, I looked at the little violet spot in the middle; then grasping with both hands the plump firm flesh, I pressed it with my fingers till the blood came and went. She never made a movement, but I could feel her body quiver every now and then. I turned her over on to her back again, and burying my face in the warm valley between her titties, I kissed them all over; and taking in my mouth one of her little nipples, I nibbled it, at the same time inhaling with pleasure, the sweet, subtle, feminine odour which always emanates from the body of a clean, healthy young woman. I then looked at her small, virgin cunt, kissed it, and laying my hand upon it, gently put my forefinger between its lips, making the girl shrink convulsively, and utter a startled little cry; and at the same time, she instinctively pulled my hand away from the "spot."

I prepared for action. "Frances," I said, "the moment has come. What I am going to do to you, will give you a little pain at first; but afterwards, you will experience nothing but pleasure when I do it to you. Do you feel much frightened?"

"No," she whispered; but nevertheless she looked a little alarmed, as she lay before me, naked and palpitating, waiting for the stroke.

I stretched out her legs as widely as possible, then, after placing myself in position to make the assault, I separated with my fingers the tightly-closed lips of her little cunt and inserted the tip of my prick; the girl, as she felt the stiff member entering her body, shrunk away from me slightly, and uttered a little cry. I pressed my lips upon her mouth, and laid my breast upon her naked, heaving bosom; then putting my hands under her, and taking hold of the cheeks of her bottom, I began to fuck her with long, slow strokes, each thrust forcing my prick a little deeper into her tight cunt which clipped my member closely in a warm embrace. The sensation was delightful! With a few vigorous movements of my loins, I gradually drove the weapon further and further into the sheath; the pain making the girl wince and groan; but she could not help moving her bottom briskly up and down to meet my thrusts. I worked away, till at last the tip of my tool touched the maidenhead which barred the passage. And now, the increased pain she felt as I battered away at the tough membrane, caused her to utter little squeaks, but she did all she could to help me; wriggling, arching her loins, heaving up her bottom, and pressing me to her bosom. I poked away as hard as I could, and she bounded under me, groaning, and squeaking. I thought the membrane would never yield. I paused for a moment to recover my breath; then taking a fresh hold of her bottom, I recommenced fucking her with increased vigour, making her quiver all over; but she managed to gasp out between her squeaks and groans: "Oh! Oh! You—are—hurting—me—dreadfully!"

At last I felt the thing beginning to yield, and after a few more powerful thrusts, her maidenhead gave way; she uttered a sharp cry of pain, and my prick buried itself to the roots in her cunt. Then, a few short digs finished the affair; the supreme moment arrived, the delicious spasm seized me, and I spent profusely, pouring out a torrent of boiling sperm, while she gasped, squirmed, and wriggled her bottom furiously, uttering little squeaks of mingled pleasure and pain as the hot stuff spurted in gushes up her lacerated cunt. And when all was over, she lay trembling in my arms, her breath coming and going quickly, her bosom heaving

tumultuously, and the flesh of her bottom twitching nervously; her cheeks were scarlet, and there was a languorous
look in her moist eyes.

As Frances was "small," and as I was "great," she had
suffered a good deal of pain;—much more than a larger
made woman would have suffered,—there had been a considerably effusion of blood, and the proof of her virginity
was plentifully displayed on the hair of the "spot," on her
thighs, and on the towels under her bottom. And as soon as
she had fairly recovered herself, she noticed the sanguinary
stains. "Oh-h!" she exclaimed in a horrified tone, beginning
to cry. "I am bleeding!"

I kissed her, and soothed her, calling her all sorts of
endearing names; telling her that it was nothing, and that
every woman bled more or less, the first time she was embraced by a man. She soon grew calm, and smiled at me
faintly; then I got a basin of water and a sponge, with which
I carefully removed all the traces of my "bloody" work from
her person, and dried her with a soft towel, while she lay,
with outstretched legs, and blushing cheeks, looking up at
me; finally I got one of my nightshirts, put it on her and
made her get between the sheets.. I then washed my "gory
weapon," and got into bed beside her, where she at once
cuddled up to me, saying with a deep sigh: "I am glad it is
over. It was very painful, and it did not give me the least
pleasure."

I laughed, saying: "I suppose it was rather painful. Never
mind. You will find that it will give you great pleasure in
future."

She looked rather incredulous, and made a little face, as
she laid her head on the pillow. She appeared to be quite
worn out; her eyes closed, and in a few moments, she fell
fast asleep. Then I got up, extinguished the candles, and crept
quietly into bed again, without disturbing the sleeping girl;
and soon after I fell asleep myself.

I woke two or three times during the night, each time

experiencing a feeling of pleasure, and getting a cockstand at the contact of the girl's plump, warm flesh, but as she still continued to sleep soundly, I did not disturb her. I woke again when it was broad daylight, and on glancing at the clock on the mantelpiece I saw that it was six o'clock. Then, sitting up in the bed, I gazed at Frances, who was lying on her back, sleeping like a child, and looking exquisitely pretty. Her short, curly, golden hair was ruffled over her broad, white forehead; her blue-veined eyelids were closely shut; the long, curved eyelashes resting on her smooth cheeks, which were flushed with a delicate pink tinge like the petals of a rose; her red lips were slightly separated, showing her small, pearl-white teeth; and as the collar of the nightshirt was a little open, I could see the upper part of her titties, which looked like tiny mounds of snow. Bending over her, I pressed my lips upon her rosebud mouth in a long, hot kiss, and she woke up with a little start, looking rather bewildered, as if she could not quite make out where she was; and she gazed at me for a moment, with her big blue eyes wide open, her cheeks at the same time growing very red; then a bright smile lit up her pretty face, and, throwing her arms round my neck, she kissed me, saying: "Oh, how funny it seems for me to be in bed with you!"

"I think it is very nice," said I, feeling her bubbies with one hand, and stroking her bottom with the other. "How did you sleep?"

"Very soundly. I never opened my eyes from the time I went to sleep until you woke me. I was very tired after what happened last night," she added, glancing at me slyly.

"And sore too, I daresay," said I, smiling and pinching her thigh. "Now let me have a look at the tender spot." She laughed, and at once laid herself flat down upon her back; then I turned down the bedclothes, and pulled her nightgown up to her chin, so that the whole front part of her lovely body was naked; her delicate skin looking even more beautifully white by daylight, than it had by candle-light.

After I had sufficiently admired the charming spectacle presented by the girl as she lay naked before me, I made her stretch out her legs, and then with my two forefingers, I separated as widely as possible the outer lips of her cunt, and examined the inside of it; finding that it was rather inflamed; the inner lips being a bright pink colour, and also a little swollen; and, on looking up the vagina, I could plainly see the lacerated edges of the ruptured maidenhead. "Carunculæ myrtiformes," they are called by surgeons.

"The 'spot' looks rather sore," I said.

"It smarts a little, and I have a feeling as if something was still sticking in it, and stretching it."

Taking her hand, I placed it on my rampant prick. "There, Frances," I said. "Feel and examine the thing that did all the damage."

She sat up in the bed, clasped her little white hand round my tool, and gazed at it with eyes round with astonishment, exclaiming: "Oh! what an enormous thing it is! No wonder it hurt me!"

Then, with her fingers, she measured its length, and pulling back the foreskin, exposed the ruby tip; the appearance of which seemed to amuse her, for she laughed softly. "Oh, what a funny-looking thing it is, with its big red knob! I never should have believed that such a great thing as that could have got into my little"—she stopped and looked comically at me. She really did not know what to call her thing.

"Do you know what the things are called?" I asked her.

"No, I don't. I wish you would tell me," she replied eagerly.

I laughed, and told her the names of the various parts of man and woman, and also all the terms in the vocabulary of love; and in addition, I explained to her the different positions in which a man may embrace a woman. She listened with rapt attention, her cheeks flushing, and her eyes sparkling at my graphic descriptions; and during the whole time I was speaking, she kept hold of my tool, occasionally squeezing it, and making me feel intensely randy. So I said: "That is a very different 'thing' to the one you felt between little Tom's legs when you spanked him."

She let go her hold, blushing very red, and gazing at me in speechless astonishment, and looking so utterly mystified, that I burst out laughing and told her how I had seen her spanking the boy, and also putting her hand under his belly.

"Oh, dear me! Did you see me do that?" she said, looking a little shamefaced for a moment; then she added, with a gleam of merriment in her eyes:

"It was such a funny little morsel. It felt just like a worm. But you must have been surprised to see me do such a thing?"

"No, I was not," I replied laughing. "You had the boy lying across your knees with his trousers down, and it was quite natural that you should have wished to feel what he had between his legs. You were a big girl at the time, and all big girls like to touch little boys' things." And, I added, "all big boys like to touch little girls' things."

She looked at me for a moment, with a demure expression on her face, but with a twinkle in her eyes; then she remarked: "Do they really?"

I rolled her over, pulled her nightgown up, and played with her; paddling with her bubbies, pinching the cheeks of her bottom in turn; pulling the soft, silky hair which covered the "mons veneris," and tickling the "spot," till she got very excited. Her bosom heaved, a sensuous look came into her eyes, her cheeks flushed, and she stretched out her legs; evidently wishing me to poke her. I was quite ready for the job, so, clasping her in my arms, I got into her; this time without much difficulty, as there was nothing to bar the passage, though it was very tight.

She winced, uttering a low cry as my prick again stretched her sore, little cunt, but she braced herself up, clenching her teeth, and holding her breath for a moment. I began to fuck her vigorously, but as slowly as I could, for I wanted to make the pleasure last as long as possible.

My lips were on hers, my breast was on her bosom, my

hands gripped the cheeks of her bottom, and at each thrust I drove my prick into her, as far as it would go; then, drawing it out again through the clinging folds of her cunt, till only the tip of the weapon remained in the sheath, I again forced it in up to the hilt, with powerful movements of my loins; making Frances bound and wriggle in voluptuous pain.

It was delicious! She worked her loins vigorously, heaving up her bottom to meet my downthrusts, groaning a little, but embracing me tightly, and evidently enjoying the poke. In a very short time I was obliged to come to the short digs; she wriggled, and squeaked; the spasm seized us both at the same moment, and as I discharged, she "came," uttering a long, shuddering sigh, squirming under me, and wriggling her bottom in a most lively fashion;—hugging me tightly, and actually biting my shoulder in her delicious ecstasy, till she had taken in every drop of moisture from my still stiff prick, round which the lips of her cunt clung tightly, as if loath to let go.

It had been a most delightful poke. I do not think I had ever enjoyed a woman more. I held her in my arms till she had done panting and sighing; then giving her a kiss, I asked her how she had liked her second lesson in the "art of love." "Oh," she replied, "it was rather painful at first, but after a few seconds, I had no sense of pain, my only feeling being one of pleasure; and at the last, the sensation was quite delightful, when I felt a peculiar thrill pass over me, and the hot stuff gushed out of you. It seemed to go right up me in a burning stream, and I could not help twisting myself about. Oh! it was nice!"

I did not poke her again, but we had a little amorous dalliance, which she entered into with spirit, thoroughly enjoying the fun, and showing that she had a decidedly voluptuous disposition.

At last I told her to go to her room, and rumple her bed, so that it should look as if it had been slept in as usual. She laughed, and jumping out of bed, huddled on her clothes; then she picked up the blood-stained towels, saying: "I will take these away, and when I am having my bath I will wash them, and leave them in the bathroom." Then she added, looking with a meaning smile at me: "I have had to wash many a towel before now."

"By Jove! Frances," I exclaimed. "It is lucky you thought of the towels. I should have forgotten all about them, and left them lying on the floor. Now give me a kiss, and run away."

She came to the bedside, and bending over me, pressed her soft lips on mine in a long kiss; then she left the room, and I turned over on to my side, and went to sleep; not waking until my man brought in my bath.

# ❦ VIII ❧

THE DAY AFTER.——A FULL CONFESSION.——
"FRANK'S" SCHOOLDAYS.——DECOYED.——LIFE IN
THE KENSINGTON BAGNIO.——INNOCENCE DIS-
PELLED.——THE REFUSAL AND WHAT CAME OF
IT.——THE MYSTERIOUS SPANKING REVEALED.
——THRICE SEVERELY SLAPPED WITH A
SLIPPER.——HARRY'S CLOTHES.——THE
METAMORPHOSIS AND THE ESCAPE.
——THE FLIGHT TO SOUTHAMPTON.
——THE FUGITIVE'S LUCKY FATE.
——THE SECOND NIGHT
OF LOVE.

I went down to breakfast at the usual hour, but Frances did
not make her appearance until I had nearly finished my meal;
then she came running into the room, smilingly apologized
for being late, and took her seat at the table. She was dressed
in a well-made suit of light clothes, and it was hard to believe
that the well-groomed, good-looking young "gentleman"
sitting opposite to me, was the girl whose maidenhead I had

taken only a few hours previously. Her face was rather pale, and her eyes were a little heavy, but she looked cheerful, and was apparently quite unconcerned at the loss of her virginity.

"Well, Frances," I said, helping her to a devilled kidney, "I hope you have a good appetite. How do you feel? Is the spot sore?"

She smiled and blushed slightly, but replied with perfect coolness: "My appetite is not quite so good as usual. I feel rather languid; and the 'spot' is still a little sore; though I bathed it well with cold water when I was taking my bath."

"Never mind. The soreness will soon pass off," I said, going over to her and kissing her cheek. "Oh, I don't mind it a bit. I love you!" she exclaimed; throwing her arms round my neck, and returning my kiss with interest. I was pleased with the girl's affection, for I had become really fond of her; so I took her in my arms, and gave her a good hug.

Then, as I had some business to do in Winchester, I ordered the dog-cart to be got ready, and I asked Frances if she would like to come with me. But she said with a little smile, that she preferred to remain quiet for the day; so giving her a parting kiss, I went away.

My business occupied me till late in the afternoon, and when I got back home, I went straight up to my room, so that I did not see Frances until we met at dinner. And then I was glad to see that she was looking quite herself again; her cheeks had regained their delicate pink colour, and her pretty, blue eyes were as limpid and bright as ever. We were both hungry, and as the cook had sent up a nice little dinner, we did full justice to it, and we drank a bottle of champagne. Throughout the meal, Frances was in high spirits, and full of fun, making me laugh several times with her humorous remarks.

After I had smoked a cigar, we went into the drawing-room, and I sat in an easy-chair near the open window, while Frances sat on a stool beside me, resting her arm on my knee;

and it suddenly struck me that she ought now to tell me all about the mysterious ladies who had kept her for six months, and then turned her out.

So I said: "Frances, I wish you to give me all particulars about your life with the ladies who took you from the school; and you must tell me the true reason why they ill-treated you, and why they told you to go away from their house. I also want to know what put it into your head to pass yourself off as a boy."

She took my hand and pressed it, saying: "I will tell you everything. There shall be no secrets between us now."

She began—"I have never told you a lie, though, as you know, I acted one for years. My full name is Frances Howard, and, as I long ago informed you, my father and mother both died in India, when I was a little over nine years of age. A month after their death, I was sent to England, and put to school in an establishment at Highgate, where there were about twenty other girls of various ages. We were well treated, and well taught, and though the mistress—whose name was Blake—was strict, she was just and kind. She sometimes used the rod, but the punishment was inflicted in private; no girl ever being allowed to see another girl birched. I myself, never received a blow of any sort during the whole time I was at the school; Mrs. Blake was kind to me, and I was fairly happy. Five years passed over quietly. I was fourteen years of age, and had never been away from the establishment for a day; when one morning, Mrs. Blake called me into her private sitting-room, and told me that she was sorry to say she could not keep me any longer in her school, as she had not received any money to pay for my board and education, for six months past: and she also informed me, that the banker, with whom my money had been lodged, had written to say that my account was overdrawn, and that there was no more cash coming to me.

"Then she went on to say that she had mentioned my case to a lady whom she knew; and the lady had most kindly

said that she would take me into her house as a companion
to her little daughter: and she finished up by telling me to
get all my things ready, as the lady was coming for me next
day.

"I was not much troubled at hearing that my money was
all gone. As I had never had much to spend, I had very little
idea as to its value, and therefore I could not grasp the full
significance of what had happened, and as I was very tired
of the monotony of my life at the school, I was glad to hear
that I was going to have a change. So I left the room, and
spent the rest of the day arranging and packing my clothes,
for I had a good wardrobe for a girl of my age.

"Next day, after I had had my dinner as usual with the
other girls, Mrs. Blake told me to put on my things, then to
go to the drawing-room, and wait there for the lady, who
might come at any moment.

"I obeyed: and at about three o'clock, Mrs. Blake came
into the room accompanied by two handsomely dressed
ladies, whom she addressed as Mrs. Leslie, and Miss Dundas,
and who, as I afterwards found out, were sisters. Mrs. Leslie
was a tall, dark, good-looking woman about thirty-five years
of age. Miss Dundas, who was twenty-five years old and very
pretty, was always called 'Kitty' by her sister.

"Mrs. Blake introduced me to the ladies, who shook me
by the hand, both of them speaking kindly to me; and I
thought to myself that it would be very pleasant to live with
such nice people.

"In a short time, Mrs. Leslie asked me if I was quite
ready to go. I replied that I was. My old schoolmistress bade
me good bye, kissed me, and gave me a sovereign; then she
shook hands with the two ladies, who immediately left the
room, taking me with them. At the door of the house, a
brougham was waiting; the ladies and I got in; the coach-
man touched the horses with his whip, and in another
moment I was rapidly being driven away from the house in
which I had passed five dull, but not unhappy years. I felt a

little sorrowful, and the tears rose to my eyes; but I soon recovered my spirits; the novelty of the whole thing was very pleasing; I had never before been in such a fine carriage, and I leant back against the soft cushions, feeling very comfortable, and thinking that my new friends must be very rich people. The two ladies conversed in low tones, glancing occasionally at me; and after a long drive, the brougham stopped at a house in a broad street; the name of which I have forgotten; but it is, I know, somewhere in Kensington.

"The house, which was a large one, stood back a little from the street, in a garden surrounded by a high wall. We got out of the carriage; Mrs. Leslie touched the button of an electric bell, and in a moment the garden gate swung open, then we walked up a short path and entered the house. Mrs. Leslie at once took me upstairs to a prettily furnished bedroom, and told me to make myself at home; then she gave me a kiss, and went away. A minute or two afterwards, my box was brought in by two smartly dressed servant girls, one of whom remained in the room and assisted me to unpack my things; and when we had put everything away in the chest of drawers, and wardrobe, she brushed my hair, which then was very long, hanging loose over my shoulders nearly down to my waist."

Here Frances paused for a moment in the telling of her story, and said, "I have always regretted the loss of my beautiful hair."

"It will grow again, whenever you choose to let it," I said, playing with the short curls on her forehead.

She continued her narrative. "The servant girl showed me downstairs, and into a most charming . little drawing-room, where I found Mrs. Leslie, Miss Dundas, and five other young ladies, sitting on low easy-chairs, or reclining on couches, having afternoon tea. These young ladies were all pretty, and young; the eldest not being more than twenty-five years old, and they were all elegantly dressed. On seeing me, they all got up from their seats, and crowded round me,

looking at me with great interest, admiring my hair, and
saying I was a pretty girl; and when I blushed at their out-
spoken compliments, they all laughed at me. But they were
kindly in their manner, and I soon found myself comfortably
seated in an easy-chair, eating a piece of cake, and sipping a
cup of tea, such as I had never before tasted in all my life.
The time slipped away rapidly; I felt very jolly, and quickly
got on intimate terms with the young ladies, who did not
treat me as a schoolgirl, but quite as if I had been a grown-up
woman. They chatted freely with me, and much to my surprise, I heard that they all lived in the house.

"At half-past seven o'clock a bell rang, then we all went
into a handsomely furnished dining-room and sat down to a
flower-decorated table; Mrs. Leslie presiding at the head,
while Miss Dundas sat the foot.

To me, a young girl who had been accustomed to dine
at one o'clock off a roast, or boiled joint, and a plain pudding; the repast seemed sumptuous, and very long; but I
heartily enjoyed the delicate, well-cooked dishes, and I drank
a glass of claret which was given to me, but I did not like it;
though I did like the glass of sweet port I was given at
dessert.

"After dinner, the six young ladies went away, leaving
me alone with Mrs. Leslie, who talked to me kindly, saying
she hoped I would like living with her: then she asked me
if it was a fact that I had no relations? I told her that I did
not know of any. I then asked her when I should see her
little daughter, to whom I was to be a companion. She
laughed heartily, saying that there had been some mistake;
as she had no daughter, but only a son, Henry, who was
about my age, and who was at school in the country. I
wondered how the mistake had arisen, but I did not bother
my head about the matter. After a little more talk, she took
me back to the small drawing-room, and gave me a book of
stories to read; then, telling me that I could go to bed whenever I felt inclined, she went away. I read for a time, then I

began to feel sleepy, so I went up to my room, finding the gas lit, the curtains drawn, and everything neatly arranged. I sat down in an easy-chair, feeling quite proud at having such a pretty room all to myself; then, after a short time, I undressed, put out the gas, got into the big, soft bed, and soon fell asleep.

"Next morning, I woke at my usual early hour, and I got up and dressed; then I went downstairs, but there was not a soul to be seen anywhere about the place, so I amused myself walking through the passages, and looking into the numerous rooms, all of which were beautifully furnished in different styles. In about an hour's time, the servants came down and began sweeping the rooms and passages, casting curious glances at me, as I roamed about; and at last one of them told me that I had better go back to my room, as breakfast would not be ready until ten o'clock.

"I took the woman's advice, went back to my room, and lay down upon my bed, feeling very hungry; and I was glad when I heard a bell ring, which I guessed meant breakfast, so I went down to the dining-room, where I found everyone assembled. They bade me good morning, and we sat down at the table, which was spread with an excellent breakfast, to which I did full justice; but I noticed that some of the young ladies looked tired and sleepy, and they did not seem inclined to talk much.

"After breakfast, Mrs. Leslie and Miss Dundas went out in the brougham, and the other ladies and myself went into the little drawing-room, where we amused ourselves in various ways until lunch, which was served at two o'clock. Later on, Mrs. Leslie took me out for a drive in the park; and at half-past seven we all again met at dinner; the ladies being attired in evening dress. And, as on the previous night, they all went away when the meal was over, leaving me by myself; so I took the book I had been reading and went to my room.

"And so the weeks passed. After the first few days, Mrs. Leslie did not take much notice of me, but the young ladies were always kind to me. I had no duties of any sort, and I amused myself by reading or sewing; and as I was allowed to come and go just as I liked, I often went into Kensington Gardens, and I used also to wander about the streets, looking at the shop windows. I thus gained confidence in myself, and never felt the least afraid of going about alone.

"I had very soon noticed that a great number of gentlemen called at the house every day, and frequently some of them remained to dinner; but on those occasions I was not allowed to dine at the table. I also discovered that the gentlemen sometimes stayed all night; and long after I had gone to bed, I often heard the ladies and gentlemen talking, laughing, and singing in the big drawing-room downstairs.

"I thought it strange, but being young, and perfectly innocent, I did not then understand what it all meant. But now that I am a woman, and have read novels, and books of all sorts, in which descriptions are given of the various queer things that go on in the world, I know what the ladies were, and why the gentlemen came to the house."

She stopped speaking, and looked up in my face, with a little smile curving her lips; then she said: "I suppose you have already guessed what sort of an establishment it was that Mrs. Leslie kept."

"Yes, indeed I have, Frances. But go on, I am very much interested," I replied. She continued. "Well, the time went on, till I had been six months in the house, and though I had a vague idea that things were not quite right, I never saw anything improper, as I was never allowed in the large drawing-room when gentlemen were there. The girls never let me into their secrets, though I knew they used to laugh and joke with each other about what went on in the house; but they always stopped talking if I happened to go into the room where they were.

"I did not then know why they were so careful of what they said before me, but now I feel certain, that the reason of their not speaking openly, was because they respected my

innocence. I had always got on well with them, and I think
they were all fond of me, with the exception of Miss Dundas,
who never seemed to take the least interest in me.

"Mrs. Leslie, I think, took it for granted that I understood the meaning of all that went on, though she never
said anything to me on the subject.

"However, I was destined soon to know more. For some
time past, I had been very much bothered with the attentions
of an old gentleman whom I knew as Mr. Wood, and who
was a frequent visitor to the house. He was constantly bringing me presents of fruit, and sweets, and he also occasionally
gave me a sovereign. I took all his gifts, but I hated him, and
always tried to get away from him as soon as possible, though
he was perfectly civil, never once attempting to take the
least liberty with me. But nevertheless he was the cause of
my being turned out of the house.

"One afternoon, Mrs. Leslie called me into the drawing-
room, and said, that as she had kept me in luxury for six
months, and as I was fourteen years and a half old; it was
time for me to do something for her in return. Not dreaming
for a moment of what she was going to ask me to do; I said
that it would give me great pleasure to oblige her in any
way. She then, in the coolest manner told me that Mr. Wood
had taken a great fancy to me, and that he was going to
remain in the house all night, and that I was to sleep with
him. At that time, I had no very definite idea of what would
happen to me if I slept with a man; but the very thought of
doing so, turned my blood cold, and filled me with an intense
feeling of horror and ·disgust. I burst into tears, and abso-
lutely refused to sleep with the man.

"Mrs. Leslie flew into a violent passion, upbraiding me
for my ingratitude to her, and she asked me scornfully if I
did not know that all the young ladies in the house slept with
gentlemen when required to do so. I felt myself blushing
scarlet, and I trembled all over, but I stammered out that I
did not know they ever did· such a thing. I really had been

ignorant of the fact. She stormed at me worse than ever, saying that I was a greater fool than she had thought; and she wound up by telling me, that if I did not consent to sleep with Mr. Wood, she would give me a sound whipping. Then she told me angrily to go to my room and think over what she had said. I went to my room, feeling dazed and miserable, and throwing myself on my bed, wept bitterly; but in spite of her threat, I was fully determined not to sleep with Mr. Wood.

"In about an hour's time, Mrs. Leslie and her sister came into the room: I jumped off the bed, and stood before them, feeling very frightened, but firm in my resolve. Mrs. Leslie asked me if I would do as she had told me? I replied with the tears streaming down my cheeks, that I could not; then I implored her not to whip me, saying that I had never been whipped in my life.

"She made no reply, but seized me and laid me across the bed: Miss Dundas immediately taking hold of my wrists and holding them tightly. Then Mrs. Leslie turned up my short frock and petticoats to my shoulders, and unfastening my drawers, pulled them down to my knees. I did not struggle to escape, nor did I again beg her not to whip me, as I knew it would be no use; but I felt very much ashamed at being turned up in such a degrading manner; I also dreaded the pain before me, and a sort of creeping sensation passed over the flesh of my bottom as I lay on the bed, in dire suspense, waiting for the punishment to commence. Mrs. Leslie leisurely took off one of her slippers, then she held my legs with her left hand, and began to spank me very severely; and as I had never before received a blow, I felt the pain acutely, but I tried to bear it quietly. The stinging slaps fell in quick succession all over my bottom; the pain grew sharper and sharper; I could no longer contain myself, and I began to struggle and cry. She went on spanking me relentlessly; my bottom seemed to be burning, and I screamed loudly at each slap.

"At last she stopped, and put on her slipper; then she and her sister left the room, locking the door on the outside, leaving me lying on the bed, with my petticoats up and my drawers down, crying with shame and pain. When the smarting of my bottom had somewhat subsided, I wiped the tears from my eyes, got off the bed, and fastened up my drawers, then I lay down again, and buried my face in the pillow, feeling very wretched.

"About an hour after, Miss Dundas brought me a cup of tea and some bread and butter, telling me that I should get no dinner that night; and she added that I was a young fool. She then went away, leaving me locked up.

"Next morning, after I had dressed, I sat waiting to be let out; but I was not. Some breakfast was brought to me, and later on, some lunch. At five o'clock, Mrs. Leslie and her sister made their appearance, and I was again asked if I would consent; and again I refused. Then for the second time I was laid across the bed and severely spanked; and as my bottom was still sore, I felt the stinging pain of the slaps more acutely than before, and I struggled more violently, and screamed louder than on the previous day.

"When the punishment was over, I was again locked up.

"At five o'clock next day, for the third time, they came into the room, and for the third time the question was put to me. Trembling, crying, and wringing my hands in utter despair, I exclaimed that I would never consent. Then, for the third time, my sore bottom was laid bare, and the spanking was begun. That time the pain was most intense; I winced, writhed, and shrieked at each stroke of the thick slipper. I struggled hard to get off the bed, and I tried to kick; but Miss Dundas held my wrists tightly, and Mrs. Leslie held my legs down, at the same time spanking away, without paying the least attention to my shrieks and entreaties, until she was quite out of breath. Then she put on her slipper, and went away with her sister: locking me in the room as on the previous days.

"My flesh tingled and throbbed painfully: I was hoarse

from screaming; my cheeks were furrowed with tears, and I lay on the bed, crying and sobbing in abject misery for quite ten minutes. Then I got up, and bathed my burning, still smarting bottom with cold water, which greatly allayed the pain. I then gathered my short petticoats up above my waist, and standing in front of the glass, I looked over my shoulder at my bottom, and saw that it was very much swollen, the skin being shiny in appearance, and a dark purple colour; it was also so tender that I could not sit down comfortably. It afterwards turned black and blue.

"I was kept locked up, and scantily fed, for three more days, but I was not again spanked. On the fourth day of my imprisonment, Mrs. Leslie came into the room, and said that if I would not do as all the other girls did, she would turn me out of the house. The threat startled me a good deal, but I again said that I would not sleep with a man.

"She glared angrily at me; then, after telling me that I was to leave her house within twenty-four hours, she swept out of the room, leaving the door open.

"I was extremely agitated, as well as frightened, and I sank down on a chair trembling all over, but I did not intend to yield, and after a time I grew calm, and then I began to think what I should do.

"It seemed to me very hard, that the fact of my being a girl should make me liable to be subjected to all sorts of indignities. At that moment I heartily wished I could change my sex. Then a sudden inspiration came to me. I would dress myself as a boy, and in that guise endeavour to get some employment. It was a splendid idea; and as I thought over it, I actually laughed, for it at once struck me that I should never be asked to sleep with a man, when I was got-up in male attire. And there would be no difficulty in completely dressing myself up in boy's clothes. The room next to mine was occupied by Mrs. Leslie's son Henry, whenever he was at home; I had never seen him, but I had heard that he was about my size and age; and I knew that there was plenty of clothing of all sorts in his room.

"I would take all that was necessary, dress myself, and then go to Southampton, and be a sailor. The whole scheme was, of course, utterly impracticable, but I did not think so at that moment. I thought it would be perfectly easy to hide my sex."

Here Frances again stopped speaking for an instant; then said, with a laugh: "And perhaps I could have kept my secret, if you had not taken down my trousers."

"Oh, I should have found out you were a girl, sooner or later; even if I had not taken down your trousers," I observed, laughing.

She went on: "No one came near me that afternoon, except the servant who brought me my tea; and I did not leave the room, so I had plenty of time to arrange my plans, and when I had settled in my mind exactly what I intended to do, I went to bed.

"Next morning, as soon as it was light, I got up, went into the boy's room, and took out of the chest of drawers, a complete suit of clothes and all the necessary under-garments; I also was lucky enough to find a pair of boots, and a straw hat. I went back to my room, dressed myself in the clothes, which fitted me very well, and then I cut off my hair. I had in my possession four pounds, and a few shillings, the remains of the money given me at various times by Mr. Wood; and as I did not wish to steal the clothes, I resolved to pay for them with the four pounds. So I wrote a note in pencil on a scrap of paper, addressed to Mrs. Leslie, telling her what I had done, and enclosing the money.

"Then I slipped quietly downstairs—no one in the house was stirring at that early hour—opened the hall-door, and ran away as fast as I could. I knew my way about, so I soon found an omnibus which took me to Charing-Cross, and from there I made my way to Waterloo station, where I had a cup of coffee and some bread and butter.

"I felt very awkward and uncomfortable in trousers, but as no one seemed to notice anything strange in my appearance, I soon got quite bold. I had not money enough for a ticket to Southampton, so I took one for Farnborough, which I knew was nearly halfway to where I was bound. When I got to Farnborough, I inquired for the Southampton road, and started off at once, walking all day, and as I had only eighteenpence, and a long distance yet to go, I could not put up at an inn. I spent sixpence on bread and cheese and a glass of beer, at a wayside public-house, and when it got dark, I crept into a haystack which fortunately happened to be at hand; but as I was rather frightened, I did not get much sleep, though I was very tired. Next morning I continued my tramp, after getting some tea and bread at a cottage; and when I had paid for my breakfast, I had only sixpence left. I I had walked about fifteen miles, and was beginning to feel very depressed, when you overtook me and spoke so kindly to me. I have nothing more to tell. You know all that has happened from the moment you took me into this dear old house where I have been so happy."

As she finished speaking, she jumped on to my knees, threw her arms round my neck, and kissed me passionately; exclaiming: "Oh, my sweetheart! How good you have been to me! I love you!"

I kissed her, and petted her, for she had got quite excited in telling her long story; but she soon calmed down, and sat quietly on my lap, with her cheek against mine.

"You are not afraid of sleeping with a man now?" I said, smiling.

"Not when you are the man," she replied laughing, and giving me a hug. Then she added earnestly: "But I would not sleep with any other man in the whole world. Nothing would induce me to do such a thing." Then, laughing again merrily: "Not even a spanking every day for a week would make me consent."

"Now," I said, "tell me how it was that your old schoolmistress knew Mrs. Leslie."

"I believe they had been schoolfellows," she replied.

"Do you think she knew the sort of house Mrs. Leslie kept?"

"No, I do not think she did. She must have been deceived in some way or other by Mrs. Leslie, who, having found out that I had no friends, took me into her house to make what she could out of me."

"Yes. I think that is the true explanation of the matter," I said, giving her a kiss. "But you must be tired after all the talking. I am sure you would like to go to bed. It is very late."

She replied that she was rather sleepy; so we went upstairs together, and Frances walked past her room into mine without the least hesitation.

I laughed; and she made a saucy little face at me, her eyes sparkling with fun; then she undressed and got into bed.

I did the same; and in a few moments my lips were pressed to her mouth, my breast was on her bosom, and my prick was stretching her still rather sore cunt; and she was heaving up her bottom, and squeaking a little, under my powerful thrusts.

## END OF FIRST VOLUME

# "Frank" and I

Volume Two

# IX

DIFFERENT STYLES OF ENJOYMENT.——"EN LEV-
RETTE."——FRESH ARRANGEMENTS.——LUCY'S
LIPS AND HOW SHE USED THEM.——HOW THE
HOUSEMAID GOT WHAT SHE WANTED AND A
LITTLE MORE.——MAUD'S APPROACHING
MARRIAGE.——BIRCHING FUN AND THE
USUAL SEQUEL.——JEALOUSY.——
THE DEPARTURE TO LONDON.——
MAUD AND FRANCES.——A
COY SCOTCH LASS.

A couple of months passed over rapidly. Frances now always
called me "Charley,"—my name is Charles Beaumont—and
as I had expected, she turned out to be a most voluptuous
girl, becoming the most charming bedfellow I had ever come
across. She insisted on sleeping with me every night,—I never
objected—but she always went back to her room to bed early
in the morning, and so no suspicion was ever aroused among
the servants. I taught her practically, much to her astonishment and amusement, all the various positions in which a man
can enjoy a woman; and she was always ready for a poke,

either by night, or by day. Often on a rainy afternoon, when we were sitting in the drawing-room, not knowing what to do with ourselves, I would make her lean over the back of an easy-chair, so that I could "have" her "en levrette" as the French call it. But I must say it was rather absurd to see what was apparently a young man in his shirt sleeves, bending well over the back of a chair, with his trousers down to his heels, displaying a big, white, feminine bottom.

She liked being poked "en levrette," for she said I always seemed to get deeper into her in that position than in any other.

It was all very pleasant, but I had begun to think that I should be obliged to make some other arrangements with regard to my sweetheart, for I was afraid that sooner or later she would betray herself. She had let her hair grow much longer than was befitting a "man"; moreover, since she had become a warm, loving woman, she did not keep such a strict guard upon herself as she had hitherto done; and I was in constant dread that the servants would notice her manner towards me.

I was rather bothered too, just at that time, by Lucy; who was still in my service, and who was plumper than ever. As I had as much poking as ever I wanted with Frances, I entirely neglected my buxom housemaid, whom I had formerly poked pretty regularly, and who was, I think, fond of me. She could not understand why I had suddenly given her up: so she used frequently to come to my room on some pretence or other, when she knew I was there. On those occasions, I always had a little talk with her, and sometimes gave her a kiss, but nothing else; so, when she saw that I was not going to "have" her, she would go away, looking very disappointed. However, she was a persevering woman, and one day, she regularly forced me to satisfy her desire.

I had gone up to my room shortly after breakfast to change my coat, and having done so, I sat down in an easy-chair to read a letter which I had received that morning from Maud. She wrote telling me that she was going to be married in a month's time; and she asked me to come and see her as soon as possible, so that we might settle all our little affairs. I was not surprised at the news; for she had before hinted that she was thinking of leaving me.

I had just finished reading the letter, when Lucy came into the room; looking, as usual, very nice in her neat print frock, white apron, and cap with long streamers. She went through the form of arranging the things on the dressing-table; then coming to where I was sitting, she looked at me wistfully with her big hazel eyes, and said: "You never give me a proper kiss now. Have I offended you?"

"No, Lucy, you have not," said I, stroking her plump cheek, but not kissing her, as I did not feel the least inclined to make love of any sort at that moment, owing to my having poked Frances several times during the night and morning.

"Why, you haven't even kissed me!" she said, pouting her full red lips and holding her face up invitingly. I smiled, but did not touch her.

"Well, I'll kiss *you*, till you give me a proper kiss." So saying, she dropped on her knees in front of me, and to my astonishment,—for she had never done such a thing to me before—she unbuttoned my trousers, took out my tool, and began manipulating it with a skilful touch, saying with a laugh, as she noticed its very limp condition: "Oh! how miserable and flabby it looks; but I'll soon make it stiff." Then, bending down her head, she took into her mouth my drooping prick, and began tickling the tip of it with her hot tongue, and drawing the foreskin backwards and forwards over the nut with her lips; soon causing the member to spring up in full erection, and giving me an intense sensation of lascivious pleasure: so much so, that I felt the premonitory symptoms of the discharge. I exclaimed hurriedly: "Stop! Stop, Lucy! or you will make me go off in your mouth. Put it in the right place. Quick!" She let it go, and jumped up, with flushed cheeks, and sparkling eyes, laughing gaily; and at once pulled all her clothes up above her waist; and as she was wearing no drawers, I had a full view, for a moment, of her massive thighs, her big legs, and the forest of curly, brown hair which hid her cunt. Then she turned round, and striding over me backwards, as I sat in the chair, she put her hand between her legs, and taking hold of my prick, guided it into its proper place: then she gradually lowered herself down till every inch of the stiff column of flesh was buried in her cunt, and her naked bottom rested on my thighs. I then unfastened the whole front of her dress; and as she had no stays on, her luxuriant bubbies were only covered by her chemise, which I soon pushed down out of the way; then holding one of her big titties in each hand, I said: "Now Lucy, you must do all the work."

"All right," she replied, giggling. Then she began moving herself up and down on the points of her toes; at one moment raising her bottom till only the nut of my tool was left between the lips of her cunt, then at the next moment letting herself down with a flop upon my thighs; each time driving the weapon up to the hilt in the sheath; while I sat still, enjoying the exquisite sensation, and playing with her large, red nipples. Up and down went her bottom, her movements gradually becoming more rapid, and when she felt the "moment" was at hand, she worked with increased vigour, her titties undulating like the waves of the sea. In another instant I "spent," and the spasm seized her: I could feel a thrill pass over her body; her nipples seemed to stiffen in my fingers, her thighs gripped mine tightly, and she wriggled on the dart that was impaling her, till all was over. Then she leant back against my breast, the pressure of her thighs relaxed, my limp prick dropped out of its place, and the thick, white stuff trickled out of the orifice, down between the cheeks of her bottom as she sat straddled on my lap. She burst out laughing, and said: "I thought I could make you do it to me!" I also laughed, remarking: "I did not do it to you. You did it to me, you naughty young woman. In fact you have committed an indecent assault upon me, and I am going to give you a good spanking for your misconduct." Then I placed her in position to receive the punishment.

"Spank away. I like having my bottom warmed," she said, pulling her chemise and petticoats well up out of the way, and settling herself down across my knees.

It always delighted me to feel my hand rebounding from her fat buttocks; and as she had said she liked having her bottom warmed, I determined to spank her in right smart fashion.

Raising my hand high in the air, I laid on the hot slaps in quick succession all over the broad expanse of white skin, which first became pink, then red, and then crimson: her flesh twitched involuntarily under the resounding smacks of my hand; but for a time she bore the smart, which must have been sharp, without moving, or uttering a sound. At last, however, she could stand it no longer; and turning her head, she looked at me, with an expression of pain on her face, saying, in a quavering voice: "Oh, stop! Stop! I can't bear any more. My bottom is too sore."

It must indeed have been sore, for my hand was tingling! I let her get up, and she heaved a sigh of relief; the tears were standing in her eyes and she looked at me rather reproachfully, saying: "You-*have* warmed my bottom. That was the hardest spanking you have ever given me." She added, with a little laugh: "You have made me pay dearly for my kiss."

Then she put her cap straight, gave herself a shake, and left the room. After I had washed, and made myself comfortable, I sat down and read Maud's letter again; and while thinking over her communication, the idea came into my head that I might send Frances to live with Maud. As that young lady was going to leave my protection of her own accord, I thought she would probably be willing to take charge of Frances, and get her rigged out in the garments of her sex. Then, when Maud had married and left the villa, I could settle Frances in it, and go and live with her for a time. It was just the very thing. So I resolved to go up to London next day and arrange it all with Maud.

I then went down to lunch, and as I felt a little languid after all my various excitements, I had a bottle of champagne opened, which Frances and I soon disposed of. I told her that I had to go to London on business the following day, but I did not enter into particulars.

Next morning, as soon as breakfast was over, I drove to Winchester, caught the morning train to town, and went at once to Maud, whom I had not seen for some time. She was looking very well, and she had assumed a demure expression, as befitting a lady engaged to be married. She did not kiss me, so I laughingly took the little woman up in my arms; refusing to put her down until she had given me a proper salute. She soon gave me a kiss, and then we proceeded to business.

She told me all about her affairs, and informed me that her fiancé was a well-to-do young tradesman in the neighbourhood.

When she had finished, I related to her Frances' story, giving full details of everything that had occurred at Oakhurst since the first day the girl had come to the house. Then I asked her to let Frances live with her for a time, and I also asked her to get the girl proper attire.

Maud was greatly interested in the romantic story; and she laughed heartily at my description of the way I had discovered Frances' true sex. She was a good-hearted woman; she had always professed to be fond of me, and she was grateful to me, as I had always treated her well; so she at once agreed to take charge of Frances, and to look after her in every way, and she also promised to see that the girl was properly fitted out with everything necessary.

Then she remarked, with a sly smile: "I fancy you must have taken Frances across your knees oftener than was necessary. I know how fond you are of whipping a bottom."

"Oh, no. I assure you I never spanked her unless she was naughty. She will tell you so herself," I said, laughing.

"I suppose you will put her here in my place when I go away to be married?"

"Yes," I replied. "I have the lease of the house for some years to come; and I will take over your servants, and buy all your furniture as it stands." I had originally given her the furniture.

"Oh, that will be most convenient. It will save me the bother of having an auction here, as I had intended. My furniture would not have quite suited the establishment of my future husband." Then she added, with a grave face, but with a twinkle in her eyes: "You must not come near me after I am married. I am going to be very proper."

"No doubt you will be," I observed, laughing. "But you are not married yet, so come upstairs, and let me give you one last little touch of the rod."

"Oh, but if you birch me, you will want to poke me as well; and I don't think I ought to allow you to do that now," she said, with affected coyness.

"Come along," I said, taking her by the hand, and leading her up to the bedroom; where she at once took off everything, except her chemise, stockings and boots; then she got out the rod, and handed it to me, saying:

"Don't whip me too hard."

I made her lean over the side of the bed; then I threw her chemise up over her head, and admired her pretty little figure, naked to her garters. It was a long time since I had used the rod, and I grasped it with the feeling of pleasure that always comes over a lover of flagellation when he is about to redden a plump, white bottom.

I should have liked to birch her smartly, but I restrained my desire, and only gave her a dozen strokes, with just sufficient force to raise a bright pink blush on the cheeks of her bottom. She winced slightly at each cut, but did not remonstrate; and by the time I had finished whipping her I had a splendid cockstand; so I laid her at full length on the bed, and poked her with great gusto. She was a nice little woman, and a good poke; but she was not in her first youth; and I fancy she had been embraced by many a man; therefore she was not to be compared in any way with my fresh, young Frances. While Maud was dressing herself, I told her that I would bring Frances up to town in a few days. Then I gave her a cheque to cover all expenses; and after giving her a final kiss, I went away.

I got back to Oakhurst in time for dinner, and when it was over, and I had lighted a cigar, I told Frances that I had something serious to say to her. She looked very much surprised, but without asking a question, she drew a stool up beside me, and sat down to listen. I pointed out to her that we could not go on any longer living together at Oakhurst; as we were sure to be found out, and then there would be a great scandal, which I particularly wished to avoid.

I added that I was longing to see her dressed in her proper attire; and that I intended taking her, in a couple of days, to a lady friend of mine in London, who could see that she was fitted out in first-rate style, and with whom she could live until she had got accustomed to wearing petticoats again.

She listened, with a very sorrowful face, to all I had to say, and when I had finished, tears came into her eyes, and she said, heaving a deep sigh: "You are right. I am afraid we should get found out some day; so I had better go and live with your friend. Have you spoken to her about me?"

"Yes. I went up to London to-day on purpose to speak to her; and we settled everything. I was with her all day."

A frown wrinkled her brow, she pouted her lips, and she glanced at me with a look such as I had never seen in her eyes before—she was evidently jealous of my "lady friend."

"I suppose the lady is a sweetheart of yours?" she snapped out suddenly, in an aggrieved tone of voice.

"She was my sweetheart before I ever saw you; and she is going to be married in a month; so you needn't be jealous, you little goose," I replied, smiling.

"I believe you love her more than you love me. I'm sure I shall hate her!" she exclaimed angrily; then, with feminine inconsistency, she began to cry. I felt annoyed, and spoke sternly: "Don't be so silly, Frances. I have a great mind to give you a sound spanking for showing such ill-temper."

"I don't care if you do spank me," she replied sobbing. Then she added fiercely: "I tell you I hate her!"

"You will make me very angry if you go on like that. I have already told you that she was my sweetheart before I knew you. She is nothing to me now. Do be a sensible girl. You will like her, I am sure. She has excellent taste in dress, and you will want some one to help you when you are getting your trousseau."

Her brow cleared, she wiped her eyes and smiled; all the woman in her was stirred at the thought of buying dresses.

"Oh, how funny I shall feel when I put on petticoats again. And long ones too! The last petticoats I wore,—the ones Mrs. Leslie turned up—were short, only reaching half-way between my knees and ankles."

"You will soon get used to petticoats; and I shall be delighted to see you in a toilette from some fashionable dressmaker's. I am sure you will look charming. You know I shall often see you."

She laughed gleefully, got on to my knees, and kissed me, saying: "It will cost you a lot of money to dress me out, for I shall want to have everything of the very best description."

"So you shall. And after the lady has married, and gone away, you shall live in the house, and I will go and stay with you."

"Oh, you darling!" she exclaimed, kissing and hugging me. "I am so sorry I was cross just now; but I am so fond of you that I can't bear the idea of your being with another woman."

Then she asked me a number of questions about the lady; and I answered as truthfully as was possible under the circumstances. However, she appeared to be satisfied with what I told her, as she did not show any more signs of jealousy, and by the time she had heard all I chose to tell her, it was late, so we went to bed.

Next day, we both began to make preparations for leaving Oakhurst; as it was my intention, as soon as I had seen Frances safely settled with Maud, to go up to Scotland to stay with a friend who had invited me to shoot grouse with him. The servants were told that "Mr. Francis" was going away for good; and in a couple of days, when everything was in readiness for our departure, I wrote to Maud, telling her that we should be with her next day in time for lunch.

The morning came, and after an early breakfast, the dog-cart was brought to the door; our luggage was put in; Frances, with rather a shaky voice, bade good bye to the servants, all of whom had assembled on the terrace, apparently sorry that "Mr. Francis" was going away. Then we climbed into the trap, and I drove off.

The groom had gone on before us, so we were alone in the dog-cart, and as soon as we had got out of the avenue on to the road, Frances burst into a flood of tears, saying: "Oh, I am so sorry to leave the dear old house."

"Never mind, Frances," I said. "You will soon have a prettily-furnished little house of your own: we shall be together very often, and have lots of fun in London; and by and by I will take you abroad."

She smiled, nestled close up to me, and soon recovered her spirits. In due course, we reached London, and arrived at the villa in St. John's Wood, about one o'clock.

Maud greeted Frances in a most friendly manner, and

kissed her; then, after looking at her for a moment or two, said heartily, and without the least sign of jealousy: "Well dear, I must say you make a very good-looking young man; but when you are dressed in your proper attire, you will be a very pretty girl."

Frances laughed, looking pleased with the evidently sincere compliment. Then we sat down to a nice little lunch with champagne; and though Frances was a little shy at first, she brightened up under the influence of a glass of wine, added to Maud's cheerful talk and kindly manner; and in a short time she was chatting away perfectly at her ease.

After lunch, while I was smoking my cigar, the two young women sat together in a corner of the room, conversing in low tones and laughing merrily every now and then as they glanced at me, their eyes sparkling with fun. No doubt they were comparing notes on the various whippings and pokings they had received from me.

However, I was glad to see that they had taken to each other, and I felt sure that Maud would be kind to the young girl, for my sake.

I finished my cigar, and then I thought I had better tell Frances at once that I was going to Scotland for a short time. I said to her: "You know that Maud is going to be married in less than a month. I am going away to Scotland for three weeks, and by the time I come back you will have got your 'trousseau,' and also have learnt how to wear the garments of your sex in a graceful manner; therefore you will appear to me in a new and charming light. I shall feel that you are my sweetheart in reality then."

My communication took her completely by surprise; she gazed at me for a moment, and then began to cry, saying: "Oh, I thought you were going to stay here with me."

"Well, so I am, when I come back. In the meantime, you will have plenty of amusement in buying all the pretty things you want; and Maud will take you out driving every day. You'll find that the three weeks will soon pass." She smiled sorrowfully; and Maud said, kindly: "Cheer up, Frances. We shall have a jolly time together, with no man to bother us."

There was nothing more to be said or done; so I sent for a hansom, and when it came, my portmanteau, and gun case were put in. I gave Maud a kiss, and bade her good bye; and she promised to take the greatest care of Frances in every way. The girl clung round my neck, sobbing; I kissed her tenderly, left the villa, and drove off to King's Cross station, quite confident that my sweetheart would be true to me during my absence.

I had a long tiresome journey; as my friend lived in the wilds of Argyllshire, twenty miles from a railway station; and consequently I did not arrive at his place until late the following day.

My friend was a bachelor, and the house was merely a shooting-lodge, so the accommodation was rather rough. I need not enter into details of what happened during my stay in the North; for one day was exactly like another; though I will just remark that I had good sport with the grouse, but no sport of any kind with a woman. In fact the only female I spoke to, was a bare-legged, but good-looking Highland lass whom I met on the moor one evening when I was walking home alone. She had not "much English," as she quaintly expressed it; but we managed to talk a little, and she allowed me to kiss her pretty face several times; but when I took hold of her round the waist, and tried to put my hand up her short petticoats, she gave me a box on the ear, and scolded me volubly in Gaelic. I let her go!

## X

IN SILK ATTIRE.——THE OLD LOVE AND THE NEW.
——A JOLLY DAY AND A GOOD DINNER.——
RETROSPECTIVE BIRCHING RECOLLECTIONS.
——"DO IT AGAIN!"——A GLORIOUS
NIGHT'S WORK.

I got back to London early one afternoon, having been away just three weeks, to a day; and I drove off at once to the villa, where I knew Frances would be waiting to receive me, for we had corresponded regularly, and I had written to tell her when she was to expect me. During the long drive from King's Cross, I kept wondering how Frances would look in her woman's clothes, and I felt as excited as if I had been a young bridegroom going to meet his bride. On my arrival at the house, I was ushered into the drawing-room, where I was received by a lovely young lady, who threw her arms round my neck, and who kissed me, and fondled me, and cooed to me with all sorts of endearing terms.

It was Frances, but I should never have recognized her had I met her in the street: she appeared so much taller in her sweeping draperies, and she was far more handsome than I had ever expected. She was beautifully and tastefully dressed

• 119 •

in a frock that set off to perfection all the rounded contours of her splendid figure; there were ribbons on various
parts of the dress, and there was creamy lace round her
throat and wrists. Her hair had grown longer, covering her
well-shaped head with a wealth of little, silky, golden curls,
which came low down upon her broad, white forehead, but
did not hide her pretty shell-like ears. Her blue eyes seemed
to be larger, and more limpid than ever; her complexion was
like milk and roses; and the excitement had raised a pink
flush on her peach-like cheeks.

Her first transports of pleasure over, she sank gracefully down upon a chair; her trim ankles and tiny feet, in
smart patent leather high-heeled shoes, showed under the
hem of her dainty, lace petticoat; and she held in her small,
white hand, a filmy handkerchief scented with some delicate perfume.

Looking at me, with a languishing glance in her beautiful eyes, and with a smile curving her cherry lips, she said:
"Well, Charley, how do you think I am looking?"

I was quite dazzled by the unexpected beauty of the
girl, and I gazed at her for a short time without answering;
thinking to myself, with intense delight, that she was all my
own: no other man had ever touched the sweet, delicious,
young creature. I lifted her up in my arms and pressing her
to my breast, kissed her rapturously on the eyes, cheeks,
and lips, while the subtle perfume of her hair, flesh, and
clothes excited in me a dreamy, sensuous feeling.

She lay quietly in my arms perfectly unmindful of her
crushed and tumbled draperies; at last I answered her question: "You are looking most charming. I always thought you
were pretty when you were dressed as a man; but now that
I see you in your proper dress, I consider you beautiful."

She laughed a long low laugh of happiness. She said:
"Oh, I am delighted to hear you say you admire me! And
I am so glad to have you with me again. I have been pining
for you. I am longing to be in bed with you again. Oh, my

sweetheart! My love!" kissing me boldly, over and over again.

I sat down on an easy-chair, holding her on my knees with my arm round her waist; then I lifted up her skirts and admired her shapely legs, cased in pale blue silk stockings, held up by black satin garters; then, putting my hand up her petticoats, I opened the slit of her drawers, played with the silky hair on the lower part of her belly, and felt the cool, firm flesh of her bottom. I had a most tremendous cockstand, and I longed to poke her at that moment, as she sat on my knees; but I curbed my desire; thinking it would be better to wait till we got to bed, and then I should be quite fresh for a long night of pleasure.

So I took away my hand from the tempting "spot," rather to the surprise and disappointment of Frances, who, thinking I was going to give her a "sitting poke," had straddled out her legs so that I might be able to get my prick between her thighs. She glanced at me, with a yearning look in her great blue eyes which were moist and glistening, but she made no remark. I gave her a kiss, saying: "Let us wait till we are in bed, and then we shall enjoy our fun all the more."

Then I asked: "How have you been getting on with Maud?"

"Very well indeed. She has been most good, and kind to me in every way. I like her very much," she added, diffidently. "But she is not very well educated, and I don't think she is quite a lady, though she has very good taste in dress."

I laughed heartily, remarking: "You are a very observant young lady Maud is certainly not well-read, and I don't think her parents were what are called 'gentlefolks.' She herself started in life as a chorus girl."

A few moments after we had finished speaking, Maud came into the room and greeted me cordially. Then, looking waggishly at us, she said: "I see you two turtledoves are billing and cooing already. I hope I have not disturbed you. Shall I go away again?" she asked, with a sly smile. Frances jumped off my knees, laughing and blushing a little, and went up to Maud, who put her arm round the girl's waist in an affectionate way, saying to me: "Haven't I dressed her nicely? Isn't she a pretty girl?"

I answered both questions in the affirmative; taking a good look at my old and my new sweetheart as they stood side by side. Frances was a couple of inches the tallest of the two; and though Maud was tastefully dressed, and was pretty, and ladylike; she was not nearly so pretty, nor had she the air of distinction possessed by Frances, who looked what she was: a refined, well-bred young lady.

Maud rang the bell, and the servant brought in a tray with a pretty tea service, which she set out on a little bamboo table near Frances; who looked very charming as she busied herself in the essentially feminine task of making and pouring out the tea.

We had a long chat, and I was glad to see that my two sweethearts were on very friendly terms; there was not the least constraint between them, and they had evidently made confidantes of each other.

After a time I told them to go and dress, as I intended taking them to dine at a restaurant. They were delighted, and ran off at once to get ready, returning in about half-an-hour, charmingly attired. I never can describe a woman's dress, but I know that both my sweethearts looked very nice; though I think Frances was the more tastefully dressed of the two. We packed ourselves into a hansom, and drove to the Café Royal where we had an excellent dinner, and we drank a couple of bottles of champagne.

We were very merry, talking and laughing without cessation during the dinner. Frances was in one of her most lively moods, and her influence made Maud more talkative than usual: for, as a rule, she had not much to say for herself.

She was to be married in four days; and she informed us that her future husband was rather a slow-going fellow, and though she liked him fairly well, she did not love him. Then she said, laughing:

"I do not suppose he has the faintest idea of what men call the 'pleasures of the rod'; but even if he has, I do not intend to let him birch me."

Turning to me, and making a little grimace, she added: "I have had quite enough whipping from you, to last me my lifetime. No other man shall ever lay a rod across my bottom."

We laughed; and Frances said: "Charley is very fond of whipping, I know, and he has made me fond of it too; but I have never had a chance of whipping anyone except one little boy, years ago. I told you all about it, Maud, and also how I liked doing it."

"Yes," replied Maud, laughing. "You told me all about it; and you also told me that the boy's mother complained to Charley, and that he gave you a smart birching. But you did not tell me you liked that."

Frances laughed, saying: "I did not like it at all. I hated it. It was very painful. Charley gave me twelve hard cuts."

"Yes," I said, with a smile. "And you most certainly did not like them, judging from the way you kicked and squealed."

She made a little face at me, and then went on: "Although I do not like being whipped myself, I must say that I should very much like to whip a pretty little boy, or a big, bouncing girl."

I laughed, and Maud remarked: "It is a funny task. I have never felt the least inclination to whip, or to be whipped."

We lingered over dessert, with coffee and liqueurs, until it got late, then we drove back to the villa, where we sat in the drawing-room for a short time while I smoked a cigar. Then Maud bade us good night, and as she left the room, said to me, with a little laugh: "Let the girl have *some* sleep to-night."

Taking Frances by the hand, I led her upstairs to the "nuptial chamber," which was the largest room in the house. It was very prettily furnished, and well-lit by a soft-shaded lamp; the bed was a fine big one, in which I had many a time poked Maud; and across which I had many a time birched her.

I sat down on a chair and looked at Frances undressing herself, and I felt much more pleasure in watching the pretty creature discard her dainty, feminine garments, than I had ever felt while watching her taking off her male attire. Standing near the bed, she removed her pretty frock; then she unlaced, and took off her blue satin stays; next, sitting on a chair, she pulled off her little shoes, and then, unbuckling her garters, she drew off her tightly-fitting silk stockings; then, standing up again, she untied the strings of her drawers and petticoats, letting the garments fall to the floor; finally, she let her chemise slip from her polished shoulders, over her swelling bubbies and broad hips, down to her feet. Then, stepping clear of the pile of snowy draperies, she stood for a moment or two perfectly naked, smiling at me in a most enticing manner; but she soon hid her ravishing beauties under a pretty lace-trimmed nightdress, and got into bed. My cock was like a bar of iron; I had not had a woman for nearly a month; and I said to myself; "that it would cast her a groaning to take the edge off me. I tore off my clothes as quickly as possible, but I did not put out the light, and in an another moment I was in bed beside the lovely girl, who at once cuddled up close to me. Pulling up her nightdress to her neck, I clasped my arms round her yielding body, feeling it all over from head to foot, and I thought that her delicate skin was softer and smoother; and that her titties were rounder and firmer; and her bottom bigger and plumper; and that altogether she was more delicious in every way than when I last had her naked body in my arms.

She twined her legs round mine, and put her soft hand on my rampant prick, saying in a low tone of delight: "Oh, Charley! Isn't it delicious to be in each other's arms again?"

Then she added, squeezing my tool, and speaking with an affectation of fear: "Oh, how big it is to-night: I am quite afraid of it."

I pressed my lips to hers, and thrusting my tongue into her mouth, I kissed her that way; much to her astonishment, as I had never saluted her so before. "How do you like being kissed in that fashion?" I asked. Her breath had been taken away by the ardour of my kisses; but as soon as she could speak, she said: "I liked it very much. I will kiss you the same way now." Then she put her velvety, hot little tongue, as far as it would go, into my mouth.

Half frantic with desire, I laid her on her back, and pulled the bed-clothes down to her feet, while she at once stretched out her legs widely, and slightly arched her loins, so that I might be able to get into her with as little difficulty as possible. Putting my hands under her, I clasped the cheeks of her bottom, and extended myself on her naked bosom; her round, firm titties feeling like small elastic cushions under my breast; then pressing my lips to hers, I thrust my tongue again deeply into her fragrant mouth; at the same time forcing my prick up to the roots in her tight cunt with a few powerful movements of my loins. Then I began to fuck her slowly, but strongly; she put her arms round my neck, clasped her legs round my loins; her soft, warm thighs pressing my sides closely, and bucked up in splendid style: her whole body quivering from the violence of my thrusts. She panted, and groaned, and occasionally uttered a little squeak, as she heaved up her bottom, and bounded under me in voluptuous ecstacy, gasping out in broken accents: "Oh—Charley!—Oh—my—love! My—love!" I poked away vigorously, my strokes gradually increasing in rapidity; while she plunged and bounced so violently, that my prick was nearly jerked out of its place; but, grasping the cheeks of her bottom tightly, I held her in position, and soon was giving her the short digs. "Oh—h—h! it—is—coming! Oh—do—it—quick!—Quicker! Oh—h—h—h!"

The supreme moment arrived. I "spent" profusely;

and she gasped, sighed, wriggled, and squirmed in a most lascivious manner; the lips of her cunt tightly clipping my half-stiff prick; and as each hot jet of sperm spurted up her vagina, I could feel the flesh of her bottom quiver and twitch in my hands; and when she had drained me dry, and had stopped sighing and wriggling; she exclaimed in a tone of rapture: "Oh, that was most delicious!"

I withdrew, and lay beside her, and she pressed her naked body against mine, lying quietly for a short time. Then, raising her head, she looked in my face with a smile curving her moist red lips, and a sensuous gleam in her big blue eyes; coolly saying: "Do it again."

I laughed; but as not more than ten minutes had passed since I had taken my tool out of her cunt, I was not in a condition to go to work again.

"You know very well I can't do it again so soon. Feel how limp 'it' is at this moment," I said, pinching her bottom.

She put her hand on my member, and felt it, saying with a laugh: "It certainly could not get into me now."

Then we had a little talking; she all the time keeping her hand on my prick, and as soon as she felt it stiffening, she began to squeeze it, and to draw the foreskin backwards and forwards over the nut, so that in a short time the weapon was again fit for use. "There," she said, triumphantly, "it is quite ready; and so am I. Put it in."

I turned her on to her side; and lying close behind her with my belly against the warm cushions of her bottom, I put my prick between her thighs into her wet cunt; then, holding her in my arms, and placing my hands on her swelling bubbies, I poked her in the side position, which was a favourite one with us both. Shortly afterwards we fell asleep; but whenever I woke in the night, I always found Frances lying close to me with her soft legs thrown over mine. Then I would poke her, and go to sleep again. And once or twice, she happened to wake when I was asleep; but she soon woke me by gently pulling my tool; and then we again made "the beast with two backs." So that altogether we passed nearly the whole night in a succession of delicious amorous combats in various positions; and when morning came, I was pretty well played out, though Frances seemed to be nearly as fresh as ever.

At half-past ten o'clock we got up, had our baths, and dressed; Frances putting on a very pretty morning frock in which she looked most charming; then we went down to breakfast.

Maud received us with a smile, saying: "Well, you two have had a fine, long night of it. I suppose he did not let you have much sleep, Frances?"

She smiled, but made no reply; and I remarked: "Frances would not let me sleep when I wanted to do so; she can't reproach me for keeping her awake."

"I am not going to reproach you," she said, laughing. "I think we were both equally to blame."

Laughing merrily, the three of us sat down to a very good breakfast, to which Frances, and I, did full justice, for we stood greatly in need of refreshment after our labours.

When the meal was over, Maud went off to meet her lover; and after I had smoked a cigar, I took Frances out for a stroll in Regent's Park.

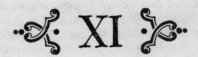

# XI

EXIT MAUD.——A HONEYMOON.——THE BEAUTY
AND QUALITIES OF FRANCES.——HER STRANGE
REQUEST AND HOW IT WAS GRATIFIED.——
SPANKED FOR LOVE.——LUSTFUL
REMEMBRANCES.

Three days afterwards, Maud was married; but neither I nor
Frances went to the wedding. However, just before my old
sweetheart left the house on the "happy day," I gave her a
cheque sufficiently large to pay for her furniture, and leave
something over as a wedding present. I also gave her a kiss,
and we parted the best of friends, after a *liaison* which had
lasted upwards of five years. I believe she made a good wife,
and she eventually became a mother, and while she lived in
the neighbourhood I used occasionally to meet her in the
streets, when we always had a little chat, but I never attempted to enter into an intrigue with her, though I have no
doubt she would have let me poke her, had I wished to do so.
After a time, she and her husband left London, and I never
saw her again. So Maud passes out of this true story.

Frances and I settled down to spend our "honeymoon"
quietly together. The servants who had remained in the villa
were two in number: a cook, and a housemaid, both of them

discreet, middle-aged women, who had been with Maud for five years, and consequently they were well-known to me; they also knew my ways, and were never surprised at anything I did.

The days slipped away pleasantly. Frances was a charming companion in every way; she was clever and witty, and, as she always read the daily papers, she could converse with me sensibly on all the topics of the day. A thing few women can do. Moreover, she was invariably good-tempered, and ready at all times to do anything I asked her; and what pleased me particularly was her extreme daintiness; she never came down to breakfast slipshod or untidy; but she always made her appearance, fresh and rosy from her bath, prettily dressed, and with her hair neatly arranged. In this respect, and in many others, she differed entirely from Maud, who had been in the habit of coming down in the morning wearing a wrapper and slippers, and with her hair twisted up carelessly.

Frances had excellent taste, and as I did not stint her in money, she soon added to her original "trousseau," a number of pretty frocks; and whenever she was out with me, her lovely face and tasteful dress always attracted respectful notice; for there was nothing "fast-looking" in her appearance. She was thoroughly ladylike, and I was proud of my sweetheart. I had made arrangements with a livery stable-keeper, so that she always had a well-appointed victoria or brougham at her service, and we used often to drive out together.

I was a member of a couple of good clubs, which I visited whenever I felt inclined; and Frances, being a sensible girl, never objected to my leaving her alone. She had plenty of resources of her own, and as she was fond of reading, she used to have a box of books sent to her from Mudie's every week. So I amused myself just as I chose, but I generally dined at home with Frances, who always dressed for dinner, and the repast was sure to be a good one, for the cook was skilful, and could always be depended upon to send up a properly cooked meal.

I was faithful to Frances; and when in London I always slept with her, and we thoroughly enjoyed our amorous gambols; so that altogether, our life at the little villa was peaceful and happy. I frequently took her out to dine at a restaurant; afterwards going to some theatre, or other place of amusement, and the girl was always delighted with the entertainments, as everything was new and fresh to her. I got her a piano, and engaged a teacher for her, and as she had a very good ear for music, she soon was able to play a little. And I found out that she had a sweet voice, so I made her learn some of my favourite ballads, and she would sing them to me in the evenings when I was at home.

While the shooting and hunting lasted, I often went down to Oakhurst for three or four days at a time; but I never once poked Lucy, although she threw herself in my way as often as she could. She did not attempt to "assault" me, and I fancy she did not like to run the risk of getting such another tremendous spanking, as was the last one she had received from me.

I was, however, always glad to go back to the villa, after a few days' absence; and I found it very pleasant to be welcomed by a smiling, handsome, well-dressed young lady, who had taken care to have a nice dinner ready for me, and who could amuse me all the evening afterwards with her lively talk. And then the delicious night that followed!

Frances seemed to become more voluptuous as time went on: in fact, she was often more eager for an embrace than I was; and even in the day-time she sometimes, by some device or other, got me to give her a poke.

I will relate how she induced me one day to satisfy her desire.

It was a cold afternoon, and we were sitting by the fire in the drawing-room having our usual cup of tea. Frances was looking very pretty, dressed in a charming, lace-trimmed, blue satin tea-gown, which fell in soft folds about her grace-ful figure. The sleeves were wide and loose, showing her beautifully-shaped milk-white arms up to her dimpled elbows.

She poured out a cup of tea, and brought it to me, then she fidgeted about the room for some time, arranging the nick-nacks on the various tables, and occasionally sitting down at the piano and striking a few chords.

At last, she came up to me, and looking in my face, said: "I feel very restless this afternoon; and I have taken a strange fancy into my head."

"What is it?" I asked.

"I want you to take me across your knees, and give me a spanking, just as you used to do when I was a naughty girl at Oakhurst," she replied, with a curious expression on her face.

I laughed. "Well, you know I am always ready to turn up your petticoats for any purpose; but I warn you that I will make your bottom smart, as I always did when I had occasion to spank you for being naughty, I do not care about pretending to spank. I like to spank in reality."

"That is what I want," she replied. "It is my fancy to be treated as a naughty girl, and spanked in the old way. Not more, but not less."

I was extremely delighted at her making this curious request. I had not spanked her for upwards of a year; and the last time I had whipped any one, was when I had given Maud her final birching, some months previously. And, as I have already stated in this narrative, whipping a bottom always gives me great sensual pleasure.

So, speaking in a stern voice, just as I had often spoken to her at Oakhurst, I said: "You have been very troublesome this afternoon. I am going to give you a sound spanking. Lay yourself across my knees."

She entered into the spirit of the thing; assuming a fright-ened expression, then with feigned reluctance placing herself in position, and as the well-dressed, handsome young lady lay across my lap, my cock sprung up against my trousers in full force.

I turned up her pretty, blue satin skirt all round, as high as I could get it, rumpling and creasing it a great deal: then, to lengthen out the pleasure, I slowly rolled up, one after the other, her lavender-scented, lace-flounced, snowy petticoats, and her delicate silk chemise. Then I stopped, and gazed at the rounded contour of her bottom, which was only hidden by her dainty lace-frilled drawers of the finest linen; and owing to the curved position in which she was lying across my knees, the thin garment clung closely to the hemispheres of plump flesh, and I thought I could see a pink tinge showing through thè filmy material. Unfastening the drawers, I pulled them entirely off her legs, and looked with glistening eyes and intense admiration, at her broad, deep, lovely milk-white bottom, displayed in all its naked beauty upon my lap. I also glanced with pleasure at her plump, well-rounded thighs, and her beautifully formed legs which were looking most charming in the tightly-fitting pearl-grey silk stockings she was wearing. Her garters were of dark blue satin, and her little feet were cased in high-heeled shoes of maroon-coloured morocco leather.

It was a ravishing spectacle! After I had satisfied the lust of the eyes, I proceeded to gratify the sense of touch. I stroked her velvet-like skin from her loins to her knees, and I paddled with the firm, elastic flesh of her bottom, squeezing it all over with my fingers, and making the blood come and go. But the most delicious part was yet in store.

I had taken care, when turning up her undergarments, to push them all well above her waist, back and front, which I had been able to do, by slightly loosening her stays. And I now unbuttoned my trousers, so that my stiff prick sprang out and pressed hard against her naked belly just above the "spot." She felt the touch of the dart, and a slight quiver passed over her body.

Everything being ready, I began to spank her; not

severely, but quite as smartly as I had ever spanked her when she had been a naughty girl at Oakhurst. She should be whipped exactly as she had desired.

I spanked her very slowly, and she winced at the hot slaps, every one of which printed a five-petaled red flower on the lily-white field; and as her bottom grew redder the smart increased and she began to wriggle in pain, quite in the old style. But I experienced a more exquisite sensation of sensual pleasure than I had ever felt before; because, on this occasion, her cool, soft, naked belly was rubbing against the uncovered tip of my upstanding prick. Placing my left hand under her, I put the end of my forefinger just inside the lips of her cunt; while with my right hand I continued to spank her smartly, each smack making her flinch sharply against my finger, and thus forcing it deeply into the warm recesses of the "grotto"; till finally the sensitive little button was touched, and then it almost immediately distilled a few drops of moisture which wetted my finger.

At last, the smarting behind, and the tickling in front, worked her up to such an intense pitch of excitement, that she could hold out no longer; and twisting herself round on my knees she looked up at me, her face flushed, her lips trembling, and her big blue eyes full of tears, yet gleaming with hot desire. "Oh, that is enough!" she exclaimed. "Don't spank me any more. Do the other thing! I am on fire! Embrace me quick! *Oh! Poke me!*"

It was the first time she had ever used such plain language.

I, also, was very hot. So, taking her in my arms, I laid her on the sofa, and threw her petticoats up to her navel; then clasping her in my arms, I opened the lips of her cunt with my fingers, and with one powerful thrust I transfixed her with the dart. And then I fucked her so lustily, that when all was over, she lay panting and quivering on the sofa, quite oblivious of everything; her petticoats up to the middle of her belly, and her legs widely separated, so that I had a full view of her cunt with its little pink lips still gaping slightly; and I noticed that the golden hair was studded with a few pearly-white drops of moisture. The randy girl had succeeded in getting the thing she wanted, though it had cost her a smart bottom. She had a shrewd idea that if I spanked her, I should be sure to get excited and poke her.

The whole affair had given me very great pleasure from first to last. I had thoroughly enjoyed spanking my sweetheart's beautiful, white bottom; and the poke which followed had been most delightful. I buttoned up my trousers, saying, with a laugh: "Now you naughty girl: you may pull down your clothes. Your pleasing punishment is over. How did you like it?"

She jumped up, and put on her drawers, smiling archly at me as she tied the strings round her waist: then she threw herself down again upon the sofa and gazed at me, with a languishing sensuous look in her great blue eyes. "I did not like the first part at all,—you hurt me dreadfully—but the second part was delicious. It was worth while going through the pain for the sake of the pleasure. And how strongly you did it to me! You seemed to be more than usually excited. Was that because you had spanked me?"

"Yes," I replied. "Whipping a bottom always excites me. And in the old days at Oakhurst,—after I had found out that you were a girl, whenever I spanked you, it was as much as I could do to prevent myself poking you when the punishment was over."

"Ah!" she said, laughing merrily, "I always thought you liked spanking me: and, as I once told you, I used rather to like getting a spanking. It made me feel queer;—though it was always very painful—and it caused me to have a curious sensation of longing for something. I did not at that time know what the feeling meant; but I understand it all now. It was the sexual desire stirring in me."

"Yes; that is what it was. And I soon found out that you were a voluptuously-inclined girl," I observed.

She laughed, saying: "Yes, I am. I must confess I am fond of the pleasures of love. But how did you manage to restrain yourself for such a time? I wonder you did not embrace me long before you did."

I laughed. "It was hard work to refrain, I can tell you; and you were very often in danger of being raped. But you know I frequently came up here to Maud; and I will tell you a secret, now that you are my only sweetheart. I used to poke Lucy the housemaid, whenever I felt inclined."

"What? that great, fat woman!" she exclaimed, laughing. "I am surprised. Why did you choose her? There were prettier women in the house."

I related to her how I had first got hold of Lucy; and I also gave a description of the way the woman had "assaulted" me, and how I had afterwards given her a most severe spanking.

Frances was very much amused. She remarked with a smile: "Poor Lucy! How you must have hurt her. You have a heavy hand when you spank, as I well know. My bottom is smarting at this moment." Then she added, laughing: "I don't think I need be afraid of your going after either of the servants in this house. They are too old and plain."

I laughed, and kissed her, saying: "You may be sure that neither of them will tempt me to be unfaithful to you."

We then went to our bedroom, and after we had washed and dressed, we drove to a restaurant and dined; afterwards going to a theatre, and finishing up with a supper before returning home.

# ❧ XII ❧

MY FRIEND FORD.——OUR VISIT TO THE "GAY"
HOUSE AT KENSINGTON.——EIGHT YOUNG ANGELS.
——LIVING PICTURES.——THE BIRCHING OF A
NIHILIST LADY.——VENUS RISING FROM THE
SEA.——THE THREE GRACES.——ONANISTIC
SCHOOLGIRLS.——GENUINE LESBIANS.——
MY RESTRAINT.——MRS. LESLIE'S STORY.
NO PLACE LIKE HOME.——A DREAM
REALISED.——SAINT GEORGE.

A few days afterwards, when we were out driving, I suddenly took it into my head to ask Frances if she thought she
could find Mrs. Leslie's house in Kensington. She replied
that she was sure she could; and at once directed the coach-
man which way to go. In a short time we arrived in a street
which Frances said was the right one, and after we had
driven a short distance down it, she pointed to a house,
exclaiming: "There it is! I wonder if the horrid woman is
living in it still? Oh! how I should like to spank her with a
thick slipper every day for three days, as she did me." Then
she smiled, and taking my hand, pressed it, remarking:

"Though after all if she had not turned me out, I should never have met my sweetheart."

"Would you like to call and see her? She may still be living there," I observed, smiling.

"No. I don't want to see her face again; though I should like to see her bottom reddening under my slaps," she replied, laughing.

We then drove home, and while we were at dinner, the thought struck me that it would be rather good fun to pay a visit to Mrs. Leslie and see what sort of an establishment she kept.

She might still be carrying on the business.

So, as soon as I had finished my cigar after dinner, I told Frances that I was going to my club, and as I should not be back till late, she was not to sit up for me. She said "very well," and gave me a kiss, for she never bothered me with questions as to where I went, or what I did. I left the villa, hailed a passing hansom, and told the driver to go to the club; intending to have a talk with a chum of mine named Ford, who was generally to be found in the smoking-room after dinner. He was there, as I had expected, smoking a cigar, with a cup of black coffee on a little table beside him.

Ford and I were old friends; he was a man about my own age, and like me, a bachelor, and we had had many queer adventures together.

I sat down beside him, lit a cigar, and asked him if he knew whether a certain Mrs. Leslie still kept a "gay" establishment in Blank-street, Kensington. "Yes," he replied, "she does. I have never been there, but I have heard that it is a first-class house of its kind. Patronized by the nobility, and I believe occasionally by royalty," he added with a laugh.

"I am going there to-night to have a look round," I said. "Will you come with me?"

"Yes, I will. I am feeling rather inclined for a spree to-night. Come along." Leaving the club, we took a hansom, telling the man to drive to Blank-street, Kensington. When we reached the corner of the street, I stopped the cab, and we got out, paid the driver, and then walked the rest of the way to the house. I touched the electric bell, and the gate was soon opened by a smartly-dressed maid-servant; whom I asked if we could see Mrs. Leslie. The woman smiled at such an unnecessary question, and merely saying: "Step this way, gentlemen," preceded us into the house and ushered us into a large, brilliantly-lighted drawing-room, where she left us, saying that Mrs. Leslie would be with us in a short time.

"A well got-up shop," observed Ford, laughing, and seating himself in a luxurious easy-chair.

I walked round the room which was handsomely furnished in a most tasteful style; the only thing about it at all suggestive, being the number of broad, low softly-cushioned couches and ottomans which were ranged round the walls, and also in the middle of the floor.

At one end of the apartment, there was a deep, broad recess, apparently opening into another room; but I could not be certain, as the place was screened by heavy curtains of dark crimson velvet.

I had often been in establishments of the same sort in London, and also in Paris, Vienna, and other cities on the Continent; but I had never seen a better appointed drawing-room, than the one I was in.

In about five minutes time, Mrs. Leslie came into the room, and greeted us as if we had been old friends, smilingly telling us to sit down and make ourselves comfortable. Then she sank down on one of the couches, displaying a pair of neat feet and ankles, cased in black silk stockings. I took a good look at the woman who had treated my pretty Frances so cruelly. She was by no means bad-looking; being a tall, dark-haired, well-preserved woman about forty years of age; she had a buxom, but shapely figure; she was handsomely dressed, and she was quite lady-like, both in speech and manner.

After a little chat, Mrs. Leslie smiled, saying: "Well, I suppose you two gentlemen did not come here merely to talk to me. Wouldn't you like to see my young ladies? None of them are engaged at this moment, so you will be able to see them all."

We both intimated that we should be delighted to make the acquaintance of the young ladies. She rose from her seat, and going to the end of the apartment, touched the button of an electric bell three times; and in about five minutes, no less than eight young women and girls came trooping into the room from behind the curtains. They were all introduced to us, their names being Alice, Kate, Edith, Fanny, Rose, Helen, Ethel, and Clara. They were beautifully dressed, and they were of various ages: two of them, Clara and Ethel, who were wearing short petticoats, and who had their hair flowing loosely over their shoulders, were not more than fourteen or fifteen years old. But these two, I afterwards found out, were not available for poking.

The other young ladies ranged in age from eighteen to twenty-five years; some were slim, and some were plump; some were dark, and some were fair; some were tall, and some were short; but all of them were more or less pretty, and one or two were rather handsome.

We ordered plenty of champagne, and sat down on the comfortable couches surrounded by the pretty girls with whom we intended to have a regular bit of sport—though personally I did not intend to poke one of them.

They were full of fun, and by no means shy, so we all soon got very merry, and there was a great deal of laughter, and no end of chaff; a little broad sometimes, but nothing indecent was said or done by any of us, just then. I began to enjoy myself thoroughly, as it was a long time since I had gone in for a spree of that sort. Ford also appeared to be very jolly. After a time, Mrs. Leslie beckoned us aside, and taking us to the end of the room out of earshot of the girls, said: "Now gentlemen; what would you like to do?

Have either of you any particular fancy? We can give you plenty of variety in this house. You can go to bed with one or more girls if it pleases you to do so. If either of you is fond of the rod, I have a room fitted up with everything necessary, where you can tie up and strip any girl you fancy and give her a little birching; or if you like it better, you can see a girl birched by another. Or would you prefer to see some Tableaux Vivants? I pride myself especially upon them.

"I can show you tableaux with scenery, and with the girls dressed in character; and I can show you some tableaux of statuary, with the girls naked; and I can also show you some very naughty tableaux."

Ford and I consulted together for a moment, then I said: "We should like to see a selection of tableaux: some of all sorts."

"So you shall. Are either of you fond of seeing the rod used?"

We both admitted that we had a liking for such a sight.

"Well then," she said, "I will show you two tableaux of whipping; then a couple of tableaux from mythological subjects; and finish up with two naughty tableaux."

Both of us were perfectly satisfied with the programme she offered, and we said so.

She then told us to take our seats on two easy-chairs which were placed a few feet distant from the curtains, and she added that we should have to wait a short time, as the scenery had to be set, and the girls dressed for the first two tableaux.

Then she made a sign to the girls, and went behind the curtains, followed by the whole troop of laughing damsels.

As we sat waiting for the entertainment to commence, we could hear the girls bustling about, chattering to each other in low tones, and occasionally laughing as they dressed themselves.

At the end of about ten minutes, Mrs. Leslie called out

in a clear voice: "The first tableau will represent, 'The Birching of a Nihilist in a Russian Prison.'"

Immediately the curtains separated in the middle, drawn aside by unseen agency, and the tableau appeared, brilliantly lighted from above, so that we could see the smallest details.

The scene showed a large, bare, prison cell, with white-washed walls, stone floor, and grated window. In it were six figures, five "men" and one woman, all attired in costume, and personating, respectively: the governor of the prison; the surgeon; a prison warder; two soldiers; and the Nihilist lady. In the middle of the cell there was a long, curved wooden structure, upon which the "Nihilist lady" was bound in a bent position, her feet resting on the floor. Her arms were stretched out one on each side of the "horse," her wrists being secured to rings: and her ankles were strapped together, and fastened to a bar at the lower part of the structure.

She was dressed in prison costume, consisting of a loose, blue serge frock, the skirt of which, as well as her petticoats and chemise, being rolled up to the middle of her back, and she had been divested of her stays and drawers. The "Nihilist lady,"—whom I recognized at Edith,—was a plump, shapely damsel, with a fine big bottom, large thighs, and good legs cased in black stockings, which contrasted well with her white skin. At the left side of the "culprit" stood the "warder" who was inflicting the punishment; a bearded "man," wearing a uniform consisting of a dark green tunic, with trousers of the same colour tucked into long boots reaching to "his" knees; and a round flat cap with a peak. "He" held high in the air a thick, bristly birch rod, which seemed just about to fall on the "culprit's" bare bottom. At the other side stood the "surgeon," a whiskered, moustach-ioed "man," in a plain, dark blue uniform, and beside him was the "governor," with a fierce moustache, dressed in an imposing uniform, with medals on "his" breast. A little in rear of the horse stood the two "soldiers," with cross-belts and side-arms. The "culprit's" bottom had been most skilfully "made-up," so that the whole surface of the skin, from the loins to the upper part of the thighs, appeared crimson, and striped all over with long livid weals, and spotted with blood, which also appeared to be trickling down the "victim's" white thighs. She had her head turned to one side, and she was glaring with eyes full of intense horror at the uplifted rod; her face was scarlet and distorted with pain; her mouth was wide open, with the lips drawn back from the teeth, as if she were screaming loudly; and the tears appeared to be streaming down her cheeks. The whole scene appeared so intensely real, that I actually waited, with a feeling of suspense, to see the rod fall on the bleeding bottom, and to hear the victim's shriek. Since that time I have seen many "Living Pictures," but I have never seen one better done.

In another moment the curtains were drawn, shutting out the scene. Ford and I applauded vigorously, clapping our hands and crying out: "Brava! Brava! Well done! Very well done!" Then, turning to me, my companion whispered: "It was splendid! The illusion was perfect. I have never seen anything to equal it, in Paris or Vienna."

After a rather long interval, Mrs. Leslie announced: "The next tableau will represent punishment as inflicted in a boarding-school for young ladies." The curtains were parted, and we saw that the recess was now fitted up as a schoolroom, with desks, benches, a blackboard, globes, and maps on the walls. In this tableau there were ten figures; seven of them, dressed as schoolgirls, in short frocks, and with their long hair flowing loose over their shoulders, were sitting on high forms, so that we could see their pretty legs, cased in silk stockings of various colours; and in two or three cases where the petticoats happened to be very short, we caught glimpses of the lace frills on the girls' drawers.

In the middle of the "schoolroom," stood a stalwart young woman, who was evidently one of the servants of the establishment, in her ordinary attire, consisting of a black frock, with white apron, cap, collar, and cuffs.

She was bending forward, "horsing" in the orthodox 'position the girl named Ethel, who was certainly not more than fourteen years of age. The skirt of her short frock, and her dainty little white petticoats were pinned up to her shoulders, and her pretty lace-trimmed drawers were hanging down about her knees. She had a most lovely little bottom with round, firm-looking, plump cheeks; and her delicate skin was as white as snow, except where it had been artificially marked with pink streaks, and small red dots, representing the ravages made by the rod.

Her thighs were fairly well developed; and her small but shapely legs were clad in long, brown silk stockings, gartered with bows of black satin; and she was wearing neat, buttoned boots on her little feet.

The "schoolmistress" in a grey wig, and with spectacles, was personated by Mrs. Leslie, who held over the girl's delicious bottom, a long, slender birch rod, prettily ornamented with blue ribbons.

Ethel played her part well. She was looking over her shoulder, her face was red, she appeared to be crying loudly in pain, and her eyes were fixed with an appealing glance on the stern "schoolmistress."

The other "schoolgirls" were looking on at the punishment with various expressions on their faces; some appeared to be rather amused at the sight; others seemed to be perfectly indifferent; and others were looking very much frightened. The girls had been well drilled in their parts. This tableau, like the preceding one, looked wonderfully real, and it was also most "fetching" to Ford and myself; as we were both "lovers of the rod"; so we did not stint our applause when the curtains closed over the picture. Then he said to me, with a chuckle: "What a beautiful, white, chubby bottom that little girl has! I have never before seen so young a one turned up. I wish we could see her being birched in reality."

"So do I. But if I had my choice, I would rather spank her smartly across my knees. I think that way of whipping a little girl gives a man the greatest pleasure," I observed.

"Now we shall have the tableaux with naked figures," said my companion, digging me in the ribs, and rubbing his hands.

In a short time, Mrs. Leslie called out: "The next tableau will be, 'Venus Rising from the Ocean.'" And the curtains were again drawn aside.

This time there was no scenery, but the walls of the recess were draped with light blue gauze. In the centre, there was a circular platform covered with sea green velvet, and on it were five female figures perfectly naked.

Venus was personated by Rose, who was about twenty-two years of age, and who was the tallest and best-looking of all the girls. She stood resting the weight of her body upon her left foot, which was slightly advanced, her right leg being bent so that only the toes touched the floor: her pretty, rounded arms were raised, and gracefully curved above her head, the palms of her hands were inclined inwards, the tips of her fingers almost meeting. Her long fair hair was hanging in artistically arranged disorder over her shoulders and bosom, partly veiling her swelling bubbies. She had large, liquid-looking gray eyes; a very white skin, a broad smooth belly; sturdy, well-shaped thighs, and good legs; her ankles were neat; her pretty feet were without blemish, and her cunt was shaded with a curly growth of very light brown hair. The four attendant sea nymphs were personated by Helen and Fanny, who were fair girls; and Kate and Edith who were dark; their hair was loose, and they were lying in graceful attitudes round the central figure. After a moment, the platform began to revolve slowly, so that we saw every part of the girls' naked bodies; their pretty, pink-tipped titties, their cunts, each one shaded with hair of a different colour; their plump, round bottoms,—"Venus" had a very big one—their variously shaped thighs and their legs of different sizes. It was a charming spectacle of naked feminine beauty, but the tableau was not in the least suggestive, and at that moment I had no more feeling of desire than if I had been gazing at a group of marble statues.

Ford, however, had evidently been differently impressed; and when the curtains had hidden the naked girls from our sight; he whispered to me, smacking his lips: "By Jove! that girl who did Venus is a scrumptious creature. What a white skin she's got! And what splendid bubbies! and such a grand bottom! and the hair on her cunt looked like floss silk! I felt very much inclined to rush on to the platform and poke her. Anyhow, I'll sleep with her to-night."

The next tableau was "The Three Graces." The platform this time was covered with black velvet, and the "Graces" were represented by Kate, Helen, and Fanny, who stood with their arms wreathed round each other's waists and busts. All three girls had shapely figures, with good bubbies, and plump bottoms. Kate, an olive-skinned girl, had a profusion of black hair on the lower part of her belly. Helen's cunt was hidden by curly, brown hair; and Fanny's "spot" was shaded with auburn hair. And while the platform was slowly revolving, we had a good look at their naked charms, both back and front, until the curtains were closed.

The improper tableaux were now to come; and Mrs. Leslie announced that the first would represent: 'Two Naughty Schoolgirls.' The actresses in this tableau, were Clara, who was about fifteen years old, and Alice, a short, slim, baby-faced girl about eighteen years of age. They were supposed to be in their dormitory and they were sitting side by side on a bed, with nothing on them but their long white nightgowns.

These garments were tucked up tightly round their waists, leaving the whole of the lower half of their pretty little figures naked; and each girl had one of her fingers up the other girl's cunt. Clara's little slit was just fledged with light-coloured down; but Alice's was well covered with chestnut hair. Their cheeks were painted so as to appear deeply flushed, their red lips were slightly open, and their eyes were fixed on each other's faces with a languishing look.

They acted their parts well, and we applauded them. In another minute, we heard Mrs. Leslie say: "The last tableau is entitled: 'A Lesbian Kiss.'" Then the curtains were again drawn back, and we saw on the black velvet-covered platform, the naked figures of the girls Fanny and Kate. Fanny, with her auburn hair coiled in thick plaits, was lying on her back, with outstretched legs, and with her hands clasped over the black-haired Kate, who was lying stretched at full length upon her, but in a reversed position, so that each girl had her face between the other girl's thighs. Kate's mouth was resting on Fanny's cunt, while Fanny's mouth was pressing against Kate's cunt, and with their tongues they were tickling each other's "sensitive spot." The black velvet on which they were lying, showed off to perfection the whiteness of the girls' naked bodies, thighs, and legs; and they appeared to be thoroughly enjoying their mutual "Lesbian Kiss." Their cheeks were flushed in reality; their eyes were gleaming with lust, their bodies were quivering, their bosoms were heaving; and each girl had on her face an expression of voluptuous pleasure.

In a moment more, the curtains closed over the lascivious scene, which had excited me greatly; as it also had my companion; and we were both quite sure that there had been no "make-believe" in the tableau of "The Lesbian Kiss."

Soon afterwards, Mrs. Leslie came out, and throwing herself down upon a couch, smilingly asked us how we had liked the show?

We both assured her that we had been charmed in every way with the entertainment; and we complimented her on her skill as a stage-manager. She seemed to be gratified at our sincere compliments, and she said she hoped to see us again, when she would show us another selection of tableaux. In a short time, all the girls—except the two young ones—came from behind the curtains; dressed only in loose wrappers over their chemises, and with their bare feet in velvet slippers. We ordered more champagne, and the fun became fast and furious; the girls all crowded round us, and unbuttoning our trousers, played with us in a most lascivious manner. And in a few moments, Ford and I were sitting on couches, each of us holding on our knees a couple of the half-naked girls, while with our hands under their scanty attire we felt their plump, warm bodies all over: paddling with their titties, pinching their bottoms, tickling their cunts, and playing all sorts of pranks, till they squirmed, giggled, and laughed hysterically.

Ford soon went off to bed with Rose; but I was still determined not to poke one of the girls. They were more or less pretty, and well-made; but not one of them was so pretty or so well-shaped at Frances; nor had one of them a whiter skin, firmer bubbies, or a plumper bottom than my sweetheart. Moreover, they were all probably poked every day by different men; whereas Frances was virgin to every one but me. So, though I had a tremendous cockstand, I resisted all the girls' blandishments; thinking to myself that I would make Frances wriggle her bottom in fine style when I got home.

I disengaged myself from the clinging arms of the two girls who were still sitting on my knees; bade them all good night; and then left the room with Mrs. Leslie, who took me into an adjoining apartment, where I paid her for my share of the entertainment.

Then, merely out of curiosity to hear what she would say, I resolved to ask her about Frances. So I said, in an indifferent way: "I believe you had a girl named Frances Howard living with you a few years ago."

She tightened her lips, frowned slightly, and cast a sharp glance at me, asking brusquely: "How did you get to know that?"

"I heard it in a roundabout way," I replied with an unmoved face. Then I asked in an innocent manner: "Do you know what has become of her?"

"No, I do not," she answered, curtly.

"Will you tell me all you know about her? I give you my word that nothing you tell me shall go further."

"Oh, I don't mind telling you about the girl. She was at school with a lady whom I knew; and she told me that she could not keep the girl, as her money had all been expended, and she had no friends of any sort who could pay for her. I offered to take her into my house and keep her. I frankly tell you that I did so because she was a pretty girl, and I meant to make use of her. If I had not taken her, she would have been sent to the workhouse." Here Mrs. Leslie paused for a moment, then said with a smile: "The schoolmistress did not know the sort of establishment the girl was going to

"I kept her for six months, and then I asked her to do as all the other girls did; but she positively refused. I was very much annoyed, and I gave her three sound spankings, on three successive days; but she was a stubborn girl, and she would not give in. So I told her to leave my house in twenty-four hours; only meaning to frighten her; as I really had no intention of turning her out. But the silly girl took me at my word, and she ran away next morning, taking with her a complete set of my son's clothes; but leaving four pounds to pay for the things. And as she had cut off her hair, I supposed she had dressed herself up in the boy's clothes. I have never heard of her since; and I have often wondered what became of her."

I affected surprise, saying: "It was a funny thing for a girl to run away in boy's clothes."

"Yes, it was very strange. But Frances was always a queer girl in many ways. She was a clever girl, and she had a strong character."

"She must have had," I observed, smiling in a childlike manner.

Mrs. Leslie did not ask me why I had inquired about Frances, and I did not offer her any explanation. But I believe she spoke the truth when she said that she had not really meant to turn the girl adrift.

Having heard all I wanted from Mrs. Leslie, I bade her "good night," and left the house; luckily coming across a belated hansom, and reached home at two o'clock in the morning. I let myself in with my latchkey and went quietly up to the bedroom, finding Frances fast asleep, and looking so lovely that I felt delighted at knowing I was in full vigour. Her silky, golden hair was streaming over the lace-bordered pillow, one arm was thrown over her head, her cheeks had a delicate pink tinge, and her rosy lips were curved with a slight smile, as if she were dreaming pleasantly. I undressed and got into bed without waking her; then taking her in my arms, I roused her with a shower of hot kisses.

"Oh, Charley!" she exclaimed, throwing her arms round my neck, and returning my kisses. "I was dreaming that I was in your arms, and now my dream has come true. I am so glad you have come home. I was afraid you were going to stay away all night."

Then, slipping her hand on to my tool, which was in full erection, she laughed gleefully, saying: "It is quite ready for me!" Then she settled herself well down upon her back, pulled her nightgown out of the way, and extended her thighs.

I buried my face in the valley between her splendid bubbies, kissing the warm, perfumed flesh, and sucking the delicious little nipples; at the same time squeezing with both hands the plump, firm flesh of her magnificent bottom. But I was too excited to spend time in dalliance, so I placed myself in position between her legs, and gave full vent to my long pent-up passions; fucking the lovely girl with such hot lust, and with such tremendous force, that she panted, sighed, and groaned under my thrusts; and I could feel the flesh of her bottom twitching in the grasp of my hands, when she felt herself inundated with the hot torrent. When she had recovered her breath, she said: "Oh, Charley, that was very nice! What has made you so excited to-night? You have not done it so strongly to me since the afternoon you spanked me." Then she added with a laugh: "I believe you have been spanking some girl or other."

"No, I have not," I replied laughing, and kissing her. "You are the only girl I ever spank now."

She cuddled up to me, and after a little rest, began to play with my half-stiff prick in such a skilful way that in a short time it was ready for action: so I again mounted and rode another delightful course. Soon afterwards we fell asleep in each other's arms.

We did not do "it" again during the short remainder of the night, but when morning came, we woke up with renewed vigour and had a couple of good pokes. For the first one, I made her get outside the bed, and kneel down on all-fours with her legs well separated, and her head resting on the pillow; then I turned her nightdress up to her shoulders, and admired her grand white bottom stuck out so prominently; and, owing to the position in which she was kneeling, I could see the lower part of the pink lips of her pretty, golden-haired, little cunt. Kneeling behind her, I clasped my hands in front of her soft, warm belly; then I thrust my prick between her half-open thighs, deep into the tight slit, until my balls touched her bottom, and poked her in "dog-fashion," while she moved her loins backwards and forwards briskly to meet my digs.

The second poke was a "St. George." I lay upon my back with my prick pointing up in the air; then Frances knelt over me in a straddling position, with one knee on each side of my body, but with her back turned towards my face, so that I might have a full view of her bottom while the work was going on. She knew what to do; and as I opened the lips of her cunt with my fingers, she lowered herself down till she was spitted on the dart; then, moving herself up and down on her knees, she rubbed my stiff member between the clinging folds of her vagina in a most delightful way; while I, to stimulate her, slapped her bottom with both my hands, till her white skin turned rosy red. And when the discharge took place, she fell forward on her face in a transport of voluptuous excitement, thus dragging the weapon out of its sheath and causing me to sprinkle her upturned bottom with white drops.

Then I got up, went to my dressing-room, had my bath, dressed, and went down to the dining-room, where I was soon joined by Frances, looking as blooming as a rose, and charmingly pretty in a fresh, crisp morning frock. We both had good appetites, and as we ate our breakfast, we chatted gaily, but I did not tell her about my visit to Mrs. Leslie.

I remained at home all the morning, and after lunch we drove to Richmond, dined there, and arrived back at the villa about eleven o'clock.

## ❧ XIII ❧

THE WHIPPING ROOM.———A TRIP TO ITALY.———
FRANCES BECOMES A FLIRT.———SPANKED FOR
FRIVOLITY.———A WOMAN PUNISHED
LIKE A CHILD.

The months rolled on; spring and summer had passed, and
it was again autumn. I had divided my time pretty equally
between Oakhurst and St. John's Wood, and altogether I
had managed to amuse myself in a satisfactory manner.

Accompanied by Ford, I had paid several more visits to
Mrs. Leslie's establishment; on each occasion seeing a fresh
selection of tableaux; some of the whipping scenes being
exceedingly quaint, as the actresses were dressed and coloured
to represent quadroon slave girls.

And one afternoon, much to Ford's delight,—and to
my own, I must confess—we saw the little girl Ethel, who
had committed some offence, birched in reality by Mrs.
Leslie. There was no tableau arranged on that occasion;
and the punishment was inflicted in the "whipping room"
of the establishment, a large apartment situated at the top of
the house.

It was well furnished, and thickly carpeted, and there
were large mirrors on the walls, which, as well as the door
and windows, were draped with heavy tapestry; and it con-

tained everything that could possibly be required by the most enthusiastic votary of the rod.

There were cushioned "horses," and sloping benches; long and short ladders; whipping blocks, and posts with rings for securing the victim's wrists and ankles. And, hanging in rows on the tapestry-covered walls, were birch rods of all sizes, whips of various kinds, leathern tawse, straps of all lengths and breadths, and flat, round, wooden "spankers," with long handles.

No one was present but Ford and myself, and when we had taken our seats, Mrs. Leslie quickly tied the whimpering young culprit by her wrists and ankles, over one of the flogging blocks; and in another moment, her short petticoats were up, and her drawers were down. Then Mrs. Leslie gave her twelve smart cuts with a small, but stinging birch rod, reddening and wealing her plump, little white bottom all over, and making her squeal shrilly.

As Mrs. Leslie was skilled in the use of the rod, she had handled it in a most graceful way; so that altogether it had been a pretty little whipping, and Ford was so much excited that he sent for his favourite Rose and took her off at once to a bedroom.

I, however, managed to restrain myself that day. But on two other occasions when I had been more than usually excited by the lascivious play of the girls, I gave one of them a poke; but I did not enjoy either of them much, and I always returned with increased zest to Frances, to whom I had been faithful, with those exceptions.

We got on together very well; she never bothered me, and she was as loving as ever; but with all her love, I think she stood a little in awe of me; which perhaps was only natural, as she had always been so completely under my authority ever since the day I had first picked her up: moreover, I was nearly sixteen years older than she was.

Anyhow, she appeared to consider herself still subject to discipline; and therefore, on the rare occasions when she offended me, I did not hesitate to spank her soundly. She never remonstrated, but would place herself in any position I told her; and sometimes I made her let down her own drawers, and raise her own petticoats to receive her punishment, which she always took in a most submissive manner, though I generally spanked her till she cried with pain.

She did not like it, but I did!

However, she never showed any signs of anger; and when the smart had passed off, she would fasten up her drawers, wipe the tears from her eyes, and sit down quietly in a chair. In fact, she seemed to be more affectionate to me just after I had given her a good spanking. There really seems to be some truth in the saying, that: "A woman, a dog, and a walnut tree, the more you beat them, the better they'll be."

She was fond of music and had practised diligently, so that she had become a very fair player, and she had also taken a fancy for painting in water colours: so that with her piano, and her paint-box, and her books, she always contrived to amuse herself during my absences.

The time passed; and as I had promised to take Frances abroad that winter, I asked her, at the beginning of December, what part of the continent she would most like to visit. She at once chose Italy; for since she had taken to painting she was always longing to see the picture galleries in Rome and Florence. So a few days afterwards, on a raw, cold December afternoon, we left London, which was looking dreary and wretched, and began our journey to the "sunny South."

From the moment we got on board the steamer at Dover to cross the channel, Frances was in a state of exuberant delight; everything being so perfectly new and strange to her. And it amused me very much to watch the girl's unaffected pleasure at all she saw, as we made our way by slow stages to Rome. I had been there before and had "done" the place pretty well; but I enjoyed going over the ground again with an intelligent companion like Frances, who, though she was very like a child still in many ways, was thoroughly interested in all the antiquities of the "Eternal City." And as she had been reading up Roman history she had got to know more than I did about the Pantheon, the Coliseum, the Baths of Caracalla, and all the other celebrated ruins.

From Rome we went to Florence, where we "did" the Florentine and Uffizi galleries, to the intense delight of Frances, whose nature was more artistic than mine; for I sometimes got tired of the pictures. However, I did not like to check the girl's enthusiasm, so we wandered through the galleries and museums, Frances hanging on to my arm, with a rapt look on her face, her cheeks pink, and her eyes shining with pleasure. The pictures never seemed to pall on her.

Then we went to Venice, which was a fresh delight to her: and she was never tired of going about in a gondola with me on the beautiful moonlight nights. The gondolier could not see us, so she used to sit on my knees and recite bits of Byron to me, and I sometimes poked her as she sat on my lap. It was very romantic and delicious to "have" my pretty sweetheart in a gondola, on a canal in Venice, on a balmy Italian night.

We visited Naples, and the south of Italy, and finally we went to Nice, where I intended to stay for some time, as I wanted to have a little play at Monte Carlo.

I took a suite of rooms at a good hotel, and we settled down to make ourselves at home for a bit after our wanderings. The hotel was full of people of all nationalities; and my "wife" and I soon made a number of acquaintances, both male and female, but chiefly male; for Frances quite eclipsed all the other women in the hotel, and they were rather jealous of her. She certainly was far prettier, and was always more tastefully dressed than any one of them; though there were some "smart" American girls staying in the house.

The men were all very attentive to my "wife," and I soon saw that she was extremely fond of admiration, which, after all, was not to be wondered at. She knew she was a beautiful woman, and she had hitherto hardly ever spoken to any man but me; therefore, when she suddenly found herself surrounded by a number of admirers, her head was a little turned.

We went to picnics, and made up parties for drives in the country, and on all occasions Frances had a lot of young men dangling after her, and she quickly developed a talent for flirting that would have done credit to a fashionable young lady who had gone through half a dozen London seasons. I could see however, that her flirtations were quite innocent, and were merely due to her natural feminine desire to attract men to her side. And it rather amused me, to see the girl whom I had brought up, and who would at any moment submit to a spanking from me, surrounded by a circle of swell admirers. However, as I did not wish her to be too pronounced in her manner, I spoke to her quietly, telling her that I had no objection to her amusing herself with a little flirtation; but that she must be more careful in many respects, or she would get herself talked about by the other women.

She was very much surprised at what I said; for in her complete ignorance of the spitefulness of her own sex, she had never thought that they would have taken any notice of her harmless flirtations. She also said that she had erred entirely through ignorance, and because she was so unaccustomed to having a lot of men about her; and she promised to be more careful in future.

She kept her promise for a few days, then she appeared to forget all about my warning, and carried on as before in a perfectly open and innocent way. I occasionally took her over to Monte Carlo, and giving her a sum of money, let her try her luck at the tables, much to her delight, as she was fond of gambling, like all her sex.

But she always lost her money in a very short time, and then she would come to me for more in the coolest way. I, myself, had an occasional run of luck, and on the whole I came off a winner, but not of much; for I am not a gambler, though I like now and then to have a go at the tables.

So the days went on, and Frances amused herself with her admirers; but I saw that one of them, named Brooke, a handsome young Englishman about twenty-five years old, had attached himself to my sweetheart more closely than I liked. And she seemed fond of his company.

I was quite sure that the girl had not the slightest idea of anything wrong, but I felt pretty sure that the man meant mischief; therefore I determined to let Frances know that I disapproved of her being so much with young Brooke.

It was a beautiful afternoon, so I told her I wished her to come for a walk with me, and she at once put on her hat, and we left the hotel. I took her to the sea-shore where we sat down on the warm, dry sand under the lee of a large rock, which hid us from the sight of every one. The scene was a lovely one; in front of us stretched the perfectly calm sapphire sea, dotted here and there with the white sails of yachts, or coasting craft; behind us, fringing the sands on which we sat, were a number of oleanders, and a few scattered palms; while further inland, rose the purple mountains.

"Frances," I said, "you must not go about so much with Mr. Brooke. I know you do not mean any harm; but I do not like his being so constantly in your company. Moreover, people are begining to talk."

She took my hand, and looked up in my face, with her clear blue eyes. "Oh, what a shame it is for people to talk about Mr. Brooke and me! I like him better than all the other men; for he is so nice. But you don't suppose I love him as I do you, Charley," she said, nestling close up to me, and pressing her rosy mouth to mine in a long kiss.

"I believe you love me best, Frances; and I have perfect

confidence in you; but I expect you to obey me. You must not allow Brooke to follow you about in the way he does."

She earnestly assured me that she would in future keep the young man at a distance; so I kissed her, and then we took a walk through the lovely country lanes. We wandered, hand-in-hand like lovers, between hedgerows of fuchsias and roses, passing trellises of vines covered with bunches of purple grapes; and skirting gardens of orange trees, laden with golden fruit, finally reaching the hotel just in time to dress for the *table d'hôte* dinner.

Next day, I took her to Monte Carlo, where we spent several hours very pleasantly, dining at a hotel, and in the evening playing a little at the tables.

A week passed, and I was pleased to see that though Frances still flirted a little with her admirers, she no longer allowed Brooke to monopolize her company. I was quite satisfied with her, and so the time slipped away quietly.

But unfortunately the quietness did not last. Brooke had evidently taken a violent fancy to Frances, so he was always trying to get her by herself.

Then, after a few more days, I noticed that she again allowed him to be constantly with her; and, much to my annoyance, I often saw the other women shrug their shoulders, and look scornfully at her.

And one night after dinner, she sat in the dusk, out in the veranda with Brooke for such a long time, that I got quite angry; but not wishing to make a scene, I went away to our sitting-room, fully intending, when she came in, to give her a bit of my mind, and something more.

In about a quarter-of-an-hour, she came into the room; and though I was feeling very much annoyed, I could not help admiring the lovely girl. She was dressed in some arrangement of silk and lace, that fell in a filmy cloud about her graceful figure; every part of her attire being perfect in fit and taste. Her cheeks had a delicate pink colour like the petals of a rose; and her beautiful white arms and shoulders were bare; she was smiling, and her big blue eyes were dancing with merriment. She sat down on a chair, and stretching out her little feet looked at the tips of her smart shoes, saying:

"Oh, Charley, Mr. Brooke has been amusing me so much!"

"Yes," I said, angrily, "you appear to have been enjoying yourself with the young man. You know I told you not to let him talk to you so much. Why do you permit it?"

"Oh, don't speak so crossly to me. I can't help his admiring me, and speaking to me."

"No. But you need not flirt with him so openly. You have been most imprudent; and you are making me ridiculous. I am very angry with you; and I am going to give you a sound spanking. Perhaps that will make you more careful in your behaviour. You don't seem to mind what I say to you."

Her face fell, and her eyes filled with tears. "Oh! how cruel you are!" she exclaimed. "I have been feeling so happy all the evening; and I did not think I was doing anything wrong in talking to Mr. Brooke. Oh! please don't spank me!"

"Yes, I will," I said. "And what is more; I will spank you again if I catch you flirting with Brooke."

She sobbed, and looked at me appealingly; but I was unmoved.

"Let down your drawers; pull up your clothes, and lie down upon the sofa," I said sternly.

For the first time, she did not at once obey my order. Clasping her hands, she said tearfully: "Oh, it does seem hard that a woman of my age should be spanked like a child."

"You behave in many ways like a child. You require discipline. Now prepare yourself for punishment; and lie down, at once."

The big tears began to trickle down her cheeks, and she heaved a deep sigh; but, without another word, she put her hands under her clothes and unfastened her drawers; then gathering all her dainty skirts up above her waist, she extended herself at full length upon the sofa. Holding her down with my left arm across her loins, I began to spank her smartly; the tears streamed down her cheeks, and she whimpered, moaned, and wriggled with pain under the stinging slaps, which, as they fell on her firm rebounding flesh, sounded like pistol shots. But she bore her punishment with fortitude, never once screaming, nor did she attempt to get away; and when I stopped spanking her, after laying on a couple of dozen smacks, her beautiful bottom was fiery red.

I let her rise, and she pulled up her drawers, fastened the strings round her waist, and wiped her eyes with a filmy, lace-trimmed handkerchief. Then, after a moment she came to me, and held up her little, red mouth, saying: "I am sorry I offended you. But I promise to be more careful in future. Kiss me."

I kissed the dear girl's fragrant mouth; then we went to bed, and in a few moments she was again wriggling her bottom; but this time it was with pleasure; not with pain.

# ❧ XIV ❧

PARIS BY NIGHT.——THE *Moulin Rouge*.—— FRANCES TRIES HIGH KICKING.——TABLEAUX VIVANTS.——A GLIMPSE OF TRIBADISM.—— A LESBIAN RECOLLECTION,——THROUGH THE PEEPHOLE.——THE FRENCH TONGUE TAUGHT.——A REVELATION.——THE DISHONEST HOTEL CHAMBERMAID. ——ANNETTE FLOGGED BY FRAN- CES.——A GOOD STRAPPING.—— WITHOUT RUFFLING A FEATHER.

After this little incident, we remained a fortnight longer in Nice.

Whether it was the spanking I had given Frances, with the promise of others if she misbehaved; or whether it was her own good sense that made her more careful, I do not know; but anyway I never had the least fault to find with her during the remainder of our stay. She was as full of fun as ever she had been, and she laughed and joked with her admirers, but she kept them all more at a distance; and she snubbed Brooke so unmistakably, that he left the hotel entirely. And I must say, I was glad when he went; for he was a handsome young fellow, with a persuasive tongue, and therefore a dangerous man to have always about one's sweetheart.

On leaving Nice, we went direct to Paris, putting up at one of the hotels in the Rue de Rivoli. And after Frances had added some charming toilettes to her already large stock of dresses, we gave ourselves up to the delights of the gay city. First of all, she thoroughly "did" the Louvre, which took several days, and I got heartily sick of tramping through the apparently endless galleries of pictures and statuary; for my sweetheart always made me accompany her; saying that she could not enjoy herself unless I was with her. Then we visited the Tuileries, and the gardens at Versailles; drove frequently in the Bois de Boulogne, and made excursions to all the other places of interest.

Finally, when we had "done" all the ordinary sights, Frances, who had by this time learnt a thing or two, insisted upon my showing her Paris by night. I could speak French, and I "knew my way about"; so I took her to all sorts of queer places, including the "Moulin Rouge," where she saw the celebrated quadrille danced, which amused her very much. She was also greatly taken with the petticoats and drawers, and the shoes and stockings worn by the principal dancers in the "high kicking" part of the entertainment. And the very next day she went off, and bought a complete rig-out of the dainty garments; saying to me, as she laughingly showed the things: "I intend to practise high kicking. It will amuse you."

After that, nearly every morning, she used to dress herself in the flounced petticoats, and the much be-ribboned, wide, gauzy looking drawers with deep lace frills, and put on the long silk stockings, and high-heeled pointed shoes. Then, while I sat lazily in a chair, she would do her best to imitate the dancers at the "Moulin Rouge."

I enjoyed watching the pretty, graceful, well-made girl,

whirling round and round, and kicking up her shapely legs in the midst of a cloud of filmy drapery; the slit of her drawers slightly open, so that I had ravishing glimpses of her golden-haired cunt, and her lovely white bottom. It was a very "fetching" sight, and it invariably gave me a cockstand, so the performance always ended the same way. I used to seize the flushed, panting girl, pull off her dainty drawers, and then poke her in some fancy position.

Among the places to which I took her, was a certain establishment where there were about a dozen girls; and at this place we saw naked tableaux of various sorts; but they were no better than the one I had seen at Mrs. Leslie's. There were no tableaux of whipping; for in France the "delights of the rod" do not seem to be appreciated so much as they are in England.

One of the tableaux, which showed the various means by which females could mutually gratify their passions, was a perfect revelation to Frances, who had not the faintest idea that women ever amused themselves in such extraordinary ways. The girl was still quite ignorant of many things connected with the "Art of Love"; as I had never mentioned to her anything about "Tribadism," "Dildoes," or any of the occult mysteries of sexual passions. She knew that men poked women in various positions,—I had shown her them all—but there her knowledge had ended.

When we got back to the hotel that night, and were talking over all we had seen; she said she did not believe that girls ever did such things to each other, in reality. I laughed, and said: "Oh yes, they do. And more often than people think." Then I asked: "Did none of the big girls ever try to tickle you between the legs when you were at school?"

"Yes; once a big girl took me on her lap, put her hand up my petticoats and let down my drawers; then she kissed me, and at the same time put her finger up 'it,' hurting me very much and also frightening me. I did not understand what it all meant, but I ran crying to Mrs. Blake and told her what the girl had done to me. She was very angry, and I know she birched the girl, for I saw her, a short time after, come out of Mrs. Blake's room, crying and rubbing her bottom. And she called me a nasty little tell-tale."

I laughed, saying: "Well, Frances; if you would not let the big girl play with your little 'pussy'; you may be sure there were other girls not so particular. That sort of thing goes on in all girls' schools."

Then she asked me if there were any other queer sights to be seen at the house where we had been that night.

I replied that if she liked she could see a man and a woman actually engaged in the "lists of love." She laughed heartily at the idea of the thing, and said she would very much like to see such a sight. So I promised to take her to the establishment the following night; and then we went to bed.

At ten o'clock next night, we drove to the establishment, and I told "Madame" what I wanted to see. She smiled, and at once took us up to a small, but comfortably furnished room, dimly lighted by a shaded lamp. One side of the room was panelled with curved woodwork, in which, low down, and cunningly concealed, were several peepholes and through them could be seen the adjoining apartment, which was handsomely furnished and brilliantly lighted; so that the smallest details of the scene that followed were clearly seen by Frances and me.

Drawing two easy-chairs up to the panel, Madame told us to take our seats; then she left us, and we sat down and waited with our eyes glued to the peepholes.

In a short time we saw a man and a woman come into the room; the man was a tall stalwart fellow about thirty years of age, dressed in evening clothes, but he did not look like a gentleman; the woman, a big, strapping, rather coarse, though not bad-looking wench, who had nothing on but her chemise, shoes and stockings. She was about twenty-five.

I do not know whether the pair knew they were being

watched, or not, but at any rate they acted all through the affair in a perfectly natural and unembarrassed way; and they certainly enjoyed themselves.

No time was wasted. The man gave the woman a sounding kiss on her thick red lips, then he stripped to his shirt, and taking her on his knees, pulled off her chemise, leaving her stark naked, except for her shoes and her long scarlet silk stockings, which came up to the middle of her thighs, and were gartered with large bows of black ribbon. The woman's skin was fairly white; and she had immense bubbies tipped with big red nipples, her thighs were massive, and her legs were thick; and the lower part of her great belly was thickly covered with dark brown hair, which completely hid the slit of her cunt.

The fun began. The man took in his mouth, one after the other, the woman's nipples, nibbling them and sucking them with apparent relish, at the same time feeling her body all over with both hands. Next, he laid her face downwards across his knees and played for a time with her enormous bottom; he stroked it, pinched it all over, and rubbed his hands up and down the division; then pulling the fat cheeks apart, he looked at the spot between them, and grinned. He then began to spank her with no light hand; the noise of the slaps resounding through the room, while the flesh of her fat buttocks quivered like jelly, and her skin rapidly grew red. She bore the pain for a short time, then she twisted herself round and caught hold of the man's hands, exclaiming,—in French of course: "That is enough! I won't have any more spanking."

She then slipped off his knees, and kneeling at his feet, tucked up his shirt, revealing his whacking great tool standing stiffly erect with its red tip uncovered. Bending her head down, she took into her mouth nearly half the length of the man's member, and began to "gamahuche" him, at the same time tickling his balls with her fingers, while he, with his eyes gleaming with sensual pleasure, played with her great titties; and I thought he was going to finish the affair in her mouth. But he suddenly jumped up, and taking the woman in his arms, laid her on a couch, and stretched her legs so widely apart, that the loose red lips of her fat cunt gaped open and showed the pink inner lips. Putting his head between her thighs, he buried his face in the forest of hair, and thrusting his tongue up her slit, tickled her clitoris to such an extent that she squirmed about, kicked up her legs, and giggled loudly.

They certainly did spin out their pleasure!

At last, he laid himself down upon her, clasped his hands under her bottom, put his tongue into her mouth, and drove the weapon up to the hilt in the sheath. Then he began to fuck her furiously, and as his shirt was half-way up his back, we could see his bare bottom rising and falling, and his prick working up and down, like the piston of a steam engine, in the woman's cunt; while she folded her arms round him, threw her legs over his loins, and heaved her bottom up to meet his strokes. He worked quicker and quicker, the woman bounced and wriggled, her whole body quivering under the violence of his thrusts. He came to the short digs, she grunted and writhed; and at last, after a convulsive dig, the spasm seized them both; and we could see the muscles of the man's bottom stiffen, as he pressed the woman to his breast at the supreme moment; while she wriggled her bottom in grand style as the discharge gushed up her cunt; while at the same time a most ridiculous expression came to her face, and she turned up her eyes till nothing but the whites could be seen. Then, after a final wriggle, they lay in each other's arms, breathing quickly from their exertions.

He had given her a most lusty poke!

It had been a most lascivious and exciting spectacle, and my cock was aching from its prolonged erection. I rose from my chair and looked at Frances, who had also risen from her seat, and who appeared to be deeply stirred by the scene she had witnessed.

Her face was scarlet, her bosom was heaving, and her great blue eyes, sparkling with desire, seemed to be starting out of her head.

Without saying a word, she put her hands under her clothes, unfastened her drawers, and kicked them off her legs; then going to a couch she laid herself down upon it, and smiled at me invitingly.

Burning with lust, I ran to her, whisked up her petti-coats, and got between her outstretched legs; then taking her in my arms, I poked her vigorously, and with one in-tense feeling of delight. Frances also seemed to feel a very great sensation of pleasure, for she bucked up, and wriggled, even more voluptuously than she usually did.

As soon as we had made ourselves tidy, I rang the bell for Madame Leblanc and settled with her. Then Frances and I left the house, drove to a restaurant, and had a nice little supper; finally reaching our hotel at about one o'clock in the morning. But, late as it was, we sat down to have a talk over the evening's amusement. After a few general observations on the whole affair; Frances remarked: "There were two things which surprised me very much."

"What were they?" I asked.

"Why, the woman took the man's 'thing' in her mouth, and appeared to be sucking it; and afterwards the man put his tongue up the woman's 'thing.' We have never kissed each other in that way."

"No. But we will some time or other; if you think you would like it," I replied, laughing.

"I am sure I should like it for a change," she said. "Oh, it must be delicious to be tickled by a soft, warm tongue," she added, looking at me with glistening eyes, and speaking in a fervent way.

"You would think it delicious for a moment or two, but you would not find it so satisfying as the real thing," I remarked.

She laughed, saying: "Well anyhow, I'll try it some

day." Then she went on: "Did you observe what a queer look the woman put on, and how she turned up her eyes at the 'supreme moment,' and did you notice how violently she wriggled her bottom? She did look so funny in every way."

I replied that I had noticed everything. She continued: "I know that I wriggle my bottom a little when you 'do it' to me,—I can't help it, though it seems absurd—but I don't think I turn up my eyes and look as silly as that woman did."

"Oh yes, you do," I said laughing. "All women turn up their eyes and look queer when the spasm seizes them; and they all wriggle their bottoms more or less violently when they feel the 'stuff' spurting up them."

"Well," she said, "it was exciting to watch the two 'doing it'; but I must say it was a ridiculous sight to see the two bare bottoms working up and down."

"Yes, Frances," I observed, smiling. "I quite agree with you. The action looks most ridiculous, but the sensation is delightful, as you well know."

"Yes, it is nice," she said, laughing.

"Well, let us go to bed and practise the movement," I said, getting up from my chair, and passing through the folding doors into our bedroom. She followed, and in a short time our bottoms were working up and down, and her eyes were turning up as she wriggled and squirmed in the delicious spasm.

A fortnight passed, and though we did not pay any more visits to Madame Leblanc's establishment, we amused ourselves very pleasantly in many other ways. It was the middle of April; there was a balmy, spring-like feeling in the air; the trees in the Bois de Boulogne were putting forth their leaves, and the snowdrops and crocuses were in full bloom; so one particularly bright morning we made up our minds to spend the day at Versailles.

As soon as we had breakfasted, Frances arrayed herself in a most dainty toilette; then we left the hotel and walked to the Palais Royal, intending to have a look at the shops before starting on our excursion. But after we had strolled about for a short time, Frances discovered that she had left all her keys and her purse, containing upwards of five pounds, behind her in our bedroom.

So we at once walked back to the hotel, and went up to our apartments to get the forgotten articles. On opening the door of the bedroom, we saw the chambermaid who always attended us, a girl named Annette, kneeling beside one of Frances' trunks, from which nearly all the contents had been taken, and scattered on the floor. Annette had thought we had gone away for the day as I had told her that we should not be back to dinner.

When she saw us suddenly enter the room, she jumped up, turned very pale, and stood looking at us, utterly taken aback, and trembling all over. She was a tall, slim, good-looking girl about twenty-one years old; with a trim figure, black hair and eyes, red lips, and white teeth, and a saucy little *nez retroussé*. She had a clear olive complexion; and she was dressed in a well-fitting black frock, with white apron, collar and cuffs; and her luxuriant hair was covered with a white, frilled cap with scarlet ribbons.

Frances at once went to the toilet table, on which she had left her purse; but it was gone, and when she informed me of the fact, I locked the door and put the key in my pocket.

Then I went to the trembling girl and searched her capacious pocket, finding in it the purse, half-a-dozen lace handkerchiefs, the same number of pairs of gloves, and also a number of small articles which she had taken out of the trunk. And had we not happened to return unexpectedly, and thus catch the thief red-handed, we should never have known who had stolen the things.

Frances could not speak French, so I acted as spokesman; saying to the girl in her own language; which I will here translate into English: "We have caught you nicely, Annette.

You are a thief. What have you got to say for yourself before I send for the manager of the hotel and ask him to hand you over to the police?" I had no intention of giving her in charge; as the whole thing would have been a great bore; but I wanted to give the girl a fright.

She burst into a flood of tears, wringing her hands, and exclaiming in accents of entreaty: "Oh, sir! Oh, sir! Don't give me to the police. I am an honest girl, but I was suddenly tempted to do wrong when I saw the purse and the keys on the table. Oh, do not have me arrested! Forgive me! Oh! please forgive me, I have an old mother to support. Oh! do forgive me!"

She was in an awful funk, and it suddenly struck me that I might get some fun out of the affair. I thought it very probable, that rather than go to gaol, she would let me flog her. At any rate I would give her the choice of the alternatives; and I hoped she would choose the flogging. She was a clean-looking, pretty girl, and my cock stirred at the thought of turning her up, and reddening her bottom.

So, I said to her: "You are a thief, and therefore you must be punished; but I will not hand you over to the police, if you will consent to receive a flogging, in the same way that we flog naughty girls in England." She stopped crying and looked at me for a moment, with her big black eyes widely opened, as if she hardly grasped the meaning of my words; then she said in a tone of relief: "Oh, sir, rather than go to prison and lose my good character, I will consent to receive any punishment you like to inflict upon me."

"Very well," I said. "But you must clearly understand that I will flog you soundly."

She shuddered slightly, and asked in a shaky voice: "But, sir, in what way do you intend to flog me?"

"I intend to flog you upon your bare bottom," I replied.

She blushed scarlet, and again began to cry, saying in a horrified tone: "Oh, but sir; when I said I would take the punishment, I did not think you intended to inflict it on my bare person. I thought you were going to flog me over my clothes. You must not strip me. I cannot bear the exposure. It would be too shameful. Oh! I cannot suffer it."

"Well, if you will not submit yourself to me entirely, I must send for the police," I said, walking to the bell-rope and taking it in my hand.

"Oh, don't ring the bell! Wait a moment. Oh! what shall I do! Oh, don't send for the police!" she wailed in a piteous tone, stretching out her arms with an imploring gesture towards me, while the tears ran down her flushed cheeks.

"I will ring the bell if you don't consent to take the flogging on your bare bottom," I said sternly.

She wrung her hands, and wept bitterly; then after a few moments' hesitation, she sobbed out in broken accents: "Oh—sir—it is shameful to be laid bare. But—I—cannot—go to prison. I—must—submit. Oh! Oh!"

Then, turning her back to us, she covered her blushing face with her apron, and sobbed.

The girl's horror at the idea of her bottom being exposed, was deep and unfeigned; for though she was a French chambermaid, she was evidently a modest girl. But I must confess that the sight of her distress added piquancy to the whole affair. It always affords great pleasure, to a "lover of the rod," to flog a female culprit who appears to feel the shame of the exposure more than the pain of the whipping.

All the time this talk had been going on, Frances had stood looking much interested, but not understanding a word that was said; and she now impatiently asked what I had been saying.

I told her that I had given Annette the alternative of going to gaol or taking a flogging; and that she had chosen the flogging.

"She deserves it," said Frances emphatically, and with rather a grim smile. Then, eagerly: "Let me flog her. You know I have long been wanting to inflict corporal punishment; and now there is a chance for me. Do let me flog her."

I smiled; but I could quite understand her desire to whip, and I resolved to let her have her wish. "All right," I said. "I will 'horse' her on my back, and you shall flog her."

Frances looked very pleased, and at once prepared for action, by taking off her gloves, hat, and jacket. Then she said: "We have got no rod; and I am not going to make my hand sore by spanking her; so you must find something for me to flog her with."

I looked round the room for some instrument of punishment, and my eyes fell on a pair of small rug straps, each about a couple of feet long and half-an-inch wide. One of them would do very well, as it would sting the culprit's bottom sharply without bruising the flesh.

So I pointed the straps out to Frances, and told her to take one of them. Annette was still standing with her back towards us, her apron was over her head, and she was crying. Going to her, I laid my hand on her shoulder, turned her round, and drew her hands away from her face; saying: "The lady—my wife—is going to flog you. So your punishment will not be so severe as it would be, were I to flog you. Now, take off your dress and stays."

"Oh, if Monsieur would please leave the room. I promise not to resist Madame while she flogs me," said Annette, clasping her hands, and speaking in a pleading way.

"I will not leave the room. I am going to hold you while you are being punished. Remove your dress and stays; and be quick, or I will ring the bell."

She hesitated a moment; and I laid my hand again on the bell-rope; then heaving a deep sigh, she slowly, with trembling fingers took off the two garments, and stood before us, with her head averted, and with streaming eyes; and as her chemise was cut rather low at the neck, I could see the division between her small, but well-rounded bubbies.

I had made her partly undress, because when a woman is "horsed" for a flogging with her dress and stays on, it is very difficult to get her petticoats turned up high enough to bare her bottom in a satisfactory way.

At one side of the room, there was a large pier glass, and opposite it there was a wardrobe with a long mirror; and it struck me that if I stood between the two articles of furniture, I should be able to see the whole of the girl's body reflected in the looking-glass, and thus be able actually to witness the flogging.

"Now, Annette, I am going to take you on my back and hold you, while Madame flogs you." So saying, I went to the sobbing girl, who trembled and shrunk away from me, but made no attempt at resistance. Seizing one of her wrists in each of my hands, I drew her arms over my shoulders, and then stooping forward, raised her feet well off the floor, "horsing" her in proper style without any difficulty, for I am six feet in height, and though she was tall, she was not heavy.

"Now, Frances," I said, "the girl will be sure to kick and struggle when she feels the strap, so you must pin up her petticoats, so that they will not fall down in the middle of the punishment."

Frances rolled the culprit's petticoats, which were white and clean, up to her shoulders, and pinned the garments securely. She wore her chemise under her drawers, which were tightly stretched over her bottom by the curved position of her body; and as I was between the two mirrors, I could see everything perfectly.

As Frances was untying the girl's drawers, she sobbed out: "Oh, madame, don't take down my drawers!" The drawers were untied, and pulled down to her knees. Then she made another appeal: "Oh, please leave my chemise. Do not strip me quite bare."

The chemise was rolled up and pinned to the petticoats, leaving the girl naked from the middle of her back to the

tops of her stockings; and as she felt her last garment removed, she uttered a low wailing cry of shame.

She had a small, but well-shaped bottom, slender thighs,
and slim legs, cased in tight, clean white cotton stockings,
gartered at the middle of the thighs with black ribbons; her
ankles were trim, and she was wearing neat, well-polished
shoes. Her olive-tinted skin was very smooth, and it appeared
to be fine in texture.

Everything being ready, I told the weeping culprit, who
was shivering with shame and fear, that she must try and
bear her punishment with fortitude; and not attract attention
by making an outcry.

Frances took the strap and twisted part of it round her
hand, leaving a length of about eighteen inches to flog with.

"Now, Frances," I said, "give her a couple of dozen
strokes, and lay them on smartly, but not too severely. Begin
at the upper part of her bottom and flog down to her thighs,
then up again to her loins. Keep cool, and don't cross the
cuts."

Frances whirled the strap in the air, and as I looked in
the glass in front of me, I could plainly see the girl's eyes
dilate with fear, and I also noticed the cheeks of her bottom
contract, and the smooth skin assumed a rough appearance.
Crack! The long piece of leather fell smartly across the girl's
bottom, and both the olive-tinted cheeks were instantly
marked with a long red stripe, the exact breath of the strap;
the stinging pain making the culprit start convulsively on
my back, and utter a stifled cry. Crack! Crack! Crack! Crack!
Crack! Crack! Frances swung the strap with a graceful
sweep of her arm, and as skillfully as if she had been a
practised flogger; laying on the strokes with equal force, in
slow time, one below the other, so that the red stripes were
printed on Annette's skin at almost regular distances apart.
She plunged and wriggled, whimpered and sobbed; and I
could feel her body quiver, and shrink against my back each
time the stinging strap struck her bottom.

I had never before "horsed" a girl; therefore it was a novel sensation, and a pleasing one, to feel her bosom and belly rubbing against my back, and the front part of her thighs rubbing my bottom, as she writhed in pain. Crack! Crack! Crack! Crack! Crack! She bounced about, twisting her hips from side to side; her flesh twitched at each stroke; she turned her head and looked over her shoulder, with an agonized expression on her face, at the strap as it hissed in the air over her bottom, and she gasped and cried, the tears running in streams down her scarlet cheeks. By this time, Frances had flogged down to the culprit's thighs, so that the whole of her bottom was prettily marked with alternate red and white stripes.

Crack! Crack! Crack! Crack! Crack! Crack! Frances was now flogging upwards. The sharp noise made by the strap as it struck the girl's firm flesh, echoed through the room; she kicked up her heels in pain, struggling hard to free her wrists from my grasp, and though she did not scream, she moaned, and cried piteously, gasping out in choking accents: "*Oh, madame!—madame! Oh, chère madame! Pas—si—fort! Oh,—pas—si—fort! Oh—madame! Ayez pitié! J'en—ai—assez! Oh!—Oh—h!*"

Crack! Crack! Crack! Crack! Her moans changed to low, suppressed shrieks, and she threw her legs about so frantically that her drawers fell off, and in her writhes and plunges, I caught glimpses of the black hair in the cleft of her thighs; her struggles becoming so violent that I had some difficulty in holding her in position.

Crack! Crack! Frances laid on the last two strokes with a little extra force, extracting from the culprit two rather loud squeals; and now that the flogging was over, the whole surface of her bottom, from the loins to the thighs, was a bright scarlet colour, as the stripes had overlapped.

Frances threw down the strap, and stood for a moment looking with an amused smile at the marks of her handiwork; then she unpinned the girl's petticoats and let them fall. I released her wrists, and she stood on the floor, crying, and twisting her loins with the smarting pain of her well-whipped bottom. Her face was red, and she looked very much ashamed.

"Now, Annette, it is all over. You may go," I said.

She picked up her drawers, and turning aside, drew them over her legs, and tied the strings round her waist; then she put on her stays and dress, whimpering, sobbing, and wiping her streaming eyes with her apron; then she put her cap straight, and hurried out of the room.

The flogging of the girl had afforded me great pleasure; as the whole affair had been so unexpected, and also so much out of the common. I was very randy, and as a matter of course, had a tremendous cockstand.

I looked at Frances, who had evidently enjoyed the task; her eyes were bright, and she was smiling. "Well, are you satisfied now?" I asked, laughing, and pinching her ear.

"Oh, yes! And I must say that whipping a bottom is exciting work. I can quite understand why you are so fond of doing it." Then, fixing her eyes on the flap of my trousers, which bulged out considerably, she laughed, saying: "I can see that you are much affected by what has taken place, so I suppose I shall now get a taste of the 'rod.' But you must take care not to rumple my frock, as it is a new one."

"All right, I won't ruffle your plumage," I said, laughing.

Making her lean over the back of an easy-chair, I raised her dainty skirt and carefully folded it over the middle of her back; then I tucked up her petticoats, and opened the slit of her drawers, so that the plump, white cheeks of her bottom were framed in the fine linen, which was scarcely whiter than her smooth skin. I began to poke her "en levrette," but I was so excited that I "spent" almost immediately. However, as my prick remained quite stiff, I did not withdraw it, but went to work again, and after a prolonged and most delicious struggle, during which I was well backed up by Frances, I discharged for the second time a torrent of hot sperm. She almost swooned from excess of voluptuous pleasure, her legs gave way under her, and she would have fallen had I not held her up. But her clothes were not ruffled!

I got her a glass of wine, and she was soon as lively as ever; and when we had had a "wash and brush up," we went quietly off to Versailles, where we spent the day as we had originally intended.

Annette must have got herself transferred to another part of the establishment; for we never saw her again, and during the remainder of our stay, we were attended by another chambermaid.

We remained in Paris for a fortnight longer, but had no more adventures worth recording. Then we returned to London; Frances being very much pleased with her first trip abroad, and looking all the better for it. I left her at the villa, and then went down to Oakhurst.

# XV

MALTHUSIAN GOSSIP.——BROOKE REAPPEARS.——
THE MEETING IN THE PARK.——EAVESDROPPING
AND SPYING.——A STOLEN KISS.——THE LOVER'S
WRATH.——BIRCHED FOR IMPRUDENCE.——A
FEARFUL SWITCHING.——THE LUST OF
CRUELTY.——AFTER THE TORTURE.
——WHEELBARROW FASHION AND
OTHER DIVERSIONS.

I found everything in proper order at my old house, but there was some business connected with the estate, which required my personal supervision; so I settled down quietly again to perform my duties as a "country gentleman." There had been a few changes among the staff of female servants.

Lucy had married and gone to live in Winchester, so I had no longer at my disposal a woman whom I could spank or poke whenever I felt inclined for a little amusement.

There were two or three pretty young maidservants in the house, but they all seemed to be modest girls, and I did not think any one of them would let me "have" her merely for the asking. No doubt I might have seduced one if I had regularly laid myself out for one of the young virgins. She would probably have had a child; and that would have caused trouble and annoyance; as well as a great deal of scandal.

I had always thought it curious that Frances had never got in the family way; for I was in full vigour as a man, and she was a perfectly healthy girl, with a hot, voluptuous disposition; who, no matter how often I poked her, never let my prick out of her cunt till it had sucked in every drop of moisture. Of course, after each poke she had invariably taken the usual precautions; but they are not always to be depended on. In fact, as far as my experience goes, there are only three sure ways of preventing impregnation, and all three spoil the pleasure of the poke. First, there is the "French letter," which spoils the man's pleasure. Secondly, there is the "preventive pessary," which spoils the woman's pleasure. The third way, is for the man to withdraw at the moment of ejaculation, and that spoils the pleasure of both the man and the woman; besides being injurious to health. However, I am glad to say that Frances, during the whole time she was under my protection, never once missed her monthly period.

During my stay in the country, I frequently went out to dinners and parties; but whenever I dined at home, I used to miss my sweetheart's bright face and lively chatter, while I was sitting at my solitary meal.

However, I went up to see her nearly every week, always remaining at the villa for two or three days, and on those occasions we had a very jolly time, in one way and another.

And so the summer wore away quietly and pleasantly. When November came, I took Frances to Brighton, where we stayed for a month: then I sent her back to London, while I went to Oakhurst to spend Christmas there with a large house-party of relatives; as had nearly always been my custom. I wished I could have had my sweetheart with me, but that would have been impossible. While my relations were living with me, I could not leave home even for a day, but as soon as they had all gone, I went up to London and took up my abode at the villa with Frances, who was delighted to have me with her again. I, also, was pleased to be with her, so we resumed our "married" life, and were always quite happy and contented in each other's company.

But it was destined that things should not always go on so smoothly. Time had passed. It was June, and the London season was at its height, when an incident occurred which bothered me at the moment, a good deal. Frances and I were sitting in the park one afternoon, when to my annoyance, I saw Brooke,—the young man who had flirted so outrageously with my "wife" at Nice—coming towards us with a smile of recognition on his face. He raised his hat to Frances, and greeted me; then coolly dropping into a vacant chair, he entered into conversation with us. I was as curt in my answers, and as distant in my manner towards him, as I possibly could be: but Frances, apparently quite forgetting that he had been the cause of her getting a sound spanking, talked and laughed with him freely.

However, I soon cut short their talk by rising from my seat, and bidding Brooke good day; then Frances stood up, and after bowing to the young man, she took my arm, and we then strolled out of the park by the Rutland gate, got into a hansom, and drove to the villa.

I did not make any remark about Brooke, thinking it probable that we never should come across him again. I dined at home with Frances, and we spent a quiet evening together; she being quite as merry and lighthearted as usual, not seeming to have been affected in any way by her meeting with the young man.

A couple of days afterwards, I had to go down to Oakhurst; where I was detained by one thing or another for ten days. During that time I heard frequently from Frances, who always wrote in a most affectionate way, invariably winding up her letters by saying that she was looking forward to my return.

At last, when all my little affairs had been settled, I started for London, without having written to apprise Frances of my coming, as I had not been quite sure of getting away that day. I reached the villa about four o'clock, but my sweetheart was not in, and the housemaid informed me that her mistress had gone to walk in Regent's Park. There was nothing strange in that, for I knew Frances was very fond of walking or reading in the park on a fine day. So, after I had had a wash, I dressed myself in the orthodox frock-coat, and tall hat, and strolled over to the park to see if I could find my young lady.

It was a lovely afternoon, bright and sunny, but not too hot, and the park was looking at its best. There was a cool breeze blowing, and the sky was flecked with masses of filmy white clouds which sparkled like snow under the rays of the sun. It had rained during the past night, so the dust had been washed from the trees and they were looking as fresh and green as if they had been growing in the country a hundred miles from smoky London. The grass also was a vivid green, the flowers were blooming, and the water in all the little ponds looked bright and clean.

In a certain part of the park, there was a secluded arbour, in which I had often sat smoking a cigar while Frances read to me; and to this spot I directed my steps, thinking that perhaps I should find her there. The place was surrounded by a thick growth of shrubs, quite concealing the entrance, and when I got near it, I heard the voices of a man and a woman. I thought I recognized Frances' voice, but to make sure, I slipped round quietly to the back of the arbour, where the shrubs were thickest, and peeping through the crevices, I saw that it was Frances, and that her companion was Brooke. They were sitting side by side on the bench talking and laughing. I was very angry at seeing Frances in that retired spot in company with the man; it was suspicious, to say the least, but I did not think that she had actually been unfaithful to me.

Then the thought passed through my head, that it was strange that I should, for the second time, be peeping at Frances carrying on a little game in an arbour. Crouching low among the shrubs, I watched and listened. I heard nothing improper; their conversation was of the most innocent description, being chiefly about the various plays and other entertainments that were then going on in London.

But I noticed that Brooke constantly glanced at Frances, with a lecherous look, his eyes roving all over her person from head to foot; she, quite unconscious of the man's lustful admiration, and she talked to him in a perfectly unembarrassed way.

Presently he asked: "Where is your husband now?" He did not know that Frances was unmarried.

"He is in the country," she replied.

Brooke smiled, as if the information had pleased him. Then they began to talk about Nice, and all the people they had known there; and I suppose he remembered how Frances had flirted with him at the hotel, so he edged close up to her and took her hand,—which I daresay he had done before. She did not withdraw her hand, and that emboldened him; for he suddenly threw his arms around her and pressed his mouth to her lips in a long kiss, which she received without making any resistance.

I ground my teeth, and muttered a curse, but I waited to see if she would permit him to do more.

After a moment, he attempted to put his hand up her clothes, but the instant she felt him touch her ankle, she struggled out of his grasp, and pushed him away; her cheeks flushing, and her eyes sparkling with anger, and stamping her foot, she exclaimed: "Oh, you have no right to treat me so! How dare you do it! I should not have allowed you to kiss me! I hate you!"

He laughed contemptuously, saying: "Why did you come to meet me then?"

"Because I was feeling rather lonely, and wanted some-one to talk to. And I did not think you would try to take advantage of my loneliness. I thought you were a gentle-man," she said scornfully. Then she rushed out of the arbour, leaving him looking very foolish.

I felt relieved. There had evidently been nothing wrong between them, so far; but nevertheless I felt very angry with her, for meeting the man by appointment, and still more angry with her for having allowed him to kiss her. I also had a strong inclination to punch Brooke's head; but then I thought, that as no actual harm had been done, it was hardly worth while having a rough and tumble fight with the man.

He sat down, lit a cigar, and began to smoke; then I walked away quietly to the main road, where I seated myself on a bench and thought over the whole affair, which had annoyed me very much, and also rather shaken my con-fidence in Frances.

I sat cogitating for about half an hour; then I returned to the villa, where I found Frances waiting for me in the drawing-room. She showed no surprise at seeing me, as she had heard from the servant that I had been in the house a short time previously. She had not the faintest idea that I had seen her with Brooke, so she came running to me, with a smile of welcome on her face; exclaiming: "Oh! my dear, I am so glad to see you. Why did you not write and tell me you were coming, so that I might have been at home ready to receive you?" Then she held up her mouth, ex-pecting her usual kiss; but I put her coldly aside and sat down on a chair without saying a word.

The smile faded from her face, and she gazed at me, with a wistful expression in her eyes. "What is the matter with you, Charley? Why don't you kiss me?" she asked in an anxious tone.

"Why don't I kiss you?" I echoed, bitterly. "Because I do not care to kiss a woman, whose lips are hot with the kisses of another man."

She was utterly taken aback, her cheeks paled, and she

stood for a moment staring at me in speechless astonishment; then, dropping on to a chair, she covered her face with her hands, and began to cry in a hopeless sort of way. I told her what I had seen. Then I asked: "How did Brooke find you out? How often have you met him?" Removing her hands from her face, she replied, sobbing: "I met him, quite by accident, two days ago in Regent's Park, and he spoke to me; and as I was feeling rather lonely, I talked to him for a time, while we walked about the park. And when we parted he asked to meet him again to-day. I have only spoken to him on two occasions." Then clasping her hands, she said imploringly: "Oh, Charley! don't be so angry with me. I have been very imprudent, but I have done you no wrong. Surely you will believe me. I have never deceived you in my life. Oh! do forgive me. You know I have very few people to speak to when you are away."

"But I told you long ago that I did not wish you to speak to Brooke; and you have disobeyed me by speaking to him; and what is far worse, you allowed him to kiss you. You must have given him some encouragement, or he would never have attempted to take such a liberty."

"Oh, I am sure I never gave him the least encouragement!" she wailed, with the tears running down her cheeks. "I know I did wrong in letting him kiss me, but I really meant no harm. You must forgive me. I do not care for him in the very least. Oh, you know I do not love any one but you." Then rising from her seat, and coming close to me, she exclaimed: "Oh! do give me a kiss."

I believed her, but nevertheless I was very angry, and I intended to make her feel my displeasure. So I said: "I will not kiss you. I feel very angry with you. I am going to dine at the club, and shall not be back till late. I do not intend to sleep with you; so have the bed in the spare room made ready for me."

She gazed at me for a moment, with a look of deep distress, then threw herself down upon the sofa, crying bitterly.

I did not say another word to her, but at once left the house and drove to my club. I ordered a good dinner, which I managed to eat with a fair appetite, and I drank a bottle of champagne; then, feeling much better, I went up to the smoking-room, and lighting a cigar, turned over everything in my mind. And by the time I had finished my weed, I had decided to forgive Frances, for what after all, was but a slight transgression; but before taking her back to my favour, I meant to give her a sharp lesson; she should have a sound birching the following day. The rod I had used upon Maud's bottom, was still in the chest of drawers in the bedroom at the villa. Having settled what I intended to do, I went to a theatre; had some supper afterwards, and finally reached the villa about one o'clock in the morning, and, letting myself in with my latchkey, I went up to bed in the spare room, where everything had been comfortably prepared for me.

Next morning, when I went down to breakfast, Frances was already in the room, looking pale and miserable. I bade her good morning, in a cold tone of voice, then taking my seat at the table, began my breakfast. She poured out my coffee, glancing at me in a pleading way every now and then; and I noticed that she hardly ate anything. When I had finished my meal, and smoked a cigar, I went into the drawing-room, and seating myself comfortably in an easy-chair, read the morning paper from beginning to end. Then I wrote several letters, and went out and posted them; afterwards strolling about in Regent's Park until it was time to go back to lunch. After lunch I meant to give Frances her birching.

During the meal, I did not speak a single word to her, and I saw that she was struggling to keep back her tears, and as soon as she could, she left the room. I lit a cigar and began to smoke, intending when I had finished, to call Frances down and let her know her fate. But I had hardly smoked half my cigar, when she came into the room and walking up to where I was sitting, looked at me pathetically, with tears in her eyes, saying: "Oh, Charley! I am so miserable and unhappy. I can't go on like this. Will you not forgive me? Punish me in any way you like. Spank me. Birch me. I will submit; if you will only forgive me."

I was delighted to hear what she said. Her voluntarily offering to submit to punishment, showed that she still really loved me. However, I did not tell her that it had been my intention to flog her, even if she had not offered herself for punishment. I merely said: "You certainly deserve to be chastised. I will birch you; and when the punishment is over, I will kiss you, and say no more about the affair."

She looked a little relieved; then she timidly said: "Oh, I wish you would spank me instead of birching me! I do *so* dread the rod."

"I intend to birch you," I said curtly.

She gave a little shudder, but did not say anything more.

Then I went on: "Go upstairs and prepare yourself for punishment. Keep on all your underclothing, but take off your dress and stays, and put on a loose wrapper. Remain in your room till I call you, and when you come down, bring the rod with you; it is in the chest of drawers."

She went away without a word, and I made *my* preparations.

I placed the couch in the middle of the room, and got four straps with which to secure her wrists and ankles, as I meant to birch her severely. Then it struck me that she would scream so that the servants would hear her. I called the two women, and told them to get ready to go out at once. They looked surprised, and then I sent them off to buy me some trifles at shops in different parts of the town.

It would take them upwards of an hour to execute the commissions, so that by the time they returned, the whole affair would be over.

All was now in readiness, and I sat down on a chair to wait for a minute or two before beginning the task which I knew would afford me the greatest pleasure. I revelled in imagination at the thought of it! I had not touched Frances' bottom with the rod since the day long past on which I had birched her for spanking the little boy.

To some readers of this story, it may seem strange and unnatural, that I should have looked forward with great delight to flogging, in an ignominious and painful way, the girl who loved me, and of whom I was fond. But anyone who is a "lover of the rod" will easily understand, and enter into the feelings which possessed me at that moment. In every one, male or female, there is more or less, a "lust of cruelty," which shows itself in different ways, in different people. "Lovers of the rod" like to give pain to their victims by flogging them in various ways. But many a man who takes pleasure in seeing a woman writhing, and crying with pain while undergoing corporal punishment at his hands, may in all other respects be tender-hearted. It is a strange, but true fact, that when a man, who has a fancy for using the rod, finds himself birching the naked bottom of a female, he has no feeling of any sort except one of strong sensual pleasure.

But to proceed. I called to Frances telling her to come down. And in a few moments she came into the room, carrying in her hand the rod, which she handed to me, and then stood meekly waiting further instructions. She was looking very lovely, but her cheeks were pale, and there was a frightened expression in her great blue eyes. Her long, golden hair was arranged in shining coils at the back of her shapely head, and on her white forehead there was a soft fringe of tiny curls. She had put on a loose pink silk wrapper, that draped her lissom figure in straight folds from her shoulders to her little feet, which were daintily shod with high-heeled French shoes.

Taking the straps in my hand, I ordered her to place herself in position. The tears welled up into her eyes when she saw the straps; for she guessed that I would not have produced them had I not meant to flog her severely; but without a look, or word of remonstrance, she laid herself down with her arms stretched out at full length. I quickly secured her wrists and ankles to the legs of the couch; but I did not fasten her body in any way; so there would be plenty scope for her to wriggle her bottom when she felt the sting of the birch. The French call the movement, "*la danse de la croupe.*" Then I drew the skirt of her wrapper up to her shoulders, turned up her pretty, lace-trimmed, white petticoats, and rolled up her pale blue chemise. Her drawers, also of pale blue silk, had not the usual slit at the back, but were buttoned at the sides. Her beautiful legs were cased in dark blue silk stockings fastened at the middle of her thighs with pink satin garters. I undid the buttons of her drawers, and pulled down the dainty garment, laying bare her superb white bottom. It seemed at that moment to be more lovely than ever as it lay upturned, framed above by the pile of snowy drapery, and below by the blue silk of the lace-frilled drawers. I gazed at it rapturously, with my eyes glistening, and my cock as stiff as a poker, at the same time thinking that such pretty cheeks were more fitted to receive the soft kisses of a lover, than the stinging kisses of a rod. Then I passed my hand several times over the alabaster white, smooth, cool skin, which my strokes would soon make fiery red, rough, and hot. But I had no feeling of compunction; and taking up the rod, I made it hiss in the air, saying: "Now Frances, I am going to flog you severely."

She shuddered, and drew in the cheeks of her bottom till the division, between the half-moons of plump flesh, looked like a thin line. "Oh, Charley!" she exclaimed in a tone of fright. "Don't be too hard upon me!"

I brought the rod down with a drawing cut upon her broad bottom, instantly marking the delicate, white skin with many red lines; she winced convulsively, her flesh quivered, she uttered a low gasping cry, and she buried her face in the sofa cushion. Again, again, and again, I drew the rod smartly across her shrinking bottom, which grew redder and redder at each cut, and also became speckled with the dark red dots made by the hard buds on the twigs of the birch; she threw back her head with a jerk, so that her long hair came loose, and moaned piteously. I went on flogging her slowly, and laying each cut upon a different spot; the long, dark red weals rose in all directions on her quivering flesh, and she began to scream with pain. The "lust of cruelty" now fully possessed me, and regardless of her shrieks, I continued to birch her. She twisted herself from side to side as far the bonds which held her would allow, arching her loins at one moment, and then at the next moment flattening herself down upon the couch, in vain attempts to escape the stinging cuts of the rod.

Turning her head, she looked over her shoulder at me, with an imploring expression in her fear-dilated eyes; the loose coils of her hair partly hiding her pain-distorted face; the tears were streaming down her scarlet cheeks, and her lips were quivering with anguish. "Oh, stop! Stop!" she gasped out between her shrieks. "I—can't—bear it! Oh—h! I can't—bear—it! Oh! Oh! do—have—mercy—on—me! Oh! you—are—cutting—me—to pieces! Oh! Oh!! Ah—h—h!! Oh—h—h—h!!!"

I stopped for a moment. I had been flogging her from left to right, and I now went round to the other side of the sofa, in order to flog her from right to left, so that both cheeks of her bottom should receive equal punishment. She had thought that the birching was over, but she was mistaken; and when she saw me again raise the rod, she uttered a long wail of terror, beseeching me in most pitiful accents not to flog her any more.

I again began to lay the rod across her wealed, scarlet, sore bottom; her screams grew louder and louder—it was lucky I had thought of sending the servants out of the house —her struggles and contortions became more violent, and she wriggled and writhed, shrieked, and screamed; and pleaded and prayed for mercy.

I stopped, and throwing down the rod, inspected the girl's bottom. The whole surface from the loins to the thighs was covered with a network of livid weals, and speckled all over with purple dots, and there were a few drops of blood on each cheek where the skin had been broken. I had not flogged her with any great severity, but her skin was so extremely delicate that it had been easily cut by the rod; and she had suffered acutely. In fact, she was in a half-fainting state; there was a cold dew on her forehead, her face had grown pale, and her eyes were closed. I pulled down her clothes, and unfastened her wrists and ankles, with as little delay as possible; then I got a glass of water and moistened her lips.

I still had a cockstand, and would have liked to poke her; but to have done so at that moment would have been sheer cruelty. I am only cruel with the rod. My feelings towards her had undergone a revulsion; I was no longer angry with my sweetheart, but felt full of pity for her. She had paid dearly for her indiscretion! I put my arms round her, kissing and soothing her till the faintness had passed off; and after she had drunk the glass of wine I brought her, the colour began to return to her cheeks. Looking at me reproachfully, she said in a weak voice: "Oh, why did you flog me so dreadfully? I had no idea you could be so cruel." Then, whimpering a little: "Oh! how sore my bottom is! The flesh is throbbing in a most painful way."

"I will bathe it for you, and it will soon stop throbbing," said I.

Taking her up in my arms, I carried her to the bedroom, and laid her face downwards on the bed, then again turning up her petticoats, I sponged her sorely disfigured, burning bottom with cold water, until the skin had got quite cool; then I applied some vaseline.

She appeared to be quite worn out, and inclined to sleep, so I covered her up, lowered the blinds, and left the room quietly.

I went down to the drawing-room, locked up the rod and straps in a cabinet, and put everything in order; and just as I had finished, the two servants came back. At five o'clock, the housemaid brought up the usual afternoon tea; and after I had refreshed myself with a cup, I took one up to Frances, whom I found fast asleep. I stood and looked at her for a moment, but she did not wake; so I left the cup of tea on a little table at the bedside.

Our dinner hour was half-past seven, so there was still two hours before me, but as I did not feel inclined to go out, I settled myself down in an easy-chair in the drawing room with a book, and managed to pass the time pleasantly till the maid came to tell me that dinner was on the table. I did not expect to see Frances, and was just going to send her up some soup and a glass of wine, when she came into the room. She was dressed in a pretty dinner frock, and her hair was neatly arranged; but her cheeks were rather pale, her eyes were not so bright as usual, and the lids were red; and when she sat down, she did so very carefully, making a little grimace when her bottom first touched the chair. "Oh, dear me!" she said dolefully. "It is awfully tender; and I have had to put on a clean chemise, the other one was spotted with blood."

I gave her a glass of champagne, and talked gaily to her, telling her that she was again my sweetheart. That seemed to cheer her up a little; she began to eat her dinner, and by the time the dessert was on the table, she had commenced to talk, and smile a little; not appearing to be the least sulky, or angry with me for having given her such a severe flogging. But I knew her disposition thoroughly, and could pretty well guess how she reasoned. She would say to herself, that she had committed an offence deserving punishment; she had received the punishment, and I had forgiven the offence; so all was right.

After dinner, we went into the drawing-room to have our coffee and she lay on the sofa while I read to her for a time; then we had a little chat, and at half-past ten o'clock we went upstairs to our bedroom, Frances walking very stiffly.

When we were in bed, she lay on her side nestling close up to me, while I kissed her soft, warm lips, and played with her delicious bubbies.

Then, pulling up her nightdress above her waist, I laid my hand gently on her bottom, finding that it was still rough with weals, and so tender that the light touch of my fingers made her shrink. "Oh, don't touch it!" she exclaimed. I removed my hand, but I rubbed my prick against her belly, saying: "Do you think you could bear to let me 'do it' to you?"

"I am afraid not," she replied. "My bottom is too sore to bear the least pressure. And I don't think we can manage 'it' lying on our sides, face to face."

As my prick was almost bursting, I determined to have a poke somehow or other; but I was puzzled for a moment to know how I could "have" her without more or less pressing her bottom. Then I remembered the "wheelbarrow" position. It is an awkward way of poking a woman, and one that I do not care for; therefore I had never shown it to Frances, although I had "had" her in every other fancy position. However, I resolved to poke her in that way now. So I said: "I can do it to you in a way that will not put the least pressure on your bottom; you won't have to lie on it, and I won't touch it. But you will find the position rather uncomfortable."

"Oh, I don't care what position you put me in, so long as you don't hurt my sore bottom!" she said without hesitation, and at the same time squeezing my prick with her soft hand.

"We shall have to get out of bed to do it," I observed.

She at once jumped out of bed, saying, with a little laugh: "Come along then!" I followed her, and turned up the wick of the shaded lamp which we always kept burning throughout the night. The room was now well-lighted, and Frances looked very charming in her long white nightdress, her pretty little bare feet showing under the hem of the lace-trimmed garment, as she stood with a puzzled expression on her face, evidently wondering how I could possibly poke her without touching her bottom.

She was soon enlightened! Lifting her up in my arms, I turned her upside down, with her feet in the air, and with her hands resting on the floor at the full extent of her arms; her nightdress falling over her head, and leaving the whole of her body naked. Then I made her put her legs round my neck, while I held her round the waist with my hands clasped on her belly, so that I supported her weight, and took the strain off her arms. Thus her body was in a slanting position; and as her bottom was uppermost, her cunt was just on a level with my prick. Then, by slightly bending my knees, and at the same time curving my back, I easily forced the weapon into the sheath, and began to poke her by moving my loins backwards and forwards. She did the same, and we had a satisfactory though rather cramped poke; during which, her wealed, red-striped, sore bottom was never once touched, or rubbed against in any way.

When all was over, I put her on her feet, and she remarked, with a laugh: "Well, you managed it very nicely; but I must say it is a very uncomfortable position. It makes all the blood run into one's head."

Then we got into bed again, and soon fell asleep.

Next morning, before getting up, I made her lie on her face outside the bed, with her nightdress up to her shoulders, so that I might make a thorough inspection of the state of her bottom.

It was very much disfigured, and it looked very sore—as no doubt it was. Cicatrices had formed over the broken places on the skin, which was very red, and the weals still showed very plainly.

However, her flesh was healthy, and it soon healed; but it was some time before all the marks had disappeared; and her pretty bottom had recovered its lily-like whiteness.

We got out of bed and had a poke "wheelbarrow" fashion; then we dressed and went down to breakfast with good appetites.

A week afterwards, I took Frances to Boulogne where

we remained a month; bathing together nearly every day; and my pretty sweetheart looked most charming in her bathing costume. In fact, she was so enticing in it, that I often poked her in the bathing-machine after she had come out of the water dripping and rosy, looking like some beautiful sea nymph.

On leaving Boulogne, we went back to London, and I lived at the villa; occasionally paying a visit to Oakhurst for a few days, just to see how things were getting on. When the grouse-shooting began, I went to Scotland, and stayed a fortnight with my friend in Argyllshire. I spent September at Oakhurst, partridge shooting; and in October, I took Francis abroad again.

## END OF SECOND VOLUME

# "Frank" and I

Volume Three

# XVI

TIME FLIES.——A GREAT CHANGE.——FRANCES
SPEAKS.——THE DISCLOSURE.——FRANCES AND
MATRIMONY.——MUTUAL MOUTHPLAY.——
THE FIRST AND LAST TIME.——FAREWELL
PLEASURES.——THE PARTING OF
THE WAYS.——ALONE.

I will now pass over a space of three years. Frances was
twenty-four years of age, and I was nearly forty. During the
time that had passed, we had got on very well together; and
I never again had had to find fault with her for any lightness
of conduct; though she was much admired wherever we
went, and she always had men dangling after her in the
various hotels we stayed at when we were on the Continent.
However, as she never permitted her admirers to become
familiar, I did not mind her amusing herself by flirting a
little. Brooke, we had never seen again.

Though Frances had never been unfaithful to me, I
must confess that I had been occasionally unfaithful to her;
simply out of desire for a change. But I never once had
come across a woman who had a better figure, or who was
a more delicious poke, than my sweetheart.

I had not constantly lived with her, but had spent part

of my time at Oakhurst; also going once a year to Scotland. And I had always taken her to some seaside place for a month in the summer, and had also taken her abroad part of every winter. We had visited Spain, and Algiers; and one year I had taken her for a six weeks cruise up the Mediterranean in one of the yachting steamers.

I had never again birched her, though I had occasionally given her a sound spanking; which she had invariably taken without making any fuss, other than the little squeals of pain she uttered, and the tears she shed while smarting under the operation. We were still fond of each other in a placid sort of way, like old married people; and we both enjoyed our nights when we were together.

I had, however, latterly often caught myself wondering how it was all going to end: for I had an idea that sooner or later, I should find the connection irksome, and want to put an end to it. So, in view of that contingency, I had invested a sum of money in Frances' name in various safe shares and securities which were paying well; therefore in the event of our parting company, she would have a very fair income. After all, it was the least I could do for the woman whom I had seduced, and who had always been faithful to me.

I never said a word to Frances about the money I had set aside for her; and she appeared to be perfectly happy in her little house whenever I was with her; and when I was away she always wrote to me in good spirits.

But to resume the thread of my story. It was the end of November and I had just arrived at King's Cross station, after an absence of two months, which had been spent at various country houses; and during the time I had been away, I had never seen Frances, nor had I once poked a woman; consequently I was eagerly looking forward to the moment when I should hold my pretty sweetheart in my arms.

I reached the villa about five o'clock, and was received

in a most affectionate manner by Frances, who was looking
very lovely in a pretty frock of some soft, dark material,
cut square at the neck, showing the upper part of her white
bosom. We sat down cosily beside the fire, in the well-lit,
prettily furnished little drawing-room, and while Frances
busied herself making the tea, I told her all about the various
people with whom I had been staying. She poured out a
cup of tea and brought it to me, standing behind my chair
while I sipped the refreshing beverage, and every now and
then bending over to give me a kiss.

Finally she perched herself upon my knees; then, as
a matter of course my hand found its way up her clothes,
and toyed with the silky hair of the "spot,"—she had on no
drawers,—while her hand unbuttoned my trousers and let
out my tool, which was in a very rampant state, after its two
months rest. She gently, with her forefinger and thumb,
covered and uncovered the red tip several times; saying, with
a laugh: "I wonder if it has been a good boy while it has
been away?"

"Yes, it has," I remarked, smiling. "Don't you see how
stiff it is?"

"Oh, that proves nothing! It is very easily made stiff;
but anyway I am going to take the stiffness out of it now."

So saying, she got off my knees, and turned her back
towards me; then she deliberately raised all her dainty skirts
above her waist, and stood for a moment, so that I might see
and admire her beautiful white bottom and plump thighs.
Then backing close up to me, she put her hand between
her legs, and seizing my member, she guided it to the right
spot, then gradually lowering herself down, she took my
prick inch by inch into her tight cunt, till her bottom
touched my balls, and she sat on my lap, with her back resting against my chest. Putting my arms round her waist
under her petticoats, I clasped my hands on her cool soft
belly, and began to poke her vigorously, by moving my loins
up and down. My movements were ably seconded by

Frances, who raised and lowered her bottom in a most voluptuous way; so that in a very few seconds, I "spent" with a prolonged quiver of sexual excitement, depositing a copious offering in the "grotto of love."

When all was over, we retired to our bedroom and had a wash; then we went down to dinner; which Frances had taken care should be a nice one. We had some clear soup; turbot with lobster sauce; a brace of roast grouse, and a soufflé; and we drank sherry and champagne. We also had dessert, with coffee and liqueurs. Then, after I had smoked a cigar, we went into the drawing-room. It had, however, struck me all through dinner, that Frances, though lively and in good spirits, had not been quite so talkative as usual. I settled down in an easy-chair to read the evening paper, while she took up a book; but I noticed that she did not seem to be much interested in what she was reading; and every now and then she glanced at me with a troubled expression on her face. I could see she was bothered about something, and I wondered what it was. A few minutes passed; then she put down her book, and coming to me, sat down in her old way upon a stool at my feet, resting her arm upon my knees, and looking up in my face. "Charley," she said, in a serious tone of voice, "I have something very particular to say to you."

I was rather surprised at her grave manner, which was quite unusual with her. "Well, what is it?" I lightly asked; expecting to be told that she had run into debt with her dressmaker, or something of that sort.

But the communication she made to me, had reference to a matter of far greater importance than a milliner's bill.

She began: "You know I am very grateful to you for all your kindness to me since the day you took me into your house: and we have always got on well together. I love you still, and I think you are still a little fond of me; but I have often thought that some day you may get married;—though you will never find a woman who will love you more than I have.

"Or you may take it into your head to leave me, for some reason or other; and then what would become of me?"

"Oh, my dear girl," I said, bending down and giving her a kiss, "if either of the events you have mentioned should happen, your future would be all right. I have taken care that you shall never want. But why have you told me all this? I shall never marry; and I don't wish to leave you."

She gave me a grateful kiss, saying: "Ah, you may not wish to leave me just at present, but I am afraid you will get tired of me in course of time. I am young now; and you say I am pretty. But I shall not be always so."

I felt there was a good deal of truth in what she had said; so I made no remark; and she went on, hurriedly: "Now, what I have to tell you will astonish, and perhaps make you angry; but I feel that I ought no longer to keep you in ignorance of certain things which have happened to me during your absence." She paused for a moment, and I wondered what was coming. She went on: "About six weeks ago, I was sitting reading in a lovely part of the park, when a rough-looking tramp came up, and begged me to give him a copper to buy a bit of bread, as he was starving. I gave him six-pence out of my purse which happened to be full of silver. He noticed it, and when I had put the purse back into my pocket, he caught hold of me roughly and tried to rob me. I struggled, and screamed loudly; and my cries were heard by a gentleman, who came running to my assistance, and drove the tramp away. My arms were bruised, I was very much frightened, and I was trembling all over: so the gentleman made me take his arm, and when we had got out of the park, he put me in a cab, and drove me home."

I made a movement of anger, uttering the word: "Damnation!"

She placed her hand on mine, saying soothingly: "Now Charley! You needn't get angry. There was no wrong done. Wait till you have heard the rest of my story."

"Go on," I said crossly.

"Next day he called upon me; and I gave him a cup of

tea, and we had a long chat. Since then he has called several times, and I have frequently met him in the park. He is a gentleman, and has always treated me with the utmost respect. He has told me that he loves me; and to-day he asked me to marry him."

I was utterly taken aback, and inclined to be very angry. "The devil he did!" I exclaimed. "Who is he? Tell me all you know about him. Do you love him? Perhaps he is only trying to deceive you."

"I don't think he is," she remarked. Then she continued: "His name is Markham; he is about forty-five years old; a widower, with two children; a boy six years of age, and a girl nine years of age; he is a merchant at the Cape, and he is very well-off. I like him, but I do not love him."

I was silent for a short time, thinking over her startling communication. Then I said: "Do you wish to leave me, and marry him?"

"I will be guided in the matter entirely by your advice and wishes. If you want me to stay with you; I will do so: but if you think I ought to accept Mr. Markham, I will marry him. Now think well over what I have said; and then tell me what you wish me to do."

I pondered deeply over what she had told me; and I finally came to the conclusion, that though I did not at that moment wish to part with Frances; yet it would be wrong for me to stand in her way and prevent her getting married. She would never get such an offer again; and if the man was rich, and a gentleman, the marriage would be a good thing for her, and also for me; as I should be relieved of all responsibility as to her future.

So, giving her a kiss, I said: "Well, my dear girl, I shall be extremely sorry to part with you; but under the circumstances, I think you had better accept Mr. Markham. I will make inquiries about him, and find out if he is what he represents himself to be. But make sure of your own mind before you definitely accept him."

She sat down on a chair, and resting her chin on her

hand, fell into deep thought. But I fancied I could guess what she would do. She would accept the man's offer. Every woman likes to get married and have a home, which she knows she cannot be turned out of—as long as she behaves herself—even should her husband get tired of her.

After a few moments, she said: "I can't quite make up my mind yet; but I will think well over the matter to-night. I am to see him, and give him my answer to-morrow."

There was nothing more to be said, at that moment, on the subject; and we both sat silent and thoughtful: we felt upset, and we could not settle down comfortably; so we soon went up to our bedroom.

But when we were between the sheets, with our bodies in close contact, and our legs twined round each other's; our thoughts quickly turned in a lascivious direction, and we had two delicious pokes before going to sleep.

Next morning, after breakfast, I asked her if she had quite made up her mind what to do. "Yes," she replied, huskily, "I have decided to marry Mr. Markham." Then coming up to me, she threw her arms round me and strained me to her bosom in a passionate embrace, while the tears rolled down her cheeks. "Oh, Charley!" she sobbed out. "It will be an awful wrench parting with you. Oh, dear me! Oh, dear me!" Then she added, trying to smile: "But perhaps it will be better for me to leave you before I get old and ugly; and you tire of me."

I had felt sure that she would make up her mind to marry the man, but nevertheless my heart was heavy at knowing that I should soon lose my pretty sweetheart, with whom I had spent so many happy years. However, I consoled myself by thinking, that as she was leaving me of her own accord, I should never have to reproach myself for sending her away—and that was an event which most probably would have happened some day or other. At eleven o'clock she went out to meet Markham; while I stayed at home to write some letters.

She came back to lunch at the usual hour, and told me

that the whole affair was settled, and the wedding day fixed; then she showed me the engaged ring her fiancé had given her; but she did not appear to be at all elated at knowing she was soon going to be a "respectable married woman"; and during lunch she often looked wistfully at me. I spent the afternoon in the City, making inquiries about Markham; and I found out that he was a man with a good reputation; a diamond mercnant at the Cape, and he was said to be wealthy.

I was glad to hear satisfactory accounts of the man; for I had been inclined to think that he was an impostor, who was merely trying to get hold of Frances.

When we met at dinner, she seemed to be in better spirits. I told her what I had heard about Markham; and she informed me that her marriage was to take place in a month's time. Then we had a long talk about the whole affair, and I gave her some "fatherly" advice.

The time passed on. Frances met her lover every day, somewhere or other; and she began to buy such an extensive trousseau, that the villa was soon littered with trunks, bandboxes, and all sorts of feminine finery, although she already had a large wardrobe. As she was going to marry a rich man, I did not think I was now called upon to make any settlement upon her: but I insisted upon paying for her trousseau; though she did not wish me to do so. She said that Mr. Markham had supplied her with plenty of money for the purpose.

During this period she was more loving and affectionate to me than ever; the tears were often in her eyes, and she would sometimes sit holding my hand in hers, without speaking. At other times, when sitting beside me in the day-time, she would suddenly unbutton my trousers, take out my tool, and play with it till I poked her.

In fact, both by day and night, she seemed to want me to "have" her as often as possible before we parted.

At last, her outfit was completed; her trunks were

packed, and the marriage was to take place in a week's time. The wedding was to be a quiet one, and she was to be married from a hotel, to which she was to go the day before the ceremony.

The week passed rapidly. On the morning of the day she was to go away she woke early, and very soon woke me. As I thought it was the last time we should be in bed together, I determined to spin out my pleasure as long as I possibly could.

After kissing her eyes, her peach-like cheeks, and her rosy, fragrant mouth, I threw off all the bedclothes, and took off my nightgown, making Frances do the same. There was a good fire in the room. Then I played with the lovely, naked woman in every imaginable way; rolling her over and over, placing her in all sorts of positions, feeling every part of her body, and biting the plump flesh in various places. I spanked her broad, white bottom gently till a pink flush showed on the cheeks; I slapped her polished back and shoulders, her rounded thighs, and the calves of her legs; even her smooth, soft belly received a few slight slaps. When her flesh was glowing and tingling from head to foot, and we were both in a high state of excitement, I stretched out her legs, and pressing my mouth on the delicious, little pink lips of her golden-haired cunt, I thrust my tongue deeply into its warm recesses, and tickled the tiny sensitive button for a moment or two. Frances quivered all over, squirming, and writhing, and turning up her eyes in an ecstasy of voluptuous delight. I quickly withdrew my tongue, and she sat up, gazing at me; her cheeks were flushed, her eyes were sparkling, and her titties were rising and falling. "Oh—h—h!" she exclaimed, drawing a long breath. "How delicious that was! Your tongue felt like a bit of warm velvet. Oh, Charley! why did you never do it to me before?"

I laughed but did not answer, and she said: "I will do it to you now."

Then she laid herself down between my legs, and for

the first time in her life, she took my prick into her mouth, nibbling it gently with her teeth, tickling the tip with her velvety tongue, and drawing the foreskin backwards and forwards with her lips, till I was frantic with lust, and almost at the point of "spending." Plucking my tool out of her mouth, I threw myself upon her, and our bodies seemed to become one, as we mutually clasped each other in a close embrace. My naked breast was on her naked, palpitating bosom, our bellies rubbed together, my mouth was pressed to her lips, my tongue was in her mouth, and my prick was in her cunt. Tightly grasping the cheeks of her bottom, while she threw her legs round my loins, I fucked her, in a delirium of passion, twice without withdrawing, making her groan, squeak, and wriggle her bottom furiously each time I discharged. And when it was all over, she lay in my arms almost fainting from excess of pleasure, her naked body quivering from head to foot. It had been a grand poke, and we had both enjoyed it to the uttermost.

We got up, had our baths, dressed, and went down to breakfast. But neither of us had much appetite; we felt depressed; and altogether the meal was a sorrowful one, though we both pretended to be in good spirits.

As soon as breakfast was over, Frances went away to get ready; and she came back in about half-an-hour, fully equipped, with her hat on. As usual, she was dressed in perfect taste, and she looked most charming. Presently a four-wheeled cab arrived at the gate of the villa, and then the trunks and bandboxes were carried out and placed on the top of the vehicle. The moment had come for us to part; and Frances clung round me, crying bitterly, and kissing me passionately.

I had a lump in my throat as I disengaged her arms from my neck. Then, after giving her a long lingering kiss, I led her out of the house and put her in the cab. She leant back in a corner, sobbing, with her handkerchief to her eyes; and in another moment the cab was driven off, leaving me feeling rather miserable.

I spent the day at my club, and dined there, returning early to the villa; but when I got into the drawing-room, where everything reminded me much of my lost sweetheart, I felt so depressed that I left the house again, and went to a music hall, just to pass the time until it was late enough to go to bed.

Next morning, when I woke with my usual cockstand, I thought of the splendid poke I had had, twenty-four hours previously, and at that moment I would have given anything to have had Frances again in my arms.

She was married that day at two o'clock; but I did not go to see her "turned off." The newly-wedded couple spent a month in Paris; and then embarked for the Cape. Frances wrote to me from Southampton the day the steamer sailed; and in her letter—which was a long one—she told me that her husband was good and kind; but that he never would be the same to her, as her first and only sweetheart Charley, whom she would never forget.

A few days afterwards, I put the villa in the hands of a firm of auctioneers, telling them to sell the furniture; and then I went home to Oakhurst. At first, I was a little restless, but after a time, I settled down to my old way of life.

During the first year of Frances' marriage she wrote to me occasionally; then her letters ceased; and I thought I should never again either hear from, or see my old sweetheart. I fancied she had passed out of my life.

# XVII

ROUND THE WORLD.——WOMEN OF ALL NATIONS.
——SLAPPING A JAPANESE GIRL.——FLAGELLATION
IN CHINA.——MARY THE PARLOURMAID AND HER
EXPERIENCES.——CHARITY GIRLS CHASTISED.——
FRANCES A WIDOW.——UNITED ONCE MORE.——
HER TALES OF MARRIED LIFE.——A SEMI-
IMPOTENT HUSBAND.——BIRCHING THE
STEPCHILDREN.——THE HIDDEN WIT-
NESS.——THE GOVERNESS'S OPINION
OF CORPORAL PUNISHMENT.

A couple more years passed. During the whole period, I had
amused myself in various ways, but I had never set up another
establishment in St. John's Wood, or anywhere else. When in
England, I had lived chiefly at Oakhurst, but I often travelled
on the Continent; I had also made a tour round the world,
and as I was in no hurry, I had taken eight months to complete the journey. I did not meet with any startling adventures, but I saw some queer phases of life, and I embraced
many women of various nationalities. I had started westward

on the trip, and while passing through the United States, I poked American girls in all the big cities from New York to San Francisco.

In the Hawaiian Islands I had seen a bevy of dusky, nearly naked damsels dance the "hula-hula"; and when the lascivious performance was over, I fucked one of the dancers on a mat in a native hut.

I stayed for some time in Japan; and when in Jeddo, I paid a couple of visits to the "Yoshiwara"; on each occasion poking one of the highly-painted, wonderfully got-up girls. But I preferred going to the tea houses in the country, and amusing myself with the "geishas," and the pretty little, olive-skinned "mousmies," all of whom were full of fun, and up to every kind of trick. On one occasion, however, I astonished a "mousmie." She was a very young and particularly plump little creature, with whom I was playing while she was in a state of complete nudity.

After the usual toying, I suddenly laid her across my knees, and smartly spanked her fat, round little bottom. She was utterly amazed; hardly knowing whether to laugh or cry; such a thing had never been done to her before, though she was well acquainted with all the other ways by which men excite themselves with women.

When I put her on her feet, she stood gazing at me, with her black eyes full of tears, at the same rubbing her bottom with both her hands. Then, as the smart gradually passed off, she began to smile, and finally she burst out laughing. Then I poked her!

When in China, I spent several days in the city of Canton, and visited two or three "flower boats" on the river. But I did not fancy the small-footed, almond-eyed, yellow-skinned Chinese girls, so I only poked one; and I did it merely that I might be able to say I had "had" a Chinawoman.

In India I tried the merits of various Hindoo, and Mohammedan girls; and in Ceylon I sampled the Cingalese damsels. And I will here state, that in my opinion there is no better poke in the world, than a young, clean, healthy English girl.

During my stay in Canton, I managed to see the bamboo applied to a culprit. The Chinese "boy" whom I had employed as a guide was an intelligent fellow named Ah Wan. He could speak "Pidgin" English; and after we had visited all the sights which are usually shown to foreigners, the "boy" asked me one day, if I would like to go to the execution ground, and see, as he expressed it: "Two pieccy pilate mans head chopped off."

Two pirates he meant to say, but the Chinese can't pronounce the letter R. They always turn it into L.

I replied that I did not care to see that sight. But I told him that I had a great wish to see how the bamboo was used; and I added that I should like, if possible, to see a female culprit punished. Then I asked him if he could manage that for me. Not a sign of surprise showed on Ah Wan's impassive countenance, when he heard what I had said. He nodded his head, saying, "Allee light. My can do that pidgin velly easy, along Mandalin cote. One pieccy day, my takey you."

By which he meant: "All right. I can easily manage that business for you at the Mandarin's court. I will take you some day."

The Mandarin's court is somewhat analogous to an English Police-court; but the Mandarin's power is far more absolute than that of a police magistrate in this country.

A couple of days after my talk with Ah Wan, he made his appearance at my hotel, with a chair and two coolie bearers.

"Come along a me," he said briefly.

I got into the chair; he gave the coolies some directions and we started off; Ah Wan walking beside the chair. In about half-an-hour we reached the court house which was a large wooden building, to which the public appeared to have free access. The Mandarin sat at a sort of high desk, surrounded by soldiers and other officials; and there were a number of people of all sorts and conditions in the court.

Ah Wan interpreted, as well as he could, all the proceedings, and I saw several prisoners sentenced to various punishments by the Mandarin; but not one received the bamboo, and I was beginning to think of going away, when a woman was brought in to receive her sentence.

Ah Wan informed me that she was a boatwoman who had been detected setting fire to a boat. A very serious crime in Canton where thousands of families live in boats on the river.

The culprit being a working woman, was not "small-footed." she was a stout, strong-looking wench about twenty-five years old, and not bad-looking for a Chinawoman of the lower orders.

She was neatly dressed in the usual loose, blue cotton jacket, coming down over her hips; with wide trousers of the same colour and material; and her long, coarse, black hair was twisted in elaborate coils, and secured with four long, broad, brass hairpins which stuck out a couple of inches on each side of her head.

The Mandarin sternly addressed the culprit, who stood stolidly gazing at him; but after he had spoken a short time, a look of intense fear came to the woman's face; she burst out crying, and stretching out her hands, made what I supposed to be a piteous appeal for mercy.

Ah Wan whispered to me: "That piecey woman catchee plenty bamboo."

The Mandarin made a sign, and three of the soldiers seized the wailing culprit and laid her face downwards on the floor, with her arms stretched out at right angles to her body. Two of the men squatted down, each holding one of the woman's arms; the third man, also squatting down, held her ankles tightly together.

A fourth man drew her loose jacket up to her shoulders; then putting his hands under her belly, he untied the strings of her trousers, and pulled them down to her heels; thus laying bare the lower half of the woman's person to the gaze of the people in the Court.

The pig-tailed spectators looked on stolidly. To them it was no uncommon sight. Women were often flogged publicly in Canton.

The culprit had a broad bottom, with large fleshy cheeks, her thighs were very big, and her legs were thick. Her skin was smooth, and of a yellow tint which was not pretty to a European's eye.

But after all, it was a feminine bottom; and it was going to be flogged; that was enough for me; and as I gazed at the naked, fat, albeit yellow posteriors, my cock stiffened slightly.

Two men, holding in their hands the bamboos, now knelt down, one on each side of the culprit. The instruments of punishment were pieces of split bamboo about two feet long, and three inches broad; and the strokes were administered with the rounded side. At a signal from the Mandarin, the punishment commenced, one man beginning at the upper part of the woman's bottom and flogging downwards; while the other man began at the middle part of her thighs and flogged upwards. The strokes were inflicted with considerable force; each one, as it fell on the woman's plump flesh, making a resounding smack, and marking her yellow skin with a broad red stripe. She wept and screamed, and struggled violently; but the men who were holding her, kept her in position; and the men who were flogging her, laid on the strokes in rapid succession; so that the two bamboos soon met in the middle of her bottom, and by that time the whole surface of her skin had become crimson.

Then they again began to go over the woman's writhing posteriors in the same way as before; one man flogging down, and the other man flogging up. The bamboos cracked like pistol shots on the victim's quivering bottom; the big cheeks opening and shutting, as she alternately contracted and relaxed the muscles in agony; while as the punishment went on, her shrieks became louder and more piercing. When the bamboos again met, the Mandarin made a sign; then the two men ceased flogging, and the other men let go their hold of the woman's limbs; but she remained lying on the floor, squealing and twisting herself about in anguish.

She had received, in all, fifty severe strokes—I had counted them—and her bottom looked like a huge piece of liver; but not a drop of blood had been drawn. No one took any notice of her; and after a time her crying subsided to choking sobs which shook her whole body and made her fat buttocks quiver like jelly.

Struggling to her feet, she pulled up her trousers; and with some difficulty, for she was trembling all over, she tied the strings round her waist. Then two soldiers took her by the arms, and led her out of the court, sobbing, moaning, and hardly able to put one foot before the other. She was taken to prison; for in addition to the flogging, she had been sentenced to a year's imprisonment. I left the court, got into my chair, and was carried back to the hotel. Then I gave Ah Wan a good "cumshaw,"—a present—and he departed, his face looking as inscrutable as ever.

Two days afterwards, I left Canton for Hong Kong, where I caught the mail steamer, and in due course arrived in London.

Since my return to England, three months had passed; during which period I had been living quietly at Oakhurst; but I could always get a poke whenever I felt inclined, as I had at my disposal one of the parlourmaids named Mary.

This girl had not been in the house at the time I went away; but she had been engaged by the housekeeper during my absence.

Mary was about twenty-three years old, a tall, good-looking, well-made girl, with dark brown hair and neat feet and ankles. I had taken a fancy to her, a few days after my return home; and had managed to get hold of her without the least difficulty, as she had often been fucked before she entered my service. However, she was a fairly good poke, and she had a nice, white, smooth skin, firm bubbies, and a big plump bottom; moreover she was particularly clean in dress and person, so that I was never afraid of turning up her petticoats at any moment. I cannot touch a girl if she has on dirty underlinen.

Mary was also well versed in the "arts of love," and she would let me do anything I liked to her except in one respect. She would never allow me to whip her in any way.

One day, after I had given her a good poke; I asked her why she was so afraid of a little whipping. She told me the reason; and she also gave me a short account of her life.

She had been left an orphan, at the age of six years; and had been brought up in a charity institution where corporal punishment was freely applied to the girls whenever they committed an offence of any sort; the little girls being spanked, and the big girls being birched. She herself had been so often soundly spanked when she was a little girl, and so often severely birched when she was a big girl, that now the very idea of a whipping made her flesh creep.

When she was at the institution, it had contained upwards of fifty girls, who were kept until they were sixteen years of age; then they were put out to service; and every girl was liable to be birched, up to the day she left the establishment.

There was a regular "punishment parade" every morning in the schoolroom at nine o'clock, when all the culprits of the previous twenty-four hours were flogged in succession, from the youngest to the oldest, in the presence of all the other girls. Everything was carried out in a methodical manner, but the preparations for punishment did not take long, as no drawers were worn by the girls at the institution. The little culprits were, one after the other, stretched at full length on a bench, and well spanked by one of the assistant mistresses. Then the big culprits were, each in turn, held over a high desk by two of the assistants. The matron, who was the only person authorized to use the rod, would then apply the birch; never giving less than six cuts, and sometimes giving as many as eighteen, for serious offences, such as stealing, or indecent conduct. She always flogged severely, and sometimes drew blood. Nearly every morning there was a culprit to be punished, and sometimes there were two or more; and she had seen as many as eight big girls birched one after the other.

I could hardly believe that girls were treated with such severity in a charity institution in these humanitarian days; but Mary assured me that it was a fact; and she added that though it was seven years since she had left the institution, she knew that the discipline of the establishment was still maintained in the same severe way as it had been in her time.

Then she went on to tell me what had happened to her since she left the institution. When she had reached the age of sixteen, she was put out to service as an under-housemaid in a large country house, where there were three young men, the sons of the master. The three young chaps at once made a dead set at her, and a couple of months after her arrival in the house, she was seduced by the eldest son of the family.

Then she had allowed the other two brothers to "have" her, and between them she had had a lively time during the two years she lived in the house. She used to get a poke from one or other of the young men nearly every day; and often all three would poke her in one night, each man spending a couple of hours in bed with her.

She had been in two establishments as parlourmaid before coming to Oakhurst; and she wound up by telling me, with a laugh, that in both places she had been poked by the master of the house.

I laughed, gave her a kiss, and sent her away.

A few days afterwards, I was reading "The Times" after breakfast; and in glancing down the column of births, deaths, and marriages, my eye caught the name of Markham in the list of deaths. I hurriedly read the few lines which announced

that Robert Markham had died at Wynberg, in the Cape
Colony, on the 10th of April; aged 50 years.

It was now the 26th of May, so Frances had been a
widow for upwards of six weeks. I put down the paper, and
thought, with a mixture of feelings, about my old sweetheart—as I still called her in my mind—and I was surprised that she had not written to tell me of her loss. Then
I wondered what she would do now that she was a widow.
Would she remain at the Cape, or would she come back to
England? and if she did return, and I were to meet her, I
wondered what would happen. During the period that had
passed since her marriage, I had often thought of her; and
now I knew she was free, my old fondness for her revived,
and I hoped, some day or other, to again clasp her in
my arms.

For days afterwards I expected to hear from her; but
no letter came; and as the days passed into weeks without
my receiving any communication from her, I came to the
conclusion that she had remained at the Cape. The time
passed on. It was the end of June, and I was thinking of
going to the seaside; when, one morning, I received a letter;
and though it bore the London postmark, I knew by the
handwriting on the envelope, that it was from Frances. I
eagerly tore it open, and glancing at the top of the page,
saw that the address was Kensington. Then I read the letter.
It was a long one, written in affectionate terms, giving me
full details of all that had lately occurred; and asking me to
call on her any day that was convenient to me. I was delighted with the letter; as the way in which it was written
made me think she was still fond of me. But withal, I was
not quite sure that she would let me poke her when we met.
However, time would show.

I sat down and wrote a love-letter to her, finishing it by
saying that I would be with her at three o'clock next day.
I had the letter posted at once, so that Frances might receive
it by the last post.

Sending for my man, I informed him that I was going

up to London for a time, then I told him to go up to town that afternoon and get everything ready for me at my chambers.

He bowed, and went away without saying a word; but I knew that I should find everything in perfect readiness when I arrived at my rooms next day. Lighting a cigar, I sat down to smoke, with a great feeling of pleasure at the thought of again seeing, and perhaps poking Frances.

Next morning, after an early breakfast, I started for London; and on my arrival there, went first of all to my chambers where I changed my clothes. Then I went to my club to lunch; and when I had finishhed my repast, I got into a hansom and drove to the address Frances had given me. It was a pretty house in one of the best streets in Kensington. I knocked at the door, which was opened by a neatly dressed maidservant, who took my card and ushered me into a drawing-room, handsomely furnished, and decorated in the most artistic style. The apartment had two bow-windows, the recesses of which were filled with large jardinières, holding pots of flowers of all sorts in full bloom; and there were also several china bowls heaped up with freshly-cut roses; and at one side of the room there was a deep alcove screened with heavy curtains of Eastern manufacture. Frances always had good taste, and she certainly had made herself a beautiful nest.

Presently, I heard the sound of light footsteps in the passage, the door was opened, and she came running into the room. Then all my doubts as to the way she would receive me, were in a moment dispelled. I could tell by the look on her face that she was still my loving sweetheart. Throwing her arms round my neck, she pressed her lips to mine in a long passionate kiss, and strained me to her bosom in a close embrace, uttering little ejaculations of joy and addressing me by all sorts of endearing epithets. I clasped her tightly, returning her kisses hotly, and for a moment or two we clung to each other in a transport of delight.

Then we sat down side by side on the sofa, and I took

a good look at her. Frances was then midway between twenty-seven and twenty-eight years of age, and was therefore in the full bloom of ripe, luscious womanhood. She had grown a little more matronly in appearance, but she seemed to me more lovely than ever. The large limpid, blue eyes were sparkling with pleasure, and her peach-like cheeks were tinged with a delicate pink colour; her lips seemed to be redder and riper; her bosom was fuller, and the curves of her figure were more voluptuous. She was not dressed in the conventional widow's weeds; but was wearing a black satin tea-gown trimmed with rich lace round the neck, and down the front; her beautiful hair was twisted into a loose knot at the back of her head; and she had no corset. That fact I had discovered when my arms were round her waist.

Holding my hand in hers, she told me all about her life at the Cape.

Her husband had invariably treated her kindly; but they had not had many ideas in common. He had always been deeply immersed in his business; going to his office in Capetown every morning, and not returning till the evening. She had soon made a number of friends both male and female; she had always had plenty of money at her command; she had had nothing much to complain of, as far as her surroundings were concerned; and on the whole she had been fairly happy. Her husband had died a rich man; the bulk of his money was to go to his two children when they came of age; but he had settled upon her six hundred a year for life; and he had made her guardian of the two children. So her marriage had turned out a good thing.

I asked her why she had not written to me sooner. And she replied that she had wished to get comfortably settled in her house before asking me to call. She then asked me to tell her what I had been doing with myself during the past three years. I gave her a short account of how I had spent the time, and she was much interested in my descriptions of some of the things I had seen and done on my trip round the world.

Then she said, smiling, and lifting up the skirt of her tea-gown so that I had a peep at her little feet cased in patent leather shoes:

"You see I am not dressed in the orthodox garments. I hate them; but I have to wear them when I go out."

I laughed, and squeezing her waist through her soft gown, said: "I am very glad you are not got-up in crepe. It is hideous to look at, besides being very unpleasant to touch."

She smiled in an enticing way, so I at once took her on to my knees, and she leant back against my breast, looking up in my face; her beautiful eyes glistening with the look of desire which I had so often seen in them, in the old days. I pressed my mouth to her full red lips in a long kiss, with a feeling of rapture such as I had never felt when kissing any other woman. Then, lifting the skirt of her dress up to her knees, I looked at, and felt her shapely legs which were certainly stouter than when I had last seen them; the plump calves seeming ready to burst through the thin black silk stockings she was wearing.

Pouting her cherry lips with pretended anger, she exclaimed: "Sir, you are very rude! How dare you take such liberties with a lone widow!" Then, bursting into a laugh, she glued her lips to mine and put her warm velvet-like tongue into my mouth.

However, she soon took it out, and said, earnestly: "Oh, Charley! How delicious it is to feel your arms round me again."

"And I am delighted to hold you in them again," I returned, kissing her, and putting my tongue in her mouth, for a change; at the same time slipping my hand up her clothes and touching the pleasurable "spot." She had nothing on under her dress but a petticoat and a chemise. The voluptuous creature had evidently prepared herself to receive a poke. While my hand roved all over her belly and thighs, she unbuttoned my trousers, and for a few moments we played with each other; she rubbing my prick with her soft hand, while I tickled her cunt with my forefinger, making her squirm, and laugh hysterically. I next unfastened the front of her dress, and pushed her chemise down, so as to fully expose the magnificent semi-globes of her snow-white bosom. Her titties had increased in size, but they were as round and firm as ever they had been. After paddling with them a moment, I took one of the rosebud-like nipples in my mouth and sucked it till it stiffened slightly in my lips; and she seemed to purr with delight; like a cat when being stroked.

Then I stretched her face downwards on the sofa, and turning up her scanty drapery laid bare her magnificent bottom, which was broader, rounder, plumper, and more delicious than ever. I gloated over it, kissed it several times, and stroked the velvet-like, cool skin for a short time. She turned her head, saying with a smile: "Now give me a nice little spanking. Not too hard."

I was only too delighted to oblige her; so I gently spanked her firm-fleshed bottom, till a pink blush showed on the plump, white cheeks.

Then I stopped. "Oh," she murmured, "I liked that! The slight tingling sensation was most pleasant. And while you were spanking me, I almost fancied I was again a girl at Oakhurst."

I turned her over on to her back, and burying my head between her outstretched thighs, I kissed the "spot," at the same time inhaling the delicate perfume of violets with which her undergarments were scented, and which also emanated from her clean, wholesome flesh.

The subtle feminine odour was delicious, and it seemed to increase my sensual passions, which were already greatly excited. My eyes burned, the blood coursed rapidly through my veins, and my prick throbbed. It was time to go to work!

Separating the closely-shut lips of her little cunt with my fingers, I inserted my prick, and gently forced it deeply into the clinging sheath which I found to be as tight as ever it had been. It had never been stretched by anything bigger than a prick.

Then pressing my lips to her rosy mouth, and grasping the firm cheeks of her grand bottom with my hands, I began to poke her with long powerful strokes. She had always been a warm voluptuous woman, but now she seemed to be perfectly frantic with lust; and the way she bucked up to my thrusts astonished me. Throwing her arms and legs round me, she pressed me to her bosom, uttering little squeaks of pleasure, and exclaiming in gasps, as she bounded under me: "Oh, Charley! Oh—h,—dear—Charley! Oh—h—h!—do—it —slowly! Oh—h! my—love! My love!! Oh—h—h—h!!!"

She could say no more. The spasm had seized her; and she sighed, squirmed, and wriggled her bottom in a most furious way; squeezing my sides with her thighs, and biting my shoulder in a frenzy of lascivious excitement; while the lips of her cunt clung closely to my prick, until it became limp and dropped out of its warm nest.

Then we lay, for a few moments, palpitating in each other's arms. It had been a most delightful poke! I had not enjoyed one so heartily since the day she had left me, more than three years previously.

She, also, had most thoroughly enjoyed what she had received.

After a short rest, she got up, heaving a deep sigh of gratified desire: her cheeks were deeply flushed, and her great blue eyes had a languishing, sensuous look in them. Her chemise had slipped down very low, exposing her large, beautiful titties which were rising and falling quickly, and her long hair had come loose and was hanging in golden coils down to her waist.

She pulled up her chemise, fastened the bosom of her dress, and twisted up her tresses. Then, sitting down again upon the sofa, she looked at me, smiling archly, while I buttoned up my trousers, and arranged my disordered necktie.

When I had made everything as straight as I could under the circumstances, I sat down beside her and put my arm round her waist; while she nestled close up to my side. "Oh,

Charley!" she exclaimed fervently. "What pleasure you have given me! I have never had 'it' done properly to me since the day I left you." She paused for a moment, looking a little shyly at me; then she said: "Oh, I must tell you everything; and I shall have to use plain words."

"Go on. You needn't be afraid of shocking me," I observed, smiling. She began: "My late husband was fond of me; he also admired me very much, and he liked to see me well-dressed at all times, but more especially when we had a dinner party;—which was a weekly event, and I may say, without boasting, that I was always the best dressed woman at the table. But when he married me, he was in bad health, consequently his sexual power was weak; moreover he was by nature a man of very cold temperament. He had no idea of the pleasant little devices which excite the passions, and add so much to the 'delights of love.' He never played with me in any way; nor did he ever manifest the least desire to look at any part of my naked body. In fact, I do not think he ever fairly saw my legs, or my titties, or my bottom. He never once touched me in the day-time; and though he used to sleep with me every night, he would often go a week, or ten days, without poking me. And whenever he did embrace me, he would just perform the act, and nothing more; and when he had finished, he would roll over and go to sleep. Moreover his pokes were not pleasant; as, owing to his want of power, he never could get a proper erection, and therefore it was always a long time before the discharge came. And during the whole time he was grinding away at me, he used to lie with his whole weight upon my body, crushing my belly, and hurting my bosom. And often, after working violently till he was out of breath, and I was sore all over, his 'thing' would go quite limp, and he would have to stop. On such occasions, I always felt sick, and faint, and disgusted; for though he had not 'come,' I generally had 'spent' more or less, without having felt the least sensation of pleasure. So that altogether I did not care for his embraces, as they were really not worth having."

"They most certainly were not," I remarked. "No wonder you felt sick and disgusted."

She continued: "You know what a hot temperament I have"—

"Indeed I do!" I ejaculated.

"Don't interrupt me, sir," she said, giving me a playful pinch. "Well then, you can imagine how dreadfully tantalizing it was to me, to lie night after night with a man who could raise, but not satisfy my desire; or at best in a very imperfect way. I used to long for a vigorous man, who could take me in his arms without crushing me, and who could poke me in proper style. I had plenty of admirers, and I often felt very much inclined to let one or another of them have me. Not that I cared a straw for a single one of the men; but merely to slake my lust, which at times nearly overpowered me. Especially after a night when my husband had been more persevering, and more unsuccessful than usual. However, I managed to curb my passions. I was never unfaithful to my husband; and no man in South Africa ever kissed me, or touched me in any way. And now I have told you all."

"My poor Frances!" I said, giving her a kiss. "I can quite imagine how you must have been tormented. But never mind; you will not be troubled in that way now. I am going to stay in London for a time, and will come and see you as often as you like. I think I am still pretty vigorous."

"Oh, you are indeed," she said emphatically. Then laughing, and giving me a hug, she added: "I shall like to see you very often."

After a little more conversation, I asked her what had become of her step-children. She informed me that they were with her, and at present, they were both being educated by a governess; but the boy was to go to school in a year's time. Then she said: "You must see the children. For the last three years I have been their governess, and taught them nearly all they know. And I think they do credit to my bringing up."

Then she left the room; returning in a few minutes followed by the youngsters, whom she laughingly introduced to me as: "Master Robert Markham, aged nine years; and Miss Dora Markham, aged twelve years and six months."

Robert was a good-looking, chubby child; dressed in a black velvet knickerbocker suit. Dora was an extremely pretty little girl, with big gray eyes, and long auburn hair flowing loose over her shoulders nearly down to her waist. She was well, and tastefully dressed in mourning; and she looked a thorough little lady.

The children were not the least shy; neither were they forward; and after greeting me in a well-bred manner, they sat down, and we had a little chat. And I noticed that they called Frances "Mamma," whenever they addressed her.

They only remained a short time in the room; and when they had gone, I said to Frances: "They are pretty children, and they certainly do you credit in every way. They seem to be very well-behaved."

"Yes," she replied. "They are well-behaved now. I have managed to get them into pretty good order; but when I married their father, they were horrid little creatures in every way. Their mother died when they were mere babies, and they have been left entirely to servants—most of whom were natives—until I arrived at Wynberg. I at once took them in hand; and a hard job I had at first, as they had no idea of obedience; but I persevered, and I spanked them whenever they were naughty. After a few whippings, they became docile; but they are still troublesome at times. When I came to England I got a nice little rod, and now I birch them whenever they misbehave, or are idle at their lessons. I do not allow the governess to lay a hand on them. The girl is the more troublesome of the two, and I have to take her across my knees oftener than I have to take the boy."

I smiled. "Do you like whipping them?"

"Yes," she replied. "I must confess I do. Especially the boy. He is a nice little fellow, and so plucky; he always takes his punishment bravely; and he has such a pretty little bottom, and such a dear little 'thing.' I always manage to touch it when I am whipping him."

"Oh, you naughty girl!" I exclaimed, laughing. Then I added: "I should very much like to see you whipping them."

"I know you would," she observed, smiling, and making a little face at me.

"Could you not manage to hide me somewhere, and let me see you using the rod, one of these days?" I said coaxingly; at the same time putting my hand up her clothes, and gently tickling the "spot," which was still a little moist with the "dew of love."

She kicked out her legs, and laughed: then after a moment's thought, said: "I think it could be managed. I could put you in the alcove behind the curtains, and you would be able to peep between them. No one would know you were there."

"That's a good girl. I was sure you could arrange the matter for me," I said, giving her a hearty kiss.

"But you may have to wait some time before you see one of the children punished. I never give them a birching unless they deserve it."

"I am in no hurry. I should like to see either of them turned up; but of course it would give me more pleasure to see you operate upon the girl."

"Oh, I know that very well; you naughty boy," she marked, unbuttoning my trousers, and letting out my half-stiff prick. Then, gently rubbing it, she said: "You shall see them both whipped in due course. And you will admire Dora's bottom very much. She has a most beautiful white skin. I have never seen a whiter one; and it is so extremely fine, that the least thing marks it. She is a great coward, and always makes a great fuss while she is being whipped."

"All the more fun for the whipper, and also for the looker-on," said I, with a smile. Then, as my cock, under her skilful manipulation had again become ready for action, I extended her on the sofa, and gave her another rattling poke; much to her satisfaction, and also to my own.

By this time it was past six o'clock, so I made preparations to depart, but Frances would not let me go. She said she had ordered a nice little dinner, as she had fully expected me to stay.

I was delighted to remain a little longer with my old sweetheart; and I told her so. She then said: "Dinner will be ready at seven o'clock, so I must run away and dress; and I will send a maid to show you to a room where you can wash your hands."

Then she tripped away; and a few minutes after, a maid-servant came and took me upstairs to a charmingly furnished bedroom, where I found a jug of hot water, comb and brushes, towels, and various other articles for making a toilet, laid out in readiness for me. I had a good wash, and brushed my hair; then I went down again to the drawing-room, where Frances was already seated, looking fresh and lovely, in a handsome black silk dinner gown, with her hair elaborately dressed in the latest style. Presently we were joined by the governess, to whom I was introduced by Frances. She said that I was her old guardian; which was, to a certain extent, the truth.

The governess, Miss Martin, was a ladylike woman, not more than thirty years of age; she had a pleasant face and manner; and she was nicely dressed. We had a little chat, and I was glad to see that Frances treated the governess with kindness and consideration, speaking to her on all occasions as one lady should speak to another, whatever may be their relative positions. At seven o'clock, dinner was announced, and, in obedience to a sign from Frances, I gave Miss Martin my arm, and led her into the dining-room. We sat down at a round table, prettily decorated with flowers and fruit; the dinner was good, and well-cooked, the wines were of very fair quality, and we were waited on by two smart parlour-maids. It was a merry little repast. Frances had always been a well-informed woman, and an amusing talker; but that night her conversation was more brilliant and witty than I had ever known it to be in the old days. Miss Martin also, had plenty to say for herself, and it struck me that she had a bit of fun in her. However, our conversation was of the most decorous description, and we all got on together extremely well. At dessert, the children came in, prettily dressed, and looking like little pictures. Each was given a plate of fruit, and they remained in the room a short time, chattering away without restraint, but behaving with perfect propriety.

After dinner, Frances told me to smoke my cigar; and when I had finished it, we went into the drawing-room, where my charming hostess, glancing at me with a humorous twinkle in her eyes, sank gracefully down upon the sofa which had been the altar of our love a few hours previously. I drew up a chair beside her, and we had a long and confidential chat, while Miss Martin played the piano.

At eleven o'clock, I bade the ladies good night; drove off to my chambers, and went to bed, feeling much pleased at knowing that my old sweetheart would be always at my disposal whenever I wanted a poke.

The time slipped away rapidly, and pleasantly. I called upon Frances nearly every day; she being always delighted to see me; and I seldom left the house without at least one poke. I also dined occasionally with her, but she would never dine out with me, nor would she go about much in my company. She said, laughingly, that now she was a rich widow, she did not wish to have any scandal talked about her. I thought she was right. And I was quite satisfied as long as she did not make any objection to my poking her. But she never did make an objection—quite the contrary—she was always ready, and glad to receive the "stroke of love."

We revelled in our mutual embraces; and to me, it was always most piquant to poke the luscious and lovely woman fully attired in her charming toilettes, in all sorts of fancy positions; on the sofa, or sitting in a chair, and sometimes kneeling on all-fours upon the floor.

No more voluptuous woman than Frances ever wriggled her bottom in the delicious spasm of love.

I had not as yet seen either of the children birched, and

I began to think that my sweetheart had forgotten she had promised to let me see her using the rod; so one day I reminded her. She said, laughing, that she had not forgotten her promise; but that, so far, she had had no reason to whip either the boy or the girl. And she again assured me that she would not fail to let me know whenever she had occasion to apply the rod.

The day after our conversation, I had to go down to Oakhurst on business, but before leaving town, I let Frances know the day on which I meant to return. I got back to London at noon on the day specified, and on reaching my chambers, found a note from Frances. It had arrived that morning, and though it was short, it was to the point. It said:

> Dearest Charley,
> Come at three o'clock, and spend the afternoon with me, and stay to dinner.
>
> Your loving Frances.
> P.S. I am going to birch both the children.

I smiled as I read the brief, but most satisfactory epistle. I was glad she had remembered her promise; and I said to myself that the afternoon would be a pleasant and exciting one in various ways.

First of all, I should have the pleasure of seeing two pretty, little, white bottoms reddening and wriggling under the rod; and then when I was thoroughly excited, and had got a good cockstand at the sight of the whipping, I should have the additional pleasure of turning up the petticoats of the whipper, and of administering to her a taste of *my* "rod." The whole thing would be delicious! I lunched at my club; and sharp at three o'clock, I knocked at the door of the house in Kensington, and was shown up to the drawing-room, where I found Frances, with a waggish expression on her face, waiting to receive me. She was dressed in her pretty, lace-trimmed, black tea gown; and when I took her in my arms to kiss her, I found that she had on no stays, and on putting my hand up her clothes, I further discovered that she was not wearing drawers.

As my hand touched her naked bottom, she laughed, saying:

"You see I have prepared myself for the 'rod'."

"That's right," I said, sitting down upon a chair, and drawing her on to my knees. "We shall have some fun this afternoon in more ways than one. Now tell me what offences the children have committed."

She replied: "Robert has been reported to me for persistent idleness, by the governess. She tells me he does not mind what she says to him. Dora has been saucy to me; and has also told me a lie, which is a fault I never pass over. I hate a liar; so I intend to make her bottom smart. She is inclined to be untruthful, and I have had to whip her twice for fibbing."

"Do they know that they are going to be whipped? Where are the young culprits? I am longing to see Dora's bottom," said I.

Frances smiled, and said: "They know they are going to be whipped, and they are waiting in the schoolroom. I always punish them there; but to-day I will bring them down here. No one will know what is going on. Miss Martin has gone out for a couple of hours; and the servants are all in the lower regions of the house. They know I sometimes whip the children; but I should not like them to find out that I had ever allowed you to be present at the punishment." Then, laying her hand on the front of my trousers, she added, laughing: "I do believe that the very thought of seeing the girl's bottom birched, has made your 'thing' stiff. What a man you are for the rod!"

"Well, I must say my thing *is* beginning to stir," said I, with a laugh. She went on: "Now go into the alcove behind the curtains. You can peep between them; but be sure to keep them closely drawn, and don't make the least noise."

Then she jumped off my knees and left the room. I

went behind the curtains, and held them closely together where they met, but I left a narrow little space, through which I could see everything, without being seen.

In a couple of minutes, Frances returned, leading by their hands the two young culprits. Robert, dressed in his black velvet suit, had a woeful expression on his face, but he did not show any other signs of fear. Dora was looking intensely frightened; she was whimpering, and the tears were trickling down her pale cheeks.

As I have before said, she was a charmingly pretty little girl, with long, glossy, soft auburn hair flowing loose. She was handsomely dressed from head to foot, and the skirt of her black frock only reaching a little below her knees, showed her small, but well-formed legs clad in black silk stockings. On her tiny feet she wore smart patent leather shoes.

Frances locked the door; then going to a cabinet, she took out a short, slender little birch rod, tied up with scarlet ribbons; and though the rod looked like a toy, it was quite big enough to raise weals on a child's bottom, and to make it smart sorely.

Both the children knew, by bitter experience, that the small birch could sting; and at the sight of the bristling twigs, Robert's lips began to tremble a little, while Dora whimpered more loudly, and covered her face with her hands.

Frances, rod in hand, seated herself on a low chair which she had placed so close to the curtains that I could almost have touched her, by stretching out my arm. Then she ordered the culprits to come and stand in front of her. The boy at once obeyed; but the girl hesitated, and the order had to be sharply repeated, before she complied with it.

Frances now took hold of Robert, laid him over her lap, unbuttoned his knickerbockers and pulled them down to his knees; then she carefully tucked up his little shirt all round, back and front, at the same time feeling his wee tool; and as she did so, she glanced up at the curtains, with a roguish smile on her face. She had seated herself with her right side turned to the curtain, so that I had a full-length view of the boy as he sprawled over her lap, with his arms and legs hanging down; and I could see everything as plainly as if I had had the young culprit lying across my own knees.

She now lectured the boy on his idleness, and told him that she would whip him every time the governess reported him for not learning his lessons. And the whole time she was speaking, she stroked and patted the cheeks of his plump little bottom. Then she gave him a dozen slight cuts, which, however, striped his skin all over with red streaks; he winced at each cut, and wriggled about briskly, twisting his loins in pain, and crying loudly, the tears rolling down his cheeks. He certainly showed pluck while he was being birched; he never screamed, and he only once covered his bottom with his hands; but he instantly removed them, when his stepmother said sternly: "Take away your hands."

When she had finished whipping him, she ordered him to go and kneel upon the seat of a chair with his knicker-bockers down. He obeyed, and placed himself in position, with his red bottom exposed; then he rested his arms on the back of the chair, crying quietly, and occasionally rubbing his smarting little posteriors.

It was now Dora's turn! While her brother was being birched, she had stood trembling and weeping, with her big, gray eyes fixed in a horrified stare on his writhing bottom. Frances told me, when all was over, that she had never before whipped the children in each other's presence. She now laid down the rod, and took a handkerchief out of her pocket; then she seized Dora's wrists and tied them together, the girl making no resistance; and in another moment she was placed in position across her stepmother's knees, where she lay quietly, though wailing with fear. Frances then turned up the girl's short skirt, rolled up her dainty little white petticoats, and tucked up her chemise; revealing the outlines of her childish figure covered only with a tightly-fitting pair of drawers, buttoned at the sides, and without a slit. Frances unfastened all the buttons, and pulled down the flap of the small garment, laying bare Dora's bottom, and also the upper part of her thighs.

I had never before seen the bottom of so young a girl—she was only a little over twelve-and-a-half years of age—and I looked at the charming spectacle with great delight. It was a most lovely little bottom: plump, round, and per-fectly proportioned, and also well developed for the age of the girl—a delicious morsel for the rod!

But her skin! What words can I use to describe the peculiar whiteness of Dora's wonderfully beautiful skin? The ordinary terms such as: alabaster white; lily-like; milk-white; and snow white, will not do. The tint was extremely delicate, and quite different to anything I had ever seen: the tiny blue veins could be distinctly traced on the exquisitely smooth surface, and the whole skin was of such extreme fineness of texture, and so transparent, that it seemed almost to take a faint, pink tinge from the blood beneath it.

Frances glanced again at the curtains, smiling, and point-ing to Dora's bottom, as if to draw my attention to its rare beauty; but I noticed that she did not touch, or feel the girl between the legs, in the way she had felt the boy. I suppose it would have been no fun to her to handle one of her own sex.

She took up the rod—it seemed almost a pity to birch such a snowdrop of a bottom—and putting her arm over the trembling culprit's loins, held her firmly down; saying: "Now, you naughty girl; I'll make you smart for telling me a lie!"

Dora contracted her muscles, and moaned in dread of the coming cut. The little rod hissed in the air for a moment, then fell with a swish on the delicate-skinned little bottom; both cheeks of which were instantly marked with red weals, and a number of small dots of a darker red colour. The girl plunged, threw back her head with a jerk, which tossed her long hair all over her face, and uttered a long, shrill squeal. Swish! Swish! Swish! The rod, with its scarlet ribbons fluttering, rose and fell, raising more red weals on the quivering flesh of the young culprit, who screamed and writhed in agony at each cut. Frances did not, however, birch the girl with more severity than she had birched the boy; but Dora's skin was far finer than Robert's, and she felt the pain much more acutely! Swish! Swish! Swish! She squealed and wriggled, twisting her hips from side to side, and kicking her silken-clad little legs about in all directions. Swish! Swish! She turned her head round; and shaking the loose hair off her scarlet, pain-drawn, tear-bedabbled face, shrieked out piteously: "Oh! Mamma! Do do let me go!" Swish! "Oh—h! dear—Mamma!" Swish! "Yah—hah—ah—h! Oh! I—will—be —good!" Swish! "Ah—h—h! Oh! I—will never"—swish!— "Oh—h!—Ah—h—h! tell—a lie—again." Swish! "Wah— hah—ah—h!" Swish! Swish! Swish! She yelled, and struggled, and bawled, and bounced; but Frances held her down tightly, and birched her slowly; while redder and redder grew her little posteriors under the flashing switch. Swish! "Ah!—Yah —hah—ah—h—h!!!" The last cut fell on the shrieking girl's twitching flesh; and Frances threw down the rod. Dora's delicious little bottom was now crimson, covered with weals, and speckled all over with purple clots. She had received eighteen cuts, and she lay trembling, crying, and writhing with the smarting pain.

After a moment, Frances took the girl up in her arms and placed her, with her petticoats up, and her drawers down, in a kneeling position on a chair beside her brother; so that I had a good view of the two well-whipped little bottoms. Both were very red, and also much wealed, but Dora's was far more marked, and sore-looking than Robert's; and her dazzlingly white little thighs contrasted strongly with the scarlet cheeks of her bottom. The boy had ceased crying, but the girl continued to weep, her sobs shaking her plump little buttocks. I compared the two small posteriors, noticing the boy's bottom though round and chubby, was not nearly so broad or so plump as the girl's. As soon as Dora's wailing had somewhat subsided, Frances lifted her off the chair, and placed her on her feet with her face turned towards the curtains. Then she again raised the girl's petticoats above her waist, and took hold of her drawers; but before pulling them up, she paused for a few moments, glancing, with a sly smile, in the direction of the curtains,—she evidently wished to show me Dora's small "spot."

I had never seen such a miniature cunt! It was a delicious little thing, with wee pink lips without a vestige of down; and it looked just like a tiny slit in her white little belly. When Frances thought I had seen enough, she fastened up the girl's drawers, and untied her wrists; at the same time telling the boy to button up his knickerbockers. He did so; and then she sent them both back to the schoolroom, the girl sobbing, and she moved her legs stiffly when she walked.

To me, a "lover of the rod," the whole affair had been most pleasing; as it had been a charming spectacle of real birch discipline; and, as a matter of course, I had a stiff erection. Frances threw herself down upon the sofa, and I came from behind the curtains with my cock standing straight out, as I had already unbuttoned my trousers. Frances laughed when she saw me approaching her with rampant prick, and at once settled herself well down upon her back to receive the attack.

Without a word, I raised her petticoats, and stretched out her willing legs; then folding her in my arms, I pressed my lips to her mouth, thrust my prick into her cunt, and poked her with intense delight; making her bound, and squeak, and wriggle under me, from the first dig until the supreme moment when we both "spent" in the voluptuous spasm. Then we lay, hugging and kissing, and mutually pleased with each other.

As soon as we had arranged our disordered attire, Frances locked up the rod in the cabinet, and we sat down to rest, and also to talk over the affair. Frances began: "Well, are you pleased with the way I whipped the children?"

"Very much pleased," I replied. "You handled the rod gracefully and skilfully; and you birched the youngsters smartly, but not too severely." She smil˙1, pleased at my complimenting her on her skill as a "whipper." "Hasn't Dora got a delicate skin? You saw how much it got marked by the rod, and you heard how she screamed while she was being whipped, but I really did not birch at all hard. If I had, the blood would have soon come. She has not the least fortitude, and she always makes a great outcry." Then she added, laughing: "I showed you more than her pretty bottom. Did you ever see such a little 'thing' before?"

"No, never!" I answered. "Nor have I ever seen so young a girl birched. She has a lovely little bottom; and you must manage—as long as I am in town—to let me be present whenever you whip her."

"Oh, I'll always let you know when I am going to turn her up; but I am pretty sure I shall not have to do so for weeks to come. The birching she has had to-day will keep her in order for a long time. She does not much mind a spanking, but she dreads the rod."

We now had a little chat on various subjects; then at Frances' own request, I took her across my knees, and gave her a smart little spanking: and I finished up the afternoon's amusements by poking her "en levrette," as she leant over the back of an easy-chair.

She then went up to dress for dinner; and I went up to the bedroom which was always at my service whenever I wanted to wash my hands or brush my hair.

When I returned to the drawing-room, I found Miss Martin there alone. We shook hands cordially, for we had become very friendly, as I was the friend of the family, and also Mrs. Markham's "old guardian." Miss Martin was a jolly sort of woman; not exactly pretty, but she was nice to look at, as she had fine, hazel eyes, abundant brown hair, white teeth, and a plump, shapely figure; she was also very tastefully dressed. She sat down in an easy-chair, leaning back in an unconstrained position, and as her skirt was a little raised, I could see her trim ankles, cased in brown silk stockings, and her neat feet in high-heeled shoes.

She was a good talker, and had travelled a good deal on the Continent with her former employers; but I had an idea that she had not always been a governess. We conversed on sundry topics for a short time, and then we spoke about the children. Miss Martin knew that they had both been whipped that afternoon; but she did not know that I was cognizant of the fact, and of course she had not the faintest suspicion that I had been present at the punishment; nor had she any idea that I was in the habit of poking Mrs. Markham.

She informed me that they were both bright, clever children, but rather difficult to manage. Then I asked, in a most innocent manner: "Do you approve of corporal punishment for children?"

"I do most certainly," she replied without the least hesitation. "For girls as well as boys?" I queried.

"Yes. Girls should be whipped whenever they are naughty. They are often more troublesome than boys. I mean little boys. I have no experience with boys over ten years of age."

"Dear me!" I said in affected surprise, "I did not think that girls were ever subjected to corporal punishment nowadays."

Miss Martin smiled. "Oh yes, they are in some schools, and also in some families," she remarked.

It was a curious subject for us to discuss, but as she did not seem to be at all diffident, I thought I would ask a few more questions

"What, in your opinion, is the best way of punishing a naughty girl?"

"I think there is no better way of punishing a naughty girl than to give her a good whipping with a birch rod in the old-fashioned way," she replied in the coolest manner.

I had some difficulty in preventing myself laughing at the plain way in which the governess had spoken. Then I said: "I suppose you have had a great deal of experience?"

"Yes," she replied. "I have been a family governess for seven years, and during that period, I have used the rod whenever my employers would allow me to do so. But some ladies I have lived with would not permit me to whip their children; nor would they whip the children themselves."

The subject then dropped; and in a few moments Frances tripped into the room, smiling and fresh, as well as faultlessly dressed, and we went in to dinner, which was a good one, as usual.

At dessert, rather to my surprise, the children came into the room as had always been their custom, whenever I dined with their stepmother.

The boy appeared to be in his usual spirits; but the girl was a little pale and depressed. They both had become very friendly with me, and I often brought them boxes of sweets: so they now sat down, one on each side of me, and I noticed that the girl seated herself very carefully on the edge of her chair. No doubt her poor little bottom was still very tender. I filled their plates with fruit, and began to talk to them; but Dora was not at all in her usual form. So just out of mischief, and to hear what they would say, I said: "Have you been good children to-day?"

Dora coloured, and cast down her eyes in silence. Frances, and Miss Martin smiled. But Robert blurted out in child-like innocence: "No; we have not been good. We have been naughty; and Mamma gave us both a whipping. I did not scream, but Dora did."

Dora blushed very red; her modesty was offended at my being told that she had been whipped. Turning to her brother, she exclaimed angrily: "You horrid boy! You may tell people that you have been whipped, if you like; but you have no business to say anything about me." She then ran out of the room, with flashing eyes and flaming cheeks.

The boy looked astonished, and we all laughed; the governess saying: "Robert, you should never tell tales out of school."

He was soon sent to join his sister; then the ladies and myself went into the drawing-room, where we passed a couple of hours pleasantly with music and conversation. Then I went home to my chambers, and after I had smoked a cigar, and drunk a glass of whisky and water, I retired to my virtuous couch, thoroughly well pleased with my day's amusements.

I stayed in town for three more weeks, visiting Frances frequently; but I never had the pleasure of seeing Dora's pretty little bottom; as ever since the day she had been birched in company with her brother, she had behaved so well, that her stepmother never had reason to turn her up.

On leaving London I went to Scotland, where I remained for upwards of a month grouse-shooting with various friends; and on my return to England, I went to Oakhurst, where I settled down for the winter, amusing myself in the usual way; hunting, shooting, dining out, and giving dinner parties in return. Whenever I felt inclined for an afternoon poke, I could always get hold of Mary, the pretty parlourmaid: all I had to do was to give her a wink, then she would slip quietly up to my bedroom, and wait there till I came.

I also used often to run up to town for a couple of days to see Frances. And so the time went on.

# ⚜ XVIII ⚜

DRIFTING APART.——THE STORY OF MISS MARTIN.
——A CRAZE FOR PHOTOGRAPHY.——FRANCES AND
THE GOVERNESS TAKING EACH OTHER'S PHOTO-
GRAPH NAKED.——A LITTLE SAPPHIC GAME.——
WIDOWS' CONFIDENCES.——A NAKED WALTZ.——
BIRCHING REMINISCENCES.——THE BET AND THE
FUSTIGATION.——A DOZEN CUTS IN SILENCE.
PEEPING TOM AND THE FINALE.

The winter and spring passed. It was again midsummer, and
I was living in London for the season. Frances had now been
settled in her house for a year; and as her *liaison* with me was
not known to anyone; and as she was young, handsome, and
comparatively rich, she had made a number of friends and acquaintances of both sexes. She went out a great deal, and
she occasionally gave a dinner party; moreover she had a
regular "afternoon," which was always well attended; for
Mrs. Markham had got the reputation—a well-deserved one
—of being a pleasant and amusing hostess. She had many admirers, of all sorts and conditions: some of them needy
fortune-hunters, who wanted to marry her for the sake of
her money; while others were men who wanted to marry

her for the sake of her beautiful face and splendid figure. I felt very sure that she would marry again, sooner or later; but so far she had not shown any preference for any man in particular. She and I were still very good friends; she always appeared glad to see me whenever I called, she told me everything that happened to her, and she consulted me about her affairs; moreover, she let me poke her whenever I wished to do so. Therefore, as I knew that no other man touched her, I was quite content to "lay low," and watch the game that was going on all round me. The boy had been sent to a boarding-school; but the girl remained at home under the tuition of Miss Martin. She occasionally misbehaved, and whenever she did, she got a sound birching in the drawing-room, from her stepmother, who always took care to let me know the hour at which the punishment was to be inflicted; and I never failed to be behind the curtains. Dora was now over thirteen years-and-a-half old: she had grown a little, and her beautiful, white bottom was bigger and plumper. But she was still a great coward whenever she came under the rod; always screaming, kicking up her heels, and begging for mercy, from the first cut to the last. I liked seeing her being whipped!

The summer wore on: Frances, with Miss Martin, and Dora, went down to Eastbourne; while I started off to Norway on a fishing excursion; but I did not get much sport, as it was too late in the season. However, I enjoyed my tour very much, as I had never been in Norway before. I liked driving in the carioles from place to place; and I admired the magnificent scenery of the fiords; though I was disappointed with the blue-eyed, flaxen-haired damsels. Many of them were pretty, but they did not appear to have any fun in them; and the few that I poked were great big cold creatures who lay like logs under me, hardly even moving their broad fat bottoms at the supreme moment.

Frances and I got back to London about the same time; and things went on between us pretty much as before. She always had numbers of invitations, but she kept herself disengaged one night in the week, so that I might dine quietly with her and Miss Martin. On those occasions we were always merry at the table, and when the meal was over and we had gone into the drawing-room, Frances would sit beside me in a corner—while Miss Martin played the piano—and tell me what she had been doing with herself since she had last seen me: and she would frequently ask my advice on various matters. But for all that, I had an idea that she was keeping something back, and that we were gradually drifting apart.

After all, I was getting on for forty-five years of age; and she had younger admirers, any one of whom would marry her.

I never said a word; knowing that in due course of time, she would tell me everything. And I could see that she had already begun to look upon me more in the light of a guardian than a lover; though she still seemed to enjoy the pokes I gave her. She and Miss Martin had become great friends; but I know that Frances never told her true story to the governess; nor did that lady ever find out that I was carrying on an intrigue with her employer.

Miss Martin had however told her story to Frances, who related it to me one day. It was a very ordinary story; without the least touch of romance. I will give it here.

The governess was a married woman. Martin was her maiden name. She was the daughter of a poor person in Devonshire; and she had been married when she was twenty years of age, to a man who was cashier of a large bank in Plymouth; and who had a good salary. The marriage had turned out badly; her husband took to gambling and betting, and he lost a great deal of money; then he became a drunkard, and ill-treated her: finally he embezzled money belonging to the bank; and to avoid arrest he fled the country; leaving her penniless, after three wretched years of married life. Fortunately there were no children. Her father and mother were dead, and she had no rich relatives to assist her. But as she was well educated, and could get testimonials as to her character, she turned governess, and had supported herself ever since her husband had left her. She had never heard from him; and she did not know whether he was alive or dead. Frances also informed me that Miss Martin had confided to her, that she had never been embraced by any man but her husband, and that she had been longing for an embrace ever since he had left her.

The two ladies had lately taken to amusing themselves with photography. Frances had bought a complete outfit, intending to do everything herself, with the assistance of Miss Martin. So they had fitted up a dark room in which to develop their plates, and as they were both clever, neat-handed women, they soon had made themselves fairly proficient amateur photographers.

They photographed each other in various costumes and they "took" me in all sorts of attitudes; they "took" the children, and the servants; and they made excursions into the country, photographing old houses, or anything else that struck their fancy.

One afternoon, when the photography "craze" was at its height, I was having a cup of tea with Frances in the drawing-room after a very pleasant poke; when she suddenly asked: "Do you think Miss Martin has got a good figure?"

I replied: "She seems to have a good one; but when a woman has got on all her clothes and her corset, one can never tell how much of her figure is natural; half of it may be due to the dressmakers' art. The only way of finding out whether a woman has a good figure or not, is by seeing her naked. Now I have often seen you naked; therefore I know you have a most lovely figure," I added, kissing her, and feeling her bottom.

She smiled, looking very much pleased. Then she went on: "Would you like to see Miss Martin and me naked together, so that you could compare our figures?"

I laughed, thinking she was joking. "I should very much like to have a chance of making the comparison, if it were possible."

"It is possible," she said coolly. "You shall see us both stark naked to-morrow. We are going to photograph each other in a state of nudity, and you can hide behind the curtains in the alcove while we are at work. Of course, she won't have the faintest suspicion that you are there, so she will be perfectly at her ease, and you will be able to make a thorough inspection of her charms."

The idea tickled me immensely, and I lay back in my chair, laughing heartily; then kissing Frances, I said: "You are a wonderful woman to have thought of such a thing: It will be awfully good fun, and I shall enjoy the scene immensely."

"Oh, I know you will," she said smiling. "Be here to-morrow at a quarter to two. Miss Martin is going out shopping in the morning, and will not be back till two o'clock; and by that time you will be behind the curtains. She won't have the least idea that you have come to the house during her absence."

"I shall be here without fail to inspect the lady; I am sure she has not got such a good figure as you have," said I, taking Frances up in my arms, and placing her a-straddle on my thighs. Then I gave her a sitting poke.

As soon as all was over, and she had shaken her petticoats straight, she ran away to dress, as she was going out to a dinner party; and I went off to my club. I ordered a good dinner, and while discussing it, I thought of the "Living Picture" I was going to see the following day. The spectacle would be a most charming and piquant one.

It is not often that a man gets a chance of seeing a modest woman in a state of complete nudity. I do not think many married men ever see their wives quite naked. Now Miss Martin was a modest woman; she had never been seen nude by any man but her husband—perhaps he had never seen her —and she would be perfectly unconscious that she was being looked at by a man. The whole thing would be delicious! After dinner, I played a few games of billiards, and then went back to my chambers, where I read and smoked until it was time to go to bed.

Next day, punctually at a quarter to two o'clock, I arrived at the house, and on entering the drawing-room found Frances there with the camera, and all the rest of the paraphernalia, in readiness for taking the photographs. We kissed; then we looked at each other and burst out laughing. After chatting a few minutes, we heard a knock at the door of the house. "There she is," said Frances, her eyes sparkling with merriment. "Now get behind the curtain. You shall see some fun." I took up my position; then she left the room. There was an easy-chair in the alcove, so I sat down and amused myself with a paper I had brought with me. In about twenty minutes, the door was opened, and the two ladies came into the room, laughing and joking with each other; and at once began to get the plates ready. As they tripped about the room, making their final preparations, I saw that they had nothing on but their chemises and wrappers; their bare feet were cased in velvet slippers; and their long hair was flowing loose over their shoulders down to their waists.

When everything was fixed up, Frances slipped a plate into the camera, and said, laughing: "Now we will take two full length photographs of each other: one shall be a front view, and the other a back view. I will operate first; so strip, and take your place."

Laughing merrily, Miss Martin kicked off her slippers, removed her wrapper, and pulled off her chemise: then, stark naked, she placed herself in front of the camera, standing in a graceful attitude. She was two years older than Frances, and about an inch taller; and also more largely built in every way. She was what is generally called a "fine woman." Her skin was smooth, and of a delicate creamy tint, which shone in the bright daylight like polished ivory. Her arms were round and well shaped. She had a full, deep bosom, with large, round, firm-looking bubbies, tipped with big, erect, bright red nipples, which were surrounded by a ring of dark olive-coloured skin. Her hips were very wide, and her belly was broad and unwrinkled. Her cunt was completely hidden under a luxuriant growth of long, soft, brown hair, which extended between her thighs, and also covered the lower part of her belly.

I had never before seen such a thick "fleece" on an Englishwoman. The front view was quickly taken; and as soon as Frances had put a fresh plate into the camera, Miss Martin turned round, and presented the back part of her body to the lens, and also to my admiring eyes. I like looking at a naked woman!

Her shoulders were broad, and sloping, her back had a graceful curve, and she had fine loins. Her bottom was worth looking at; and as my eyes roved over its swelling contours, I said to myself: "What a bottom for a whipping!" It was very large and plump, with broad, well-rounded cheeks touching each other closely the whole length of the division. Her big thighs were well-formed, her legs were shapely; and she had neat ankles and pretty feet.

When the governess's "back settlements" had been successfully photographed; she put her wrapper on her naked body, and took her place behind the camera.

Frances then stripped, and was photographed, back and front, by Miss Martin.

As Frances had promised to show me some fun, I was curious to see what she would do next; for I had a shrewd idea that the taking of the photographs was merely an introduction to the *séance*.

The little game was soon begun. She got a tape measure, and going up to Miss Martin, said laughingly: "Take off your wrapper, and then we will measure ourselves all over, so as to find out exactly how much taller and bigger you are than I."

Miss Martin seemed much amused with the idea, and she at once threw off her wrapper. Then the two naked women stood bottom to bottom and measured their respective heights; Frances being five feet five inches, and the governess: five feet six inches.

Then, laughing and turning each other round; they measured their arms, and thighs and legs; and their busts, waists, and hips. While they were thus engaged, I was able to make a fair comparison of the charms of the two ladies.

Miss Martin's cream-tinted skin was pretty, but it did not please me so well as the lily-white skin of Frances. I preferred the slight shading of curly, golden hair on Frances' cunt to the thick growth of straight brown hair which hid Miss Martin's slit. That lady had a fine bosom, a grand bottom, and well-made limbs; and altogether her figure was good; but it was not so good as that of Frances.

Again, Miss Martin, though a graceful woman, was not so graceful in all her movements as Frances. And to sum up, I may say that both women were fine specimens of different types of ripe feminine beauty. But in my opinion, Frances had a more thoroughbred look than the governess.

After completing their measurements, they stood face to face, closely inspecting each other's charms; and the whiteness of Frances' skin seemed to attract Miss Martin! She laid her hand on Frances' bosom saying: "What a beautiful white skin you have got. I wish mine was like it."

Frances laughed. She was very proud of her alabaster-like skin; but she said:—untruthfully, I thought—"Oh, I think the tint of your skin is prettier than mine!" Then she put her left arm round the governess's waist and gave it a squeeze, at the same time feeling her bubbies, and pinching the big red nipples with her right hand; saying: "I admire your titties very much." The governess smiled, started slightly, and her eyes began to shine, but she made no remark. Frances next put her hand on the lower part of Miss Martin's belly and played with the hair; twining the long locks round her fingers; remarking: "What lovely long hair you have got here! I never saw anything like it before, on any woman."

Then she began to tickle the "spot" with her forefinger. A strong tremor passed over the governess from head to foot;

her breath came and went; her big titties rose and fell; her
face grew flushed, and her eyes sparkled; and suddenly
throwing her arms round Frances, she kissed her on the lips,
exclaiming in a hot whisper: "Oh! Mrs. Markham, you are
exciting me awfully! Oh! how I wish you were a man!"

Frances embraced her; and the two women clung to one
another; each one grasping with both hands the cheeks of the
other's bottom; their bosoms touched closely, and they rubbed their bellies together; the hair of their cunts mingling,
while they kissed each other on the lips.

Poor Miss Martin was evidently full of desire for a male;
but Frances was perfectly cool: she was merely playing with
the governess; partly out of devilment, and partly to amuse
me.

After a few seconds, she pushed her companion to the
sofa and extended her upon it on her back: then, acting the
part of the "man," she stretched out Miss Martin's legs, and
separating the lips of her cunt, inspected the pink orifice;
saying with a little laugh: "Why, the passage is almost
closed up!"

Next, she got on top of her, and clasped her hands under
her bottom. Then the pair went through all the motions of a
man and woman poking. Frances worked her bottom up and
down, pushing her cunt at each stroke against Miss Martin's
cunt; while that lady moved her bottom in the feminine way.
And I think she must have spent: for I saw a queer look
come in to her eyes, and a slight quiver passed over her. She
was evidently quite ignorant of "tribadism," and everything
of that sort. Frances, had she liked, might have enlightened
her. But she did not. After a moment, the woman sat up.
Frances was still cool and collected; but Miss Martin was
not, and was palpitating. She blushed, and exclaimed: "Oh,
dear me! What have we been doing! I'm afraid we've been
very naughty. It was nice, but very unsatisfactory, and tantalizing. Oh! I would give anything at this moment to be in
the arms of a vigorous man!"

I felt very much inclined to step out and offer myself.

After a moment, she went on: "Do you not miss your husband very much at night, Mrs. Markham?"

"I can't say I do," replied Frances demurely; but glancing up at the curtains, with a twinkle in her eye. She knew that in a very short time she would have a "husband" on top of her.

"I am surprised to hear that. You seem to be of a warm disposition," observed Miss Martin.

Frances laughed, remarking: "I think you also, have a warm temperament."

"Yes," said the governess. "Unfortunately for myself, I have. I often find it very hard to keep straight."

"It *is* very hard for us widows," said Frances, sighing, as if she was really lamenting the difficulty of keeping straight.

Miss Martin continued: "I would get married again if I were a widow. But I have never heard of my husband's death; and he said he would come back some day. Though if he does, I will not live with him. He is a bad man, and he treated me shamefully."

"But," she added shyly, after a little pause; "he was a strong man, and he used to embrace me most vigorously. Sometimes he 'did it' to me half-a-dozen times during the night! I wonder how I escaped having a child."

"Ah, my husband was a very different sort of man! He could hardly 'do it' at all," said Frances, in a sorrowful tone of voice. She was a capital actress.

"Oh, that must have been horribly tantalizing," observed Miss Martin. Then she said: "I wonder you don't get married again."

"Perhaps I will some day or other," replied Frances, laughing. Then she stood up, saying: "I feel inclined to dance. Let us have a waltz. You shall be the 'gentleman' this time, and you must hug me tightly."

Miss Martin laughed, and getting off the sofa, put her arm round her "partner's" waist in "manly" fashion; then they began to revolve briskly to a waltz tune hummed by

Frances. They were both good dancers; and it was a most charming spectacle to see the two shapely naked women waltzing gracefully round and round the room; their beautiful bubbies undulating, their broad hips swaying voluptuously, and the movements of their legs.

At last they sat down, flushed and panting; I thought that all the fun was over: but Frances had not finished her little game. As soon as she had recovered her breath, she put her hand on Miss Martin's bottom, and stroked it; saying in a tone of admiration:

"What a splendid bottom you have got; so plump and so firm. I thought I had a big bottom, but yours is far bigger in every way." The governess smiled, and looked very much pleased. "Yes. I *have* got a big bottom," she remarked complacently. "My husband used to admire it very much."

"Well, it is worthy of admiration," said Frances. "I believe men like women to have large bottoms. But, talking of bottoms, puts me in mind of whipping. I suppose, during the years you have been a governess, you have birched a good many little bottoms."

"Yes, many a one. I have birched girls up to seventeen years of age."

Frances laughed, then she asked, in the most innocent way:

"Were you ever birched when you were a girl?"

"Yes, very often."

"Were you really," said Frances, as if she were much astonished. "At a boarding-school, I suppose?"

"I never was at a boarding-school. I got all my birchings at home. I will tell you. My mother died when I was ten years old, and I was brought up, and educated entirely by my father. He was a stern, hard man; and whenever I failed in my lessons, or committed an offence, he used to lay me across a chair, bare my bottom, and birch me severely. He kept me under discipline until I was seventeen years of age; and he sometimes flogged me till the blood came.

"But I was a strong girl, and could take an ordinary birching with considerable fortitude. Of course, I used to cry and writhe, but I never screamed unless he birched me hard enough to draw blood. He used to whip me with a full-sized birch rod; a very different thing to the little toy you use when you whip the children."

"Well," said Frances, smiling, "toy as it is, I don't think you could bear a dozen smart cuts of it, without crying out."

"Oh, I'm sure I could," said Miss Martin, with a little laugh.

"I'll bet you a dozen pairs of gloves to one pair, that you don't take a dozen cuts in perfect silence," said Frances, laughing.

"I'll take the bet. I want some gloves, and I am sure to win them. Get out the toy," said the governess, also laughing.

Frances went to the cabinet for the rod, and as she passed close to the curtains she turned towards them and smiled mischievously. The artful creature, knowing how fond I was of seeing a woman's bottom whipped, had regularly humbugged the governess into allowing herself to be birched.

Flourishing the rod in the air, she said: "Now, Miss Martin, lie down. You may wriggle, and kick your legs about as much as you like while I am whipping you; but if you utter the least sound, you will lose the bet."

The governess stretched herself at full length upon the sofa, saying laughingly: "All right, Mrs. Markham! You can begin. You won't have much trouble in preparing me for punishment. But you must whip me fairly. Don't strike always on one place; and don't strike me on the thighs."

As the end of the sofa was towards the curtains, I had a splendid, full-length view of Miss Martin's plump, naked figure, as she lay prone; the swelling hemispheres of her great bottom standing out in high relief, while the cream-like tint of her skin was well shown off by the dark olive-green colour of the velvet on which she was lying.

Frances placed herself on the left side of the sofa, so

that I saw her naked figure in profile, and very lovely it looked. Her beautiful white skin glistening; her delicious, round, pink-tipped titties rising and falling quickly, a smile curving her ripe red lips, her cheeks slightly flushed, and her blue eyes sparkling with excitement at the idea of using the rod. She was fond of whipping.

She began to birch: and though the rod was but a toy, the birching was no child's play. Swinging the switch high above her head, for each stroke, she laid on the cuts slowly, with graceful sweeps of her round white arm, and with such force, that her bubbies shook, and the muscles of her bottom quivered each time she struck the blow.

The little, be-ribboned birch rod hissed as it swept through the air, and it made a sharp swishing noise as it fell on the firm flesh of Miss Martin's big bottom. The creamy skin reddened rapidly, and small weals rose in all directions on the broad, plump cheeks. She had winced sharply on receiving the first cut; the pain evidently being greater than she had expected: then she stiffened herself, clenched her fingers in the palms of her hands, buried her face in the sofa cushion, and lay perfectly still. But her flesh quivered involuntarily at each stinging cut of the little rod.

She certainly showed great fortitude. Not a sigh, or a moan escaped her lips, though the birching was a severe one; and when the twelve cuts had been inflicted, her bottom was scarlet and also considerably wealed. But she had won the dozen pairs of gloves. I thought they had cost her dear.

Frances threw down the rod, and Miss Martin got off the sofa, heaved a deep sigh of relief, and stood with both her hands pressed to her bottom. Her face was red, her lips were trembling a little, and her eyes were moist. Smiling faintly, she said in rather a shaky voice: "I have won the bet. But I must say that the 'toy' stung in a way that disagreeably surprised me. I should never have believed that it could cause such pain. It was as much as I could do to take the twelve cuts in silence." Then twisting her head round, and looking over her shoulder, she said: "My bottom is very much marked, and it is still smarting dreadfully."

Frances said, in a tone of sympathy: "Oh, you poor dear! I did not think you could have borne the birching. I fully expected you would have told me to stop, after I had given you two or three cuts. You *have* got pluck. I am sure I could not have taken one cut without screaming."

All this was to flatter her victim. She went on: "You had better go to your bedroom, and bathe your bottom with cold water. I will put away the camera, and see to the plates."

Poor Miss Martin, with a rueful face, rubbed her bottom, and said: "I shan't be able to sit down comfortably for hours. I remember that I used to rub vaseline on my bottom to allay the smarting after a flogging. I will apply some now."

Then she put on her chemise and wrapper; thrust her feet into her slippers and left the room.

Frances, still perfectly naked, threw herself down upon the sofa and burst out laughing; and I came out of the alcove, in a state of intense excitement. The whole spectacle had been most lascivious, from the moment the two ladies had stripped themselves naked, up to the moment the governess had left the room. My cock had been in full erection the whole time, and now it was positively aching from the prolonged strain; so I at once threw myself upon the lovely naked woman, and clasping her lithe, yielding body in my arms, I poked her with such vigour that I astonished both her and myself.

When she had put on her scanty attire, she sat down beside me on the sofa, and after complimenting me on the vigour I had shown; she said: "I hope you enjoyed the entertainment. I think it was quite a 'variety' show."

"It was splendid," I replied, giving her a hearty kiss. "I never enjoyed anything more in my life. You are a very clever woman. The way you worked up Miss Martin was a triumph of art."

Frances laughed merrily. "Oh, she is a perfect innocent! She has learnt more this afternoon, than she ever learnt in the whole of her previous life. Now, tell me truly what you think of her figure."

"She is a very well-made woman, but her figure is not so good as yours," I replied; and I meant what I said.

Frances was very much pleased, and she kissed me. Then she observed: "Well anyhow, she has got a bigger bottom than I have. I really do admire it; and I should often like to birch it, as I did just now."

"I daresay you would," I said, laughingly. "But I am very sure you will never be able to get her to let you birch her again. You flogged her right well, and she must be rather sore at this moment."

"I *did* lay on smartly," said Frances smiling, "and I am afraid I shall never again have the pleasure of touching her big bottom with the rod. But now you had better go away. I don't want her to find out that you have been in the house at all. Come back at seven o'clock and dine with us; but be careful not to drop a hint about what you have seen."

I accepted the invitation to dinner; then I gave Frances a kiss, and slipped quietly out of the house, while Miss Martin was still in her room—putting vaseline on her bottom—I suppose. It was then four o'clock, so I took a stroll in Regent-street, and "drew" the Burlington Arcade. Then I went to my chambers and dressed for dinner, and at seven o'clock, I was again in Frances' drawing-room, waiting for the ladies to make their appearance. In about five minutes they came into the room with their arms round each other's waists; both were prettily dressed, Frances looking handsome, and Miss Martin looking quite pretty. She shook hands with me in her cordial way; her face showed no trace of disturbance, her eyes were bright, and her manner was as calm and composed, as if nothing out of the common had occurred during the afternoon. The birching had not affected her spirits; though no doubt her bottom was still tender.

We had a very nice dinner, and when it was over we spent a pleasant evening in the drawing-room, conversing on the various topics of the day. Miss Martin talked well, and sensibly, and, as I chatted with her, I often caught Frances glancing at me with such a humorous twinkle in her eyes that I had some difficulty in keeping my countenance. How horrified the demure-looking lady would have been, had she known that I had seen her, stark naked, being birched a few hours previously! I did not get back to my chamber till midnight. I stayed in town for three weeks after that little event, then, as the shooting season had commenced, I went down to Oakhurst, where I remained until the end of the year.

# XIX

FRANCES TO BECOME MRS. GILBERT.——FAITHFUL
TO HER FIANCE.——THE PLEASANT PLOT AGAINST
THE GOVERNESS.——MISS MARTIN GIVES WAY.
——DORA GETS A WHIPPING.——HOW TO HUMIL-
ILIATE A YOUNG GIRL.——A DELIGHTED SPEC-
TATOR.——THE GOVERNESS GETS A
SLAPPING AND SOME SEXUAL COM-
PENSATION.——FRESH FIELDS AND
POSTURES NEW.

At the beginning of January I returned to London and took
up my abode at my chambers. I had not seen Frances for
some time; so the day after my arrival in town, I started off
to pay her a visit, hoping to spend a couple of hours with
her, and have a nice, quiet poke, but I was disappointed. It
happened to be Frances' "afternoon"—which I had forgotten
—and when the maid ushered me into the drawing-room, I
found it full of visitors of both sexes. Mrs. Markham shook
hands with me in the usual conventional manner, saying a few
commonplace words of welcome, and then I had to take
my seat among the chattering throng, just as an ordinary
visitor. I swore inwardly, for I wanted a poke badly, and

Frances was looking most "fetching" at that moment, both in face and figure. She had entirely given up wearing mourning, and she was dressed in a handsome, richly-laced tea-gown, and she was by far the prettiest woman in the room.

Among the men present, there was one who appeared to pay more attention to the charming hostess, than did any of the other male visitors. He hovered about her constantly, sometimes bending down to whisper to her in a confidential way; and she was very gracious in her manner towards him.

I did not know him to speak to; but I knew that his name was Gilbert. He was a tall, good-looking man, about thirty-five years of age, with dark hair, and a long, drooping moustache—I had got light hair, and I did not wear a moustache.

I drank a cup of tea, and chatted with some people whom I knew; then, seeing that there was no chance that afternoon, of getting a quiet talk with Frances, I bade her good bye, and left her, for the first time, without as much as a kiss.

I called again next day, but she was out; however, I had an interview with Miss Martin, and while chatting with her, I made a few inquiries about Gilbert.

The governess, thinking I was merely asking for information in my capacity as Frances' "old guardian," told me without hesitation that they had made Mr. Gilbert's acquaintance when at Eastbourne during the summer. She added, laughing: "I think he is in love with Mrs. Markham; he is constantly calling at the house, and he often sends her presents of flowers, and box tickets for theatres."

"Do you think she is in love with him?" I inquired.

"I don't know whether she is actually in love with him, or not; but she seems to be fond of his company. He is a very nice gentlemanly fellow, and he is very well-off. Mrs. Markham might do worse than marry him."

Having got all the information I wanted out of Miss Martin; I bade her good bye, and went home to think over what I had heard.

I was not jealous; or even surprised at the news, as I had always felt certain that Frances would marry again; but I determined, at the first opportunity, to ask her to tell me exactly the state of her feelings towards Gilbert.

I did not get a chance of speaking to her on the subject for some days; as she was either out when I called, or else there were visitors in the room. However, one afternoon I managed to catch her alone, and I questioned her about Gilbert.

She seemed to be a little confused; but she told me that ever since she had been introduced to him at Eastbourne, he had paid court to her, and that latterly his attentions had become very marked.

"Do you love him? Don't be afraid of telling me," I said, kissing her. "I am your 'old guardian,' you know; and only wish for your happiness."

"Well, Charley, I must confess that I am fond of Mr. Gilbert; and I think he wishes to marry me. If he proposes to me; I will accept him."

Then she added: "I suppose you are very much surprised?"

"No, I am not. I know that the man admires you, and he will probably soon ask you to be his wife. If you are sure you will be happy with him, I shall be quite satisfied to let you go."

"But perhaps he never will ask me to marry him."

"Then some one else will be sure to do so. A young, handsome, rich widow like you, will not be long without another offer," I said, taking her on my knees, and putting my hands up her petticoats.

She made no objection, verbal or otherwise, so, with great delight, I laid her on the sofa, took down her dainty silk drawers, and gave her a poke. And she seemed to enjoy it thoroughly, judging by the way she bucked up and wriggled her bottom.

Time passed. I did not see much of Frances; but I often saw Miss Martin, and from her I learnt that Mrs. Markham was being ardently courted by Mr. Gilbert; so I daily expected to hear that she was engaged.

Another week went by, and then one morning, I received a note from her asking me to call at three o'clock. I went to the house at the appointed time, and found her looking rather flushed and excited, but very lovely. I thought that she had something important to tell me; and so she had, but at first she only talked about the most trivial things, and she looked so "fetching," that I sat down beside her on the sofa and proceeded to feel her hidden charms. I squeezed her bottom, stroked her thighs, and played with the silky hair of the "spot"; then, as she only smiled, I attempted to place her in position for a poke. But she would not allow me to lay her on her back; she began to struggle, saying: "Don't, Charley! Please don't do that. Let me go; I have something to tell you."

I at once released her; then she sat up on the sofa and arranged her disordered petticoats, with a curious little smile on her face.

"Well, what have you got to tell me?" I asked, though I well knew what I should hear.

"Mr. Gilbert has asked me to marry him, and I have consented. I have grown to love him, and therefore I do not think I ought to let you embrace me any more. You know I have always been a faithful woman, both as a sweetheart, and as a wife. No man has ever touched me but you, and my late husband. And now I intend to be faithful to my future husband. You are not angry with me, I hope?"

"No, no," I replied, kissing her in a fatherly manner, "I am not the least angry with you. I have no right to be. I know that you have always been true to me; and I think you are quite right to be true to the man who is going to marry you."

She smiled, and pressed my hand. Then I asked: "When are you going to be married?"

"In two months' time. And I want you to do me a favour."

"What can I do for you?"

"I want you to give me away. Everyone thinks you are my guardian."

This was rather a startling request; but after a moment's thought I decided to do as she wished, when the time came. As I had to give her up, I might as well give her away. So I said:

"Very well, Frances. I will give you away."

"Oh, you dear old Charley!" she exclaimed, kissing me. "I am so happy now! I was afraid you would take the whole affair quite differently, and be cross and disagreeable. It would have made me very miserable if we had parted on bad terms. We always got on so well, when we lived together."

"Except on the occasions when I spanked you," I observed, smiling. "Oh, I didn't mind the spankings much," she said, laughing. "But I shall never forget that last birching you gave me." Then she added in a tone of regret: "After I am married I shall never have a chance of using the rod, as Dora is to go to a boarding-school."

"If you really wish to use the rod, you will manage to do so, somehow or other," I observed smiling.

"Oh, I know what I shall do," she said laughingly, but half in earnest. "I will get a nice little page boy about thirteen years old; and whenever he misbehaves I will birch him. I should like to take a boy of that age across my knees."

"I doubt if a boy thirteen years old would let you flog him. He would most probably pull your hair down," I said, laughing. Then I asked: "Has Miss Martin got another engagement?"

"Not yet. But I am going to look after her until she gets a really good situation. She is a dear woman, and I am very fond of her."

Then looking at me slyly, she went on: "Do you know, Charley, that Miss Martin admires you very much? She thinks you are such a fine, handsome man. In fact, she once told me that she would like to be kissed on the lips by you."

"Oh, indeed!" said I, with a laugh. "That is very flattering to me. But perhaps she was joking?"

"I don't think she was. Why don't you make love to her? You know she is a well-made woman, and you heard her say, the day I whipped her, that she would like to feel herself in the arms of a vigorous man. Take her in your arms some day, and kiss her well. I know she is voluptuous, and I am almost certain she will let you 'have' her."

"Well," said I, laughing, "there is an old saw, which says, 'Never kiss the maid when you can kiss the mistress.' But as you won't let me 'kiss' you any more, I may perhaps try for the governess some day. However, if she shows any coyness, I will let her alone. I won't bother myself to regularly make love to her."

Frances smiled, saying: "Think over what I have told you. And call on me whenever you like. I shall always be glad to see my 'guardian.' But," she added with a laugh, "he must not attempt to take any more liberties with his ward." Then she added: "I must run away and dress, as I am going out for a drive with Arthur."

So saying, she shook hands with me, and tripped out of the room, leaving me feeling rather forlorn. But, after all, I really had nothing to complain of. Frances had always treated me fairly; and in the present case she had acted in a perfectly straightforward manner. I went off to my club, and I played a rubber of whist; then I had a good dinner, with a bottle of champagne; and by the time I had smoked my cigar, I felt much better, and quite reconciled to the idea of Frances' marriage. Then I began to think about Miss Martin. I had sometimes been inclined to get up an intrigue with her; but had hitherto refrained, out of a feeling of faithfulness towards Frances. But now that all was over between us, I said to myself that I would have a try at the buxom governess before she left her present situation. She had a nice face; her figure was undeniable, and she had a grand bottom.

A few days passed uneventfully; then I received a note from Frances, written in her brief style. It said:

"Dear Charley,
I shall be out all day. Call at three o'clock, and ask for me
as usual. Miss Martin will be at home alone. Make the
attempt! I think you will succeed.

Yours, Frances."

P.S. "She knows nothing about this little plot."

I laughed and at once made up my mind to try my luck. At
three o'clock I called at the house and asked for Mrs.
Markham.

The maid told me that her mistress was out, but that
Miss Martin was at home. I said that I would see her, so I
was shown up to the drawing-room, where I found the lady
comfortably seated in an easy-chair beside the fire, reading
a novel.

She appeared to be glad to see me, shaking hands with
me warmly, and informing me that she was all alone, as Mrs.
Markham had gone out to spend the day. I feigned surprise
at hearing that; then I sat down beside her and we began to
chat. I do not think she meant to attract my attention to her
figure; but my eyes *were* attracted, and I thought she was
looking very desirable. She was leaning back in her chair in
an attitude which displayed the swelling contours of her
luxuriant bosom, and the curves of her broad hips; her feet
were on the fender, and she showed her neat ankles clad in
black silk stockings.

After a few ordinary remarks, we began to talk about
Mrs. Markham's approaching marriage, and also about matrimony in general. Then we got upon the subject of love, free
and untrammelled, and I quoted some rather erotic passages
from Swinburne's "Songs before Sunrise"; at the same time
taking her hand, and squeezing it. The pressure was slightly
returned. Keeping possession of her hand, I bent over and
kissed her cheek. She shrank away slightly, but did not appear to be offended; so I sat down on the floor at her feet
and put my left arm round her waist; then, pressing my
mouth to her full red lips, I put my right hand up her

petticoats and took hold of her plump leg just below the frill of her drawers. She closed her eyes, a blush rose to her cheeks, and her bosom began to flutter; but she never moved; so, thrusting my hand higher up among the flounced draperies, I opened the slit of her drawers and touched her cunt. She started, and uttered a little ejaculation; then throwing one leg over the other, she gripped my hand tightly between her warm thighs; but she did not say a word. I had taken the outworks without any trouble, so I knew that I should soon occupy the fortress!

Taking her up in my arms—she was no light weight—I carried her to the sofa and laid her down upon it; then putting both my hands up her petticoats, I unfastened her drawers and pulled them down to her heels. Then my hand strayed all over her most secret charms. I stroked and squeezed her great big bottom, the flesh of which was firm, and I played with the long locks of soft hair which covered the lower part of her belly; and finally I tickled the "spot" with my forefinger. When she felt it, she squirmed, and covered her blushing face with both her hands; but she lay quite still.

I unbuttoned my trousers; raised her petticoats, stretched out her legs, and got between them; then clasping my hands under her bottom, I began to poke her. But I had actually to part with my fingers, the long, thick hair which completely hid the lips of her cunt, before I could get the weapon into the sheath.

She struggled a little, for form's sake, exclaiming in a low tone:

"Oh, don't! What are you doing? I won't have it!"

However, when I had fairly got into her; she abandoned herself entirely to me, and settled down on her back.

As she had not been poked for upwards of eight years, her cunt had contracted, so that it was wonderfully tight and small, for a woman of her age.

I fucked vigorously, but as slowly as possible; and she

seemed to be rather tender; for she winced a little as my big prick stretched the "spot," which had been virgin for so long a time. But, nevertheless, she liked the embrace; meeting my thrusts well, and heaving up her bottom in a brisk and lively way, uttering little cries of pleasure and pressing me tightly to her bosom.

When the end came, and I sent the hot stream up to her womb, she gave a squeak, and wriggled herself about under me; gasping out: "Oh! Oh! Oh!—h—h—h!" till she had received the whole of the discharge. Then she laying panting, and sighing; with her bosom palpitating against my breast, and her bottom quivering in my grasp.

I buttoned up my trousers, and she fastened up her drawers: her cheeks were flushed, her eyes were shining, and she appeared to be perfectly satisfied with what I had done to her. Throwing her arms round my neck she gave me a hot kiss, saying fervently: "Oh! that was *so* nice. I have been longing for years for such an embrace."

Then she added, coolly: "But I must run away, and take the necessary precautions. I won't be long. Wait till I come back."

So, nodding and smiling at me, she left the room, and I made myself comfortable in an easy chair, feeling very well satisfied with the plump governess. She was not Frances. But she was a voluptuous woman, and she had proved to be a luscious poke.

I determined to "have" her as often as possible in future.

She came back in about a quarter of an hour, looking fresh and nice. She gave me a cup of tea; then we had a confidential chat; and she promised to let me know what day she would be alone again in the house. Thus everything being settled to our mutual satisfaction, I kissed her, and went away.

Next morning, while I was dressing, it struck me that Frances would like to hear how I had fared with the governess.

So, at four o'clock, I called at the house, and for a wonder, found the mistress at home alone. After the ordinary greetings had passed between us; she asked, eagerly: "Did she let you 'have' her?"

"Yes," I replied.

She laughed, saying: "I knew she would. Was she nice?"

"Yes. But not so nice as you," I answered, smiling, and bowing.

She rose to her feet, swept a profound curtsey, and then sank down again into her chair, laughing heartily.

I remained chatting with her quietly till our *tête-à-tête* was interrupted by the entrance of some visitors whom I did not know; then I shook hands with her, and took my departure; without having seen Miss Martin.

A few days passed, but I did not pay a visit to Kensington. If I *had* gone, I should not have got a poke. I knew that Frances would not let me touch her; and I also knew that Miss Martin would not allow me to "have" her if Frances was in the house. The buxom governess had not the least idea that her intrigue with me was known.

However, I daily expected to hear from her that the "coast was clear." At last the note arrived; telling me that she would be at home alone, all the afternoon; and that she hoped to see me. As soon as I had lunched, I started off, intending to spend a few hours with her, as I had taken quite a fancy to her opulent charms. At half-past two o'clock, I reached the house, and was shown into the drawing-room, where I found her waiting to receive me. She was looking very nice, and I at once gave her a hearty kiss, which she returned warmly; her eyes sparkling, and a pretty pink colour rising to her plump cheeks.

I took her on my knees, and putting my hand under her petticoats, I unfastened her drawers, and played with her in the usual way till my cock was in a full state of erection. Then I lifted her up, and was just going to lay her on the sofa for a poke; when she said, smiling: "Wait a little. I have something to do first. It won't take me long. I will soon be back, and then we will have a long afternoon together, with nothing to disturb us."

"What are you going to do?" I asked.

"I am going to whip Dora," she replied in a matter-of-fact way, going to the cabinet and taking out the rod. Then she walked towards the door, saying: "I shan't be more than ten minutes."

"Stop a moment," I said. "Why, I thought Mrs. Markham herself always punished Dora?"

"So she does. But to-day she was in a hurry to go out, so she asked me to whip the girl. I have never hitherto whipped her."

"What has she been doing?" I asked; taking the rod from Miss Martin, and examining the little article as if I had never seen it before.

"She has been saucy and insubordinate to her step-mother. The girl has been very troublesome lately; as she has been allowed to have her own way a great deal too much since Mrs. Markham has been engaged. However, she shall smart to-day. Her stepmother has told me to whip her soundly. And I intend to do so."

"What a tiny little rod this is!" I observed, holding it up. "I should not think it could hurt much."

"Oh yes, it can," said Miss Martin emphatically. No doubt she remembered how much it had made her own bottom smart.

I laughed, as I thought of the day when I had seen her naked under the rod. Then I said: "I should very much like to see how a governess whips a refractory girl. Could you not let me see you punishing her? I could hide behind the curtains in the alcove, and she would never know that I was there. Come now, Kate,"—her name was Catherine—I added, kissing her: "do let me see you at work. It will give me great pleasure; and I assure you that no one shall ever hear anything about the affair." She laughed; and after a little hesitation, said: "Very well, dear. If it will really give you pleasure; I shall be delighted to let you see me whip the girl." I gave her another warm kiss by way of thanks.

Then she went on: "When Mrs. Markham punishes Dora, she merely whips her. But I will humble her as well as whip her. You shall see how a strict governess punishes a rude, saucy girl."

So saying, she placed three chairs close together in a row. Then, turning to me, she said: "Now hide yourself, and I will go for the girl."

She then left the room; and I put the rod on the table, and went into the alcove behind the curtains, which were closely drawn.

In a short time, the governess returned with the culprit, who was looking pale and frightened, though not actually crying. Dora was over fourteen years old: she had grown rather tall, and her budding bosom was just beginning to show its rounded contours; but she was still wearing rather short petticoats. She was prettier than ever, and her long auburn hair now reached below her waist. As I gazed at her, I thought what a lovely woman she would be in a few years' time.

The governess seated herself on a chair, and addressed the delinquent, in a stern voice: "Now, Dora, you know that your mother has requested me to whip you soundly. And I warn you that if you are not perfectly submissive, I will double your punishment. Take off your frocks, stays, and drawers; fold them up tidily, and put them on the sofa."

The tears welled up in the girl's eyes, and began to trickle down her cheeks; and she hesitated a moment; then she took off her smart little satin corset. Then, putting her hands under her petticoats, she slowly unfastened her drawers, let them slip down her legs to the floor, and stepped clear of the dainty, lace-trimmed garment. Then, with trembling fingers, she folded up the articles, placed them on the sofa, and stood, with downcast, tearful eyes, waiting for further orders.

"Now, get the rod; hand it to me, with a curtsey; say that you have misbehaved; and ask me if I will be pleased to give you a good whipping."

Dora's pale face flushed, when she heard the humiliating order, and the tears ran quicker down her cheeks; but she did not move.

"Obey me at once. Every time I have to repeat an order, I will add to your punishment," said the governess, stamping her foot.

The girl was cowed. She got the rod, and handed it to the governess, with a curtsey, saying in a low trembling voice: "I have been naughty. Please give me a good whipping."

"I will," said the governess. "Lie down at full length upon the chairs, and bare your bottom to receive the punishment."

Dora gave a choking sob, but at once walked to the chairs, and placed herself in position; then she pulled up all her drapery, exposing her lovely little naked figure from the waist downwards. It was six months since I had last seen the girl turned up. Her delicious bottom was as dazzlingly white as ever; but it had become more developed; it was broader and deeper, and the cheeks were plumper; her thighs had increased in size, and so had the calves of her well-made legs. Her small feet were cased in patent leather shoes, and she was wearing long black silk stockings, which showed off the whiteness of her skin to perfection. Altogether, the half-naked girl was a charming spectacle.

My cock sprung up, my eyes grew moist, and my mouth watered, as I gazed at the pretty bottom; and I heartily wished that I had been going to birch it.

Miss Martin now rose from her seat, and rod in hand, walked over to the culprit, and looked down at the "field of operations" for a moment.

Then she said: "Pull your petticoats up higher, and tuck them under your body."

The girl drew up all her garments as high as she could,

and pushed them underneath her belly; then, covering her face with both hands, she awaited the stroke. But her suspense was prolonged.

The governess laid down the rod, and took out of her pocket some straps, with which she coolly began to fasten Dora's wrists and ankles to the bars of the chairs; and as the girl had never before been tied up for a whipping, she became dreadfully frightened, and began to whimper.

When she was securely fastened, Miss Martin gave her a long lecture on her bad behaviour; winding up by saying: "I am going first of all to spank you; then I will birch you."

Dora shuddered, uttering a low groan, and her smooth bottom became quite "goose-skinned" with fear.

The governess sat down upon a chair; so that she was just at the right level to administer the punishment, without having to stoop.

She began the spanking: laying the slaps only on the right cheek of the girl's bottom, taking care not to touch the other cheek. The smacks sounded loudly as they fell in slow succession on the plump, firm flesh; and at each smack the marks of the governess's fingers were printed in red on the delicate, white skin. Dora bore two or three slaps pretty quietly, then she burst into a loud fit of crying, and winced at each smack.

When the governess had applied a dozen smart slaps, she stopped spanking, and leisurely inspected the sufferer's bottom which looked very funny, the bright scarlet colour of the spanked cheek, contrasting strongly with the snow-like whiteness of the untouched cheek. Then she set to work on the white left cheek, giving it also a dozen sharp smacks, which made it match the other in colour. Dora was crying, and wriggling her bottom the whole time, but she did not scream.

"Now, miss; you shall have twelve cuts with the birch," said the governess, taking up the rod and making it whistle in the air over Dora's red and smarting bottom. She turned her head round, and fixed her eyes, with an agonized look, on the threatening twigs, while the tears streamed down her cheeks. "Oh—h! Miss Martin," she cried out in piteous tones: "Please don't birch me!—Oh! please—don't—whip me—any more. Oh! I—have—had enough. My bottom—is—burning. Oh! Oh! Oh!"

Swish! Swish! Swish! The birching was begun; each cut extracting a loud, shrill squeal from Dora, and making her twist about in anguish, while small purple weals rose in all directions on the red skin. Miss Martin birched away calmly: and I saw that she was well skilled in the use of the rod. She did not swing the birch high in the air, she merely raised her arm from the elbow, and laid on the cuts with a peculiar sort of "flicking" stroke from the wrist. She never struck twice in the same place; the cuts were all applied with the same degree of force, and she never allowed the ends of the twigs to curl over on to the side of the culprit's bottom. The flogging was fairly administered from beginning to end.

Dora, throughout the birching, squealed and writhed; cried and plunged; and begged abjectly for mercy. But she was not let off a single cut. The governess threw down the rod, and unfastened the girl's wrists and ankles; saying: "Do not attempt to pull down your petticoats, or to get up until I give you permission."

She then went back to her chair and seated herself; leaving Dora lying on the chairs, crying and twisting her hips in pain; and with her wealed, scarlet bottom exposed. When her crying had died away to sobs, Miss Martin said: "Get up; come to me, and thank me for your punishment."

Dora got on her feet; her cheeks were nearly as red as her bottom; the tears were running from her eyes, her lips were quivering, and her face was full of pain. She walked stiffly up to the governess, and sobbed out, in choking accents:

"Thank—you—for—the—whipping—you—have—given me."

"Now, pick up the rod; kiss it, and put it away in the cabinet. Then dress, and go to your room."

The girl picked up the rod, kissed it meekly, and returned it to its place in the cabinet. Then she drew on her drawers, put on her corset and dress, and slunk, still sobbing, out of the room.

I stepped from behind the curtains, and gave the governess an appreciative kiss, as I was much pleased with the way she had administered the chastisement. She smiled, saying: "Now you have seen how a governess can punish a naughty girl, morally as well as physically. Dora may soon forget the whipping, but she will remember the degradation she has undergone. In having been obliged to ask me to give her a whipping; then, having had to prepare herself for the punishment; then having been compelled to thank me for whipping her; and finally having been forced to kiss the rod. She is a saucy girl, but she is now thoroughly humbled; and I am certain that she will not need another whipping for a very long time."

"You did the whole thing splendidly," I said. "The way you spanked one side of her bottom, and then the other, amused me very much; and you applied the rod in a most skilful way. I had no idea that a whipping could be inflicted in such an artistic style."

She laughed, and appeared to be highly delighted at my compliments, saying: "There is an art both in spanking and birching, as there is in everything else. I have had plenty of practice, and I flatter myself that I can whip a bottom with a fair amount of skill."

"You can, indeed," I remarked. Then I added: "Now, Kate, I want you to let me have a good look at your bottom."

She smiled, and blushed slightly, but answered without hesitation: "Very well. You may look at it."

I made her lean well over the back of an easy-chair; then I turned her skirt, petticoats, and chemise up to her shoulders; and unfastening her drawers, let them slip down to her feet. Then, with a stiff prick, and glistening eyes, I inspected her grand bottom, which swelled boldly out in high relief as if inviting a spanking.

I passed my hand over the creamy-white hemispheres of plump firm flesh; stroking them up and down; squeezing them, and playing with them in all sorts of ways, while she looked over her shoulder, smiling.

"You have a magnificent bottom, K~te," I observed, pinching one of the cheeks with my finger and thumb.

"Yes, I believe I have rather a good one," she said, thrusting her head round, and glancing down at her big posteriors.

"Will you let me spank you?" I asked.

She hesitated a moment; then said: "Yes. But not too hard."

"All right, I won't be too hard. I'll only raise a blush on the pretty white cheeks, and make them tingle a little."

She braced herself up, stiffening the muscles of her bottom and thighs; and bending well over the chair. Then I began to spank her; and it was a very pleasing task. I laid on the smacks pretty smartly, my hand rebounding from her firm, elastic flesh; and in a very short time the great white half-moons had turned a rosy red, and she had begun to flinch under the hot slaps.

I stopped spanking; then unbuttoning my trousers, I let out my tool, intending to poke her "en levrette." But when she saw me advancing to the attack, she looked surprised, and was going to stand up. So, I said: "Don't move, Kate. I am going to enjoy from behind."

She gazed over her shoulder, with her large, hazel eyes wide open in utter astonishment—she had evidently never been poked "en levrette"—but she stood still. Taking hold of her massive thighs, I slightly separated them; then clasping my hands in front of her belly, I stooped a little, and thrust my prick between the lower part of the cheeks of her bottom, deeply into her cunt. I began to work vigorously, and she appeared to thoroughly enjoy the novel sensation of being poked from behind. She moved her loins backwards and forwards briskly to meet my digs, squeaking with pleasure; and when the discharge came, she received it with a quiver of voluptuous delight, wriggling her bottom furiously, and heaving a deep sigh of satisfaction.

When all was over, and she had fastened up her drawers, and I had buttoned up my trousers, we sat down on the sofa.

Glancing rather shyly at me, she said: "I have never been embraced in that way before. It quite astonished me. I had no idea there were more ways than one of doing it."

"It can be done in many other ways, and I hope to show them all to you, in time," I observed.

She laughed; her eyes gleamed, and her cheeks flushed. She was decidedly a voluptuous woman, and the thought of future pokes in strange positions, was evidently pleasing to her.

We had a short chat, then she rang for tea; and after we had refreshed ourselves with a cup, she sat down on the floor at my feet, coolly unbuttoned my trousers, and took out my limp prick, which she began to handle in a skilful manner. She was up to that trick! When she had got my tool ready for action, she laughed and looked up in my face, her eyes shining with a sensuous expression of desire. I said: "Now, I'll show you another way of doing it. Stand up with your back towards me." She instantly rose to her feet and placed herself in the required position, laughing and looking over her shoulder.

"Pull open the slit of your drawers as widely as possible, and then hold your petticoats well above your waist." She did so: and as soon as the big semi-globes of her bottom —still pink from the spanking—were fairly exposed, I drew her close up to my knees, and made her lower her bottom down upon my upstanding prick, which I guided with my fingers into its proper place, until the weapon was up to the hilt in the sheath. Then I told her to move herself up and down on the "dart," and she did so, while I gently worked my loins; so, in a short time, the affair was finished; and she had been again poked in a new position, much to her amusement and satisfaction. She remarked, as she lay back against my breast:

"That is a capital way of doing 'it,' when a woman has got all her clothes on. The position is comfortable, and it does not rumple her dress."

"Yes," I replied. "It is a most convenient position. A man can 'have' a woman that way, in a moment, in any quiet corner; or in a railway carriage, or even in a hansom cab."

She laughed, and asked me a number of questions about the various ways of poking. I gave her full descriptions of the different methods, and by the time I had satisfied her curiosity, it was also time for me to be going, as I had an engagement to dinner. So I gave her a kiss, telling her that I had to go home and dress. She got off my knees, where she had been sitting ever since I had poked her, and arranged her rather disordered attire; saying, with a laugh: "Well, we have spent a pleasant afternoon. I hope to see you soon again, and then you must show me practically some of the other positions."

I laughed, and replied: "I will show you, in due course, all the other positions."

Then I shook hands with her, and took my departure, feeling very well pleased with what I had seen, and also with what I had done.

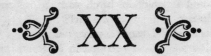

# XX

CONCLUSION.——DORA AND THE "MARTINET."——
FRANCES MARRIED AGAIN.——REGRETS.——THE
BRIDE'S GOOD-BYE.——FRANCES A HAPPY
MOTHER.——THE PUPPETS SATISFAC-
TORILY DISPOSED OF.——"ALL'S
WELL THAT ENDS WELL."

The time passed. In another week Frances was to be married.
She had introduced me to Gilbert, whom I found to be a
very good sort of fellow in every way, and very much in
love with Frances. She also loved him, so there was every
chance of the marriage turning out well. I was glad to know
that my "ward" would have a good husband, and I felt quite
sure she would be a faithful wife, if she was well treated, and
also well poked. During the past weeks, she had very frequently been out with her *fiancé;* so I had been able to spend
pleasant afternoons with Miss Martin whom I showed practically—as she had desired—all the various positions in which
a man may poke a woman.

Dora had been sent to a boarding-school which had been
recommended by Miss Martin; and that lady, one afternoon,
told me that the principal of the establishment was a strict

disciplinarian, and a firm believer in the salutary effect of a good whipping applied in orthodox fashion to the bottom of a naughty girl. Miss Martin also informed me that the mistress of the school did not use a birch rod, as she considered it too apt to cut the tender skin of a girl's bottom.

So, instead of a rod, she always used a small whip with six thin leather thongs—it is called in France a "martinet"— which stung sharply, and left scarlet stripes on the culprit's bottom, but never broke the skin. The delinquents were flogged privately, and were strapped to a padded "horse" while receiving their punishment.

The governess added, laughing: "Dora will soon find herself on the 'horse,' and then she will feel what a real flogging is like. She has never had a severe whipping in her life."

"Poor Dora!" I remarked in a tone of sympathy.

"Oh, you needn't pity her! It will do her good. You have no idea what a troublesome girl she has lately become."

We then dropped the subject, and proceeded to business. That afternoon I spanked her once, and poked her twice.

The last few days before the marriage slipped away rapidly, and uneventfully; the wedding day arrived, and then, according to my promise, I gave Frances away. She was exquisitely dressed, in the most perfect taste; and though she was thirty years old, she was still a very beautiful woman, and I felt a pang of regret at knowing that I should never again poke her, or even have the pleasure of feeling her plump bottom or her firm bubbies.

At the wedding breakfast there was a large party of guests, including a number of the bridegroom's relatives; the usual speeches were made, and everything passed off well.

Frances was in good spirits; and just before she left the room to put on her travelling-dress, she drew me aside out of sight of the guests, and giving me a kiss, said: "Charley, I love my husband and I will be faithful to him; but I shall never forget how kind you have been to me, from the day you took me into your house, up to the present moment."

I clasped a bracelet on her wrist, as a wedding present, and kissing her for the last time, bade her good bye; then she ran upstairs to her room.

In a short time she came down, dressed for her journey; and then the newly-married couple got into their carriage, and were driven off, amid showers of rice, to Charing Cross station, *en route* for Italy, where they intended to spend their honeymoon.

And so, for the second and last time, my sweetheart passed out of my life.

Next day I went home to Oakhurst, and settled down to my old life as a country gentleman.


Five years have passed since the last lines were written, and I again take up my pen to put the finishing touches to the story.

Frances is now a buxom matron, thirty-five years old, with two little children. She and her husband are perfectly happy; they are very well-off, and they live in London half the year; and I am always a welcome guest at their house whenever I choose to go there. Gilbert and I are very good friends; as he has not the faintest suspicion that I ever was anything to Frances but her "guardian." She has quite a daughterly affection for me, and whenever we meet we talk and laugh about the old days.

Miss Martin, after leaving Frances, got a good situation as governess in a family, where she remained until she heard of her husband's death in South America. Then she married again. I have never seen her since.

Frances' two step-children live with their father's relations: but they often visit their stepmother, and I have frequently seen them. Robert is sixteen years old, and is studying for the army. Dora is nineteen years old, and has grown— as I knew she would—into a magnificent young woman, tall and shapely, and most "divinely fair." She is engaged to be married.

My story is finished, and though I am fifty years of age, I am in good health, and I can still "look upon the wine when it is red," and I can also still enjoy a pretty girl.

But often, in the long winter evenings, when I am sitting all alone in my big dining-room after dinner, I think of the "boy Frank" whom I had picked up on the road twenty years before, and who had eventually turned out to be a loving, faithful woman.

## END OF THIRD VOLUME